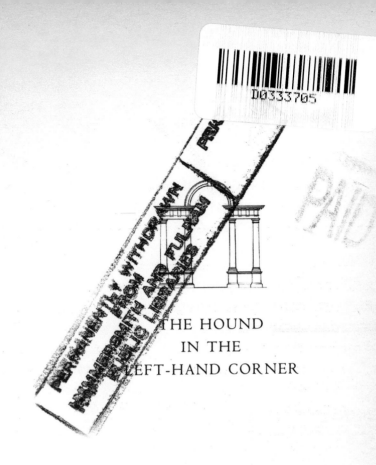

THE HOUND
IN THE
LEFT-HAND CORNER

ALSO BY GILES WATERFIELD

The Long Afternoon

GILES WATERFIELD

The Hound
in the
Left-Hand Corner

review

First published in 2002
by REVIEW

An imprint of Headline Book Publishing

10 9 8 7 6 5 4 3 2 1

British Library Cataloguing in Publication Data

Waterfield, Giles
The hound in the left-hand corner
I. Title
823.9'14 [F]

ISBN 0 7472 6885 1

Designed by Peter Ward
Typeset by
Letterpart Limited, Reigate, Surrey
Printed and bound in Great Britain by
Clays Ltd, St Ives plc

Headline Book Publishing
A division of Hodder Headline
338 Euston Road
LONDON NW1 3BH

www.headline.co.uk
www.hodderheadline.com

For Caryl and Coral
two terrific trustees

ACKNOWLEDGEMENTS

I would like to thank a number of people for their help and advice in writing this novel, and particularly Charles Anyia, Rupert Christiansen, Jeff Fuller, John Hardy, Lucy Hughes-Hallett, Giles Ockendon, Sophie Plender, Paul Ryan, Luke Syson and Martin Wyld; my agent Felicity Rubinstein; the designers of this book, David Grogan and Peter Ward; at Headline, Hazel Orme, Ros Ellis, Mary Anne Harrington, Janice Brent and my ineffable editor, Geraldine Cooke. For advice on various aspects of the book, Glynn Woodin and James Robins at Mustard Catering; Rob Van Helden, Robert Salter and their colleagues at Rob Van Helden Floral Design; Jon Campbell and Sandra Patterson at the National Gallery, London; for her advice on evening clothes, Katherine Goodison, and on jewellery, Judy Rudoe.

THE CHARACTERS

Trustees and Staff
of BRIT: *The Museum*
of British History

THE CHARACTERS

EXHIBITIONS DEPARTMENT
Lucian Bankes (Head of Exhibitions)
Louisa (PA to Head of Exhibitions)
Diana Stanley (Deputy Head of Exhibitions)
Hermia Bianchini (Exhibitions Assistant)
Suzette (Exhibitions Assistant)
Mirabel Thuillier (exhibition designer – freelance)

CONSERVATION DEPARTMENT
Friedrich von Schwitzenberg (Head of Conservation)

EDUCATION DEPARTMENT
Melissa (Head of Education and Community Outreach)

SECURITY DIVISION
John Winterbotham (Head of Security)
Ian Burgess (Deputy Head of Security)
Anna (warder)
Bill (warder)
Ralph (warder)
Norman (warder)

PRESS AND PUBLIC RELATIONS DEPARTMENT
Mary Anne Bowles (Head of Press and Public Relations)
Julia (Special Events)
Ben (Press Office Assistant)
Luke (Press Office Assistant)

Guests at the Dinner

HRH The Duke of Clarence
Police Sergeant Ted Hoskins (Personal Protection Officer
to Duke of Clarence)
Tanya (lecturer, Queen Mary's College, London;
Auberon Booth's girlfriend)
Lady Burslem
Sir William and Lady St John
Mr Kobayashi (Chairman of Japco; sponsor of
exhibition in Japan)
Ronnie Smiles (picture restorer)
Valentine Green (journalist)
Denzil Marten (art dealer)
Lord Willins of Plympton (Chairman of Trustees,
The Bloomsbury Museum)
Jonathan (Diana's boyfriend)
Ranald Stewart (Director, South London Museum)
Baroness Shawe and Mr William Shawe
Gregory Noble (novelist)
Ms Margaret Mills (Minister of State, Department
of Cultural Affairs)
Mrs Ferdinand Hill (lender to the exhibition)

* * *

George Evans (architect, Trusty Owen)
Imogen (Diana's hairdresser and friend)
Sergeant Major Jenkins, Corps of Commissionaires

Angel Cooks

'Mr Rupert' Burnham (General Manager)
Leonore (Mr Rupert's Personal Assistant)
Gustavus (Head Chef)
Fred (Head of Operations)

The Hound
in the
Left-Hand Corner

THE MUSEUM,
THREE A.M.

At 0300 hours the guard on patrol duty on the first floor is due to walk through Exhibition Suite One. In his central control room in the basement, with its cameras watching every public gallery, the staff corridors and meeting rooms and potential entry points (though not quite yet the offices), the exits, the delivery yard, the stores, the four streets around the building, John Winterbotham, Head of Security, can survey everything always. Now he turns to the camera covering Exhibition Suite One. He trusts his men, more or less, but Ralph, who is patrolling the ground floor at this moment, is a new boy. At 0300 hours precisely the door to the first room opens and Ralph, small, neat and dark, appears. He looks conscientious but nervous, as though an assailant might emerge from behind a showcase. He knows he's under surveillance. He looks around the whole room in the approved manner and presses the security button, which records his time-keeping. John Winterbotham is reasonably satisfied, though it's a pity none of his young recruits has his own military background.

On the morning of Midsummer's Day of 2001, BRIT is asleep. It was called the Museum of English History until last year, but with the millennium it was felt that a livelier name was needed and that 'English' had exclusive connotations, so 'BRIT' (sub-titled 'The Museum of British History') came in instead.

At least, it seems asleep from outside: no passer-by could sense the dim security lights glowing in all the rooms, or the sound of solitary steps along the marble and parquet floors. Anyone glancing at the portico, with its ten enormous columns and monumental staircase, might think it the temple of an abandoned cult. Only a set of cords above the front door, waving in the night breeze, suggests it's ever inhabited.

Anyone who could enter the closed double bronze doors with their reliefs of Britannia and St George would reach a completely still entrance hall. It is a vast domed room, with screens of columns on four sides and a stone coat-of-arms above each screen. Opposite the entrance a gigantic staircase leads to the upper floor. Each corner of the room is occupied by a massive statue: Art, Industry, Learning and Valour. During the day this is the busiest part of the building, constantly filling and emptying, babbling with a thousand tongues and a dozen languages, with enquiries for the lavatories and the cafeteria and Michelangelo's David and the Magna Carta, with hordes of near-rioting French schoolchildren and attentive Japanese. At night, empty and lit by pale security lights, its cavernous heights offer no welcome.

The room has perplexed generations of museum directors and designers. 'So imperialistic,' they said after the Second World War, 'so huge, how can we persuade ordinary people it's a place for them?' 'How *can* we make it look swinging?' they had cried in the sixties as they tried to disguise the dimensions under false white ceilings and walls. At the beginning of the new century, the management team agonises over its authoritarianism and social élitism.

At the back of the building, Ralph walks slowly into the first exhibition room, apparently surprised at its transformation since the previous night. Though not quite finished, the exhibition, which is to open later that day, is almost in place. It's the museum's major event of the year, indeed its biggest exhibition ever, and has kept the place in turmoil for weeks. ELEGANCE, it's called, 'The Eighteenth Century Revisited'. *What a to-do*, thinks Winterbotham. The installation staff were work- ing there until an hour ago under the supervision of Diana, highly professional woman that, and left in an unruly bunch, shouting and giggling as though they'd been drinking – though he kept a close eye on them and spotted no irregularities. *The big problem was the arrival of a huge painting by Gainsborough or somebody like that, it's all over the posters and stuff, came in at ten p.m. in an unmarked van with a police escort, God, what a business, a Mr Marten and a Mr Smiles in attendance with their own crew of technicians, wouldn't let anyone from the museum near it, took it into the exhibition and hung it themselves. They seem to have had a bit of aggro with that German bloke, head of Conservation, who wanted to inspect it, wouldn't let him near the thing. He was furious, said it was his duty, but they wouldn't listen to him. Apparently it's worth an amazing amount of money, star of the show. Belongs to the Chairman of the Trustees, apparently it's the absolute prize of his collection; good man, Sir Lewis, knows how to handle authority, unlike some who are always asking your opinion when it's their job to lead . . .*

Young Ralph seems tempted to linger. He must be spoken to. A good guard concentrates on the job in hand. That job's about security, not looking at objects. The only reason to look at any specimen on display is to check that it's in place and undamaged. After a pause or two, Ralph walks through the room at the correct speed and reaches the second exhibition room at 0302, the scheduled time. John glances at the camera covering the ground floor front. His man there is Norman, long-established, no problem, an ex-Welsh Guardsman like John himself.

Ralph is currently patrolling the Gallery of Early English History: from the Stone Age to the Norman Conquest. It was the first gallery created when the museum was founded. A shaky government was persuaded that the museum would kindle patriotic fervour by celebrating England's political liberty, maritime endeavour, industry and science, literature and the arts, agriculture, trade, warfare. By the beginning of the twenty-first century it is one of the largest and most popular museums in the country, visited by over two million each year.

There's a great deal to see. Even the building, long derided as pompous, is now admired. On the South Bank of the river behind Lambeth Palace and Waterloo Station, it was paid for in 1902 by an ambitious purveyor of wine and spirits. He hoped the building might turn him an earl but not being a gentleman had to be satisfied with a viscountcy. Viscount Haringey wanted a proper building like the Natural History Museum, but up to date. He commissioned, from the architects Lanchester and Rickards, a palace in the quintessentially English Wrenaissance style. Built in red brick and Portland stone, its twenty-five-bay façade boasts a tower at each end, adorned with balconies at three levels, and unexpected finials on the hipped roof. The huge coat-of-arms of England over the main entrance has been a favourite target for paint-throwing political protesters ever since the museum opened.

The Gallery of Early English History is long. Having walked its eighty yards at a steadily increasing speed and glanced at some of its four thousand exhibits, visitors imagine they've seen the whole museum. They don't realise that beyond its marble doorcase, over three floors, stretch the Gallery of Medieval History, the Gallery of Early Modern History, the Tudor and Stuart galleries (sponsored by a firm of interior decorators), the Georgian and Regency galleries, two Victorian galleries, the Gallery of the Industrial Revolution (sponsored by a Japanese car production company), the Gallery of English

Painting and Sculpture (supported by a major American trust), the London Gallery, the Gallery of Empire, the Gallery of World War (no sponsorship available here), the Gallery of Women's History, the Gallery of Technology and Science, the Discovery Room, and a number more, quite a number. The attendants are used to comforting visitors who, turning the corner and gaining their first view of the apparently eternal Gallery of Medieval History, turn pale, grip their bags convulsively, plead for escape. But there is none. 'Museum fatigue can be a problem,' admits the Director.

At three in the morning nobody's suffering from museum fatigue. Only, perhaps, the security staff, who've been patrolling the building since midnight. In the Gallery of Early English History the slowly pacing Norman sees the yards of gallery stretching into a distant penumbra, interrupted only by the security lights glowing every few yards. The axe heads and sherds, the fragments of old shoes and fruit, the busts of Roman emperors, the illuminated manuscripts, slumber like rocks on the ocean bed.

When John arrived at the museum he had a great deal to do: a spot of tyranny was essential. Discipline had gone out of the window: the attendants would lounge around in gabbling groups ignoring the public, morale was rock bottom. One pair of attendants, a man and a woman and both married, were suspected of mistaking night duty for night pleasure. ('Too right those two like to be on the same floor,' somebody said in the mess room, and everyone guffawed.) At night some of the men drifted completely out of control. While they were supposed to check the offices of the senior staff, they were not meant to settle down on the furniture or peer at confidential memoranda. The curators hated having their space invaded by unseen strangers at night. It was realised that rules had to be tightened when someone scrawled 'Old Jenkins likes shagging goats' in the trustees' lavatory (Sir Hubert Jenkins, authority and frequent lecturer on Agriculture in Early Medieval England, was director until three years ago). There's no more nonsense under John's rule. He keeps a tight grip on everything that goes on.

The control room is the heart of the institution. Unless the plant and the objects are safe, none of the activities the curators are so proud of (which personally he often finds a waste of time) could take place. Few of the staff know how intimately he surveys their activities, and might not like it, but the system is essential for good security. One day he hopes to be able to hear what is being said in all these public and staff spaces, to ensure that there are no breaches of confidence in conversation, but nonsense about civil liberties makes this difficult. He's mentioned once or twice to the Head of Admin irregularities of conduct he's noticed on the screen or on his walks around the building but the man's never seemed receptive.

When John left the Army he doubted any civilian job (outside the police force) was worth doing and was sceptical about the museum. But when he realised that though the staff numbered only three hundred, there were over a million objects with a total value of £400 million for which he'd be responsible, his interest quickened. Now in his newly modernised control room, known to his staff as the Pentagon, he can survey his banks of cameras, the line of computers recording the action, the electronically guarded record files, the constant presence of a uniformed man, and feel that here at least, in this disordered muddle they call England's capital city, discipline and order rule.

He'll be going home shortly for some kip before returning for one of the busiest days in the museum's year. No family now that June's moved to Lichfield and the children have left home, so no need to spend time with them. His new girlfriend's pretty understanding about his irregular hours (though she was a bit too eager to be invited to the dinner that night, which of course was not possible, really went on about it). He looks at the day schedule for 24 June 2001, shaking his head.

0800   *Final exhibition installation begins — technical staff and exhibition staff arrive*
         Great Hall closed to public all day
1030   *Press view begins (NB beige press cards)*
1130   *Press conference in Lecture Theatre*
1200   *Royalty Protection Group Security Advance Party arrives*
1230   *Trustees' meeting in Board Room*
1300   *Trustees' lunch in Board Room*
1430   *Rehearsal for Grand Pageant: actors arrive via Entrance for Groups*
1600   *Industrial Revolution, Early Georgian, Regency closed for caterers*
         Caterers arrive to set up Great Hall for dinner
1700   *Entrance Hall set up for drinks reception*
1815   *Guests arrive for reception — NB no glasses outside Entrance Hall*
1930   *Exhibition closes for guests*
         (RPG Security Advance Party check exhibition rooms)
1940   *HRH arrives at main entrance. Attends reception*
         (Personal Protection Officer RJH; Close Protection Officers POC and JF)
1945   *HRH leaves Entrance Hall for exhibition galleries — main lift. Meets further group*
2002   *HRH arrives in exhibition*
2015   *Dinner guests commence move to Great Hall*
2030   *HRH leaves exhibition*
2040   *HRH arrives in Great Hall*
         Painting moved from exhibition gallery to Great Hall — to arrive after Duke is seated

2045 *Dinner served*

2215 *Speeches*

2230 *Performance of Grand Pageant*

2245 *Grand Pageant ends*

2300 *HRH departs (north entrance)*

2345 *Final guest departure scheduled*

0200 *Caterers depart*

Museum closes

All OK, at least in principle. *The thing I'm most worried about is the Grand Pageant, which involves large numbers of extras, children from nearby schools (what are they doing there anyway, still up at eleven?), complicated lighting effects and some tiresome actors and actresses. I won't be able to go home again until three the following morning, at the earliest. No problem about that. But I really must leave now — I should have left at midnight.*

Ian Burgess, his deputy, comes into the room and looks at him enquiringly as though wondering why he hasn't left. Secretly, John's never happy leaving Ian to play boss at night and is sure he'll make a bad mistake one day, but he can't be on duty all the time. Ian just isn't tough enough, too soft with the staff — and the public, too, for that matter: you have to keep them in order, especially the types you get in south London. 'Keep an eye on the new boy,' John tells him, 'and watch the screens for the exhibition galleries, especially the room where that new picture is hanging — belongs to the Chairman, absolutely vital no one goes near it.' Then he leaves.

Ian rolls his eyes at the other guard in the control room (also non-military, and his ally) and looks at the screens. Ralph has moved into the Gallery of Women's History, still on time. If he does look at one or two objects as he passes, and even stops for a moment, it does no harm, Ian considers. He and the

boss disagree on that point, as on many. It's time for Ian to
settle into the supervisor's office next door, although he'll be
off himself at four; it never seems his territory when John's
around. Ian's hoping for promotion to another institution soon,
and will be glad to be number one, free to introduce a human
working-with-the-public approach. It will be good never to
have to see John again.

John passes through the entrance hall on his way to the
staff entrance. He likes the hall at night, quiet, grand,
powerful, its majesty undisturbed by crowds, the lights
subdued, everything in order. If only, he sometimes thinks, it
could always be like this. This evening, during the royal visit,
the entrance hall and the Great Hall next door will look as
they should look. Then indeed, with the highest in the land
visiting the museum, the men in their black and white
according to the code, the ladies richly dressed and jewelled,
the movements of guests and staff prearranged, every action
planned in detail and carried out by trained professionals —
then this mighty building will be used as it should be. He's
developed a proprietorial affection for the place; it appeals to
something deep inside him. Lingering for a moment, he
savours the sense of responsibility the great empty space gives
him. He shivers a little at the thought of the day ahead.
Could anything go wrong? No, of course not. He must get
some rest.

GLOUCESTER STREET, PIMLICO,
SEVEN A.M.

The alarm rings punctually at seven a.m. It always rings at seven, winter or summer, weekday or Sunday, workday or funday. Occasionally Auberon wonders if waking at seven on a foggy Sunday morning is necessary, especially after a gruelling night out. But the habit's strong and since he's talked about it more than once in profile interviews, he is strict with himself. He sometimes wonders if the idea of a form of monastic discipline subconsciously appeals to him. Tanya hates waking up early, of course, and can be cross, but then her crossness can lead to exciting physical contact just at the moment when his energy's at its peak, so that their limbs, more or less toned, surge under and over the luxuriant duvet... Tanya's not there this morning, but in her own home a mile away preparatory to dashing out of bed and throwing on her clothes so as not to be late to deliver her nine a.m. History of Western Philosophy lecture at Queen Mary's College (she's taught there for a while). She'll stay over this coming evening, probably, if they're not too exhausted. So nice they have the choice, the variety... He's very fond of her, he thinks, though actually he's found her rather snappy lately: she keeps complaining that they always do what he wants to do, always see his friends not hers, always go to his type of difficult history seminar rather than her type of difficult philosophical forum, and attend pretentious house parties at weekends (lately she's completely refused to co-operate on that one, says it might be part of his job but it certainly isn't part of hers). Is he selfish? Hard to know — he finds it hard to assess himself, he often wonders what he's doing with his life . . . And it's hard to know about Tanya, too. Maybe it's time for a . . . Ah, well, that can take its time, there's too much to think about now . . .

'Big day,' he says to himself, caressing the sheets. 'Big, big day.' He can spend ten minutes in bed, collecting himself, doing his stretching routine before the morning's regular workout. Well, almost regular anyway, it really is such hell doing those dreary exercises. Ten minutes in bed is much more pleasant: he can shape out the day, decide which events require concentration and which he can coast through. When he wakes up he always knows what's in his diary: usually six or eight engagements plus lunch (always) and dinner (almost always), and three or four private views or receptions from which it's nice to make a selection. He loves his glamorous life nowadays, so different from teaching or his quiet youth in Bradford . . . but should he be resisting this glamour, is it superficial and ultimately worthless?

Anyway, since he's chosen glamour of a sort, he may as well do it properly. These early-morning minutes allow him to choose clothes for the day and the evening. He always changes in the evening, never keeps on his suit. Often he has to change up, into a tux, or sometimes down — although his casual clothes are carefully chosen too. Once an adventurous dandy, he's become less experimental recently, finding the people he deals with now are uncharmed by the crocodile-skin waistcoats and baggy scarlet silk trousers that made such an impact at High Table and provided his fusty colleagues with regular scandalised gossip. No more sartorial extravagances. On the other hand the chalkstripe suits he wore in the early nineties, with their red or

yellow linings and waisted look, redolent he'd liked to think of
old money subtly flavoured with new vigour, now embarrass
him. How could he have worn them? he sometimes asks
himself, looking at the one or two he's kept (they were
extremely expensive). They look so absurdly posh – what a
frump he must have been. Now he has a New Look, a New
Labour but at the same time Cool Academic Look. Dark suit,
usually Italian, though there are one or two nice English suits
around (he likes them understated, in very beautiful wool). Of
course, he needs to dress just a little English for the job – a
passing self-deprecating reference to his suit label to the right
journalist shows he's in touch with contemporary design. One
of those updated Savile Row-look suits, perhaps the dark grey,
is probably right for today's business. White shirt – successful
political figures always wear white shirts these days, but it's OK
to sport good ones. A strongly coloured tie – care's needed
here, the tie should be striking but not obtrusive, though clearly
expensive to the initiate. He cherishes his ties and owns around
two hundred, which are arranged by colour and fabric. ('It's the
museum man in you,' Tanya tells him.)

*Odd, isn't it, how much time one has to devote to self-presentation these
days in a museum? Not what I was brought up to expect. But this style
business is essential if one's to make any impact on the media . . . Do try not
to think about the interview next week for the Bloomsbury Museum. I doubt
I'll get the job – too young, too inexperienced, they'll say. And not all the
Bloomsbury trustees (cultivated derelicts, some of them) will like my style of
directing a museum, which is . . . well, what is it? Lively? Straightforward?
Modern? Caring? Socially inclusive? God knows what it is, opportunistic and
vacillating it often seems to me, trying to keep the waters from pouring in,
maintaining some academic standards when the trend is to discard them as
briskly as possible. But, then, I've had my successes and, of course, if
ELEGANCE stuns the press (as it's already beginning to do), I'll go into the*

interview room with garlands of roses round my head and cannons firing in my wake. Tonight's so important — the opening and the dinner (the Bloomsbury Museum's trustees are mostly coming) matter in all sorts of ways. The other candidates for the job, according to the papers and gossip (I've tried not to listen to it, but no success there), are a mixed bag, if gossip can be relied on. At least I'll be given a good reference by my chairman, who'll certainly not miss me.

Yes, a lot depends on today.

He turns and stretches another way. He tries not to worry but hardly succeeds. Do I truly want Bloomsbury or am I just impelled by feeling it's my duty to be ambitious? I think I want it, such a wonderful place, and after five years I could go on to a major job in the United States or a university chair, probably, if I keep up the publishing . . .

God, how pleased Dad would have been to see me in this job — from semi-detached house in Bradford to national museum directorship, and it would never have happened without all that support they gave me. I might have been running a local supermarket, and proud of it too. Pity Mum is so vague now but she's pleased when she grasps what I'm on about — loves the pictures of me in the papers . . .

Four more minutes till he has to leave his crisp white bed, with its three linen-encased pillows to the left and three to the right. Linen sheet beneath, finest linen duvet above. Never did do the stretching exercises in bed, oh, well, he can make up for that at the weekend, probably, possibly, or whatever. He loves his bed, the source of such pleasure, and often in the evening after a day crammed with activity lies contemplating the soothing sheets, and the ivory paint and pale wood of a room in which every detail gives visual and tactile pleasure. It is a place of repose, of which there's too little in his life except when he's with Tanya and they're getting on well.

The room has a united colour scheme, no strong accents, only whites, ivories and creams, pale browns and beiges, and an occasional touch of pink and green. The vase of flowers, which always adorns the window-sill in front of the translucent blind, obliquely marks the seasons, reflecting nature in this cool elegance. No untidiness here: he dresses and undresses next door, in a little room where the clothes racks slide out of the cupboard at the touch of a switch, and where forty or fifty pairs of shoes lie in suppliant rows on a miniature conveyor belt designed by one of the museum's technicians. He smiles. Very silly, really, all this dandyishness ...

Who'll get my job if I do move on? From odd dropped remarks, it might be none of them — the Chairman may have in mind one of my staff. Don't know which. Diana, could it be, beautiful Diana, though she's hardly senior enough? Jane? Too close to retirement. Lucian? ... It could well be Lucian. Lucian — that would explain why he's recently started appearing (he never used to) at functions whenever the chairman's there and is obviously establishing a humorous deferential relationship with that important individual ...

Not a nice thought, being succeeded by Lucian ...

Usually this early-morning half-hour is the time when he reads, not duty things like business reports on the museum and deconstructions of nationhood, but books he never speaks about to his colleagues or friends, and scarcely to Tanya. He's reading Pascal's *Pensées*, just at the moment. The world — which takes a great interest in him — thinks of him as a sunflower, its head turning constantly towards the sun. Auberon does indeed enjoy the media, just as they enjoy him, but people who think him superficial do him an injustice: the sunflower has no interior life. But he can't read this morning, too many teasing thoughts interrupt him. Has the big Gainsborough arrived safely? he wonders. And all this business of the loan of the Gainsborough to Japan, for example, that worries him too. Can that idea be sound, should he be taking more of an interest in the whole idea, is it wise to let the Chairman get on with it and not find out what's really going on? Lewis clearly doesn't want him to meddle, but all the same . . . God, Lewis is difficult . . .

He thinks the exhibition will be OK — better than OK, pretty splendid — and intellectually coherent, and attractive to a wide public. They've had quite a lot of trouble with it, the Chairman *would* insist on including lots of his own pictures, very hard it was to argue with him, especially when he said he wanted his Gainsborough to be the centrepiece. What really annoyed all of them was when they had to include a not very interesting picture belonging to that man Denzil Marten, the art dealer — Jane Vaughan said no art dealer's stock should be included in an exhibition, and certainly not when it was of doubtful quality, but Lewis began to look so furious when this objection was delicately mooted that they abandoned the subject . . .

Downstairs he hears the splattering of mail through his letterbox, twenty or thirty envelopes usually. He's only recently stopped counting, more from pressure of time than any loss of curiosity. He has to admit to himself that he enjoys the public recognition asserted by a groaning mailbag. Ever-increasing numbers want him to attend private views and dinner parties and book launches and conferences, and make speeches and give lectures all over the country and indeed the world. His private address is not especially private, since he is a generous communicator and at parties dispenses his card widely to strangers, only realising when they ring that he never wants to speak to them again. As the book jacket of his much-admired recent biography of the Earl of Strafford (his doctoral thesis) puts it, 'Dr Auberon Booth was educated at Cambridge and Harvard Universities and has taught at St Peter's College, Oxford, and Princeton University. After a spell in the Department of

Modern Antiquities at the Bloomsbury Museum, he became Director of the Museum of English History in 1997. He is thirty-five. Rooted academically in the study of English history, he regards himself as a citizen of the world. He has published many academic articles and a study of the cult of luxury at the Early Stuart Court.'

It's definitely time to move. As his naked body rises from the bed he glances at his six-foot-two expanse of mildly bronzed flesh. It looks OK, but it should be better: his shoulders don't look firm enough. At least there's hardly any fat on him; his thighs are as firm as ever. Thirty-six is middle age by some definitions (though he prefers to think middle age begins at forty) but he's not really concerned about that. It's time to think about acquiring some gravitas – puckish youth can't be protracted. The full-length mirror at the end of his bed reveals his fine health and hair but also forces him to look at his face. He wishes he liked his face better: it always disappoints him. Regular features. Thick brown hair, shorter than it was: long hair's so unfashionable these days. Sensitive yet powerful mouth, that's the line. Strong chin. Tanya likes the chin. The problem is the eyes, which are brown (a dull colour) and set too close together. When he was a child he overheard his mother say to his father, 'He's good-looking, our boy, it's a pity his eyes are so close together.' To which his father replied that excessive good looks never helped a man. Well, they probably didn't in Bradford in the 1970s, but they certainly do in modern London. Always the romantic, she was – typically, she chose his name, not at all the sort of name his dad liked, said it would give the boy a lot of trouble at school, and he was quite right, of course, though at King's it fitted in nicely.

Not good-looking enough, really. He wishes he were ... Well, he wishes he were better at everything. He wishes success weren't such hard work, and often so disappointing once achieved. There are so many things he wishes ... 'Stop being discontented, Auberon,' he says to himself.

He pulls his exercise mat from under the bed and unrolls it. Tanya finds his exercise sessions infuriating. He runs a little on the spot. Then he stops. He finds the idea of all this morning training boring and unattractive. He's supposed (according to his brutal and highly expensive personal trainer) to do two sets of thirty press-ups and sixty stomach crunches and fifty repetitions with the dumb bells every morning. He really doesn't want to, today. He decides that since this will be such a testing day he ought to give himself an easy start. He smiles a little at his own lack of resolution.

It's seven thirty. Time to be getting on. He goes into his bathroom and closes the door.

HAY HILL, LONDON W1,
SEVEN A.M.

S ir Lewis and Lady Burslem are asleep, and the world's
quieter for it. Their flat on Hay Hill is large for a London
flat, but it's not their home. Home is a rambling house in
Suffolk, which they bought twenty years ago when they were
first beginning to be seriously rich, and which they've handsomely remodelled and redecorated. Hay Hill is just a *pied-à-*
terre, they like to say, a *pied-à-terre* with a dining room and
drawing room, a library (for him) and a little study (for her).
They still share a bedroom and a bed, after thirty-five years of
marriage. He has a dressing room and they each have a
bathroom, very distinct in character. They discussed the designs
together with a specialist, who proposed for him an ebony and
silver room, and for her a softly lit lilac and gold boudoir,
which she loves to show her women friends after dinner. There
is a spare room where nobody is encouraged to stay since
staying with the Burslems happens at Herring Green.

The bedroom faces on to a light well, faced in white
ceramic tiles. The interior decoration compensates for the lack
of natural light. The walls are pale yellow, dragged a few years
ago in a way their daughter (who works for a laddish magazine)
tells them is completely out of date. 'Terribly Colefax and
Fowler, Mum,' she says, 'we're all going minimalist these days,'
but Lady Burslem likes it. The Regency-style curtains are so

ample that closing them is a labour. They are made of glazed chintz ('Not really an 1830s material,' said Mirabel Thuillier, the rather marvellous head of Historic Interiors who has done so much work for them and has become a friend, 'but we'll allow it'), its faintly menacing pink roses crowding together on a gold and cream background. The chintz gleams stiffly and nobody ever dares touch it.

In the *lit à la polonaise*, also by Historic Interiors, the owners of this comely apartment are lying. Sir Lewis is sleeping efficiently, on his side, an arm flung towards his wife. Above the sheets only a thick silver head can be seen. He wears dark blue silk pyjamas with white piping round the collar. Even in sleep, it is clear that he is a man of determination, accustomed to command. The bulk under the sheets suggests a firm, compact body, rather less than six feet long. On his bedside table are an adjustable light for reading (he refuses to use Historic Interiors' clever obelisk lamp), steel-rimmed glasses, and a recent academic study of the career of Benito Mussolini. He reads at least a chapter every night: however late it may be, this is a man of intellectual curiosity and self-control, who has little time to waste on sleep.

Elizabeth Burslem does not read the books her husband likes. Before they were married she did a course at Lucie Clayton and worked as a secretary while going to parties every night, but it was a brief period of her life since they married very young. On her bedside table (plain Regency mahogany, like her husband's) lie *Vogue*, *Country Life* and the most recent set of official instructions for magistrates. She wears a coffee-coloured silk nightdress with lace around the neck, Italian and expensive-looking. She lies more or less on her back in sound sleep with only an occasional twitching, and snores faintly now and again. Lady Burslem's face is soft and pink when she is asleep; it is a face that has been expensively looked after for many years: although not always rich, she has always been aware of the importance of appearance. Her curling hair invites a stroking hand; her lips are parted in a little smile. She faces her husband, secure in her marriage, her wealth, her surroundings. She comes from a much better family than he does, as she sometimes reminds herself when he is trying her patience, but she cannot complain about the material and mental comforts he has brought her.

Each morning when he wakes Sir Lewis's eyes encounter a landscape painting on the wall opposite his bed. Just now it's his favourite possession, partly because it's his most recent acquisition. It suggests a yearning for the simplicity of Nature. He must be fond of the countryside, owning twelve and a half thousand acres of it in England and a further two thousand in Portugal. The picture shows a country river between pale green and grey banks lined with willows. A prominent gold label announces that the painting is by Renoir. The other pictures in the room are more modest: a little Degas pastel, a sketch by Toulouse-Lautrec, a Seago depiction of a boat on a breezy sea, a presentation drawing by John Ward (commissioned by one of his boards) showing Sir Lewis sitting at an official-looking table. The Renoir is the prize, but only the prize in this room: it does not compare so favourably with the much bigger, more important paintings in the drawing room.

Sir Lewis is a passionate collector. He's been buying art ever since, at twenty-four when he had very little money, he bought three works at Agnew's annual watercolour sale from the allowance his father gave him. Those watercolours are now consigned to a minor spare room in the country, but even the dubious Copley Fielding has been kept, out of sentiment. His houses bulge with paintings and he's recently acquired a villa in

Portugal – primarily, his wife says, for pictures. At the private views he ceaselessly attends, gliding in his chauffeur-driven car to two or three chattering picture-rooms in an evening, he is one of the rare guests more interested in art than gossip or champagne. Every morning in the car, he spends a moment or two arranging the day's new invitation cards, by date and priority of interest, and talking to Denzil Marten, the art dealer in St James's who has given him so much advice over the years. And just occasionally he likes to sell – especially if he can make a big big profit. It gives him a thrill.

Eighteen months ago this sleeping knight was disappointed to be offered the chairmanship, not of the National Gallery (as he'd hoped) but of the Museum of English History (as it then was). He'd have liked to shape the art-acquisition policy of a great national collection. But he told himself that the museum was much admired, received £8 million grant-in-aid from government, had a large staff and a celebrated young Director, and included a fine collection of English paintings and sculpture. He finds its affairs more interesting than he'd expected. It's disappointing not to be more closely involved in choosing exhibitions and acquisitions, and he finds the Director headstrong and full of his own ideas. But at least ELEGANCE was Sir Lewis's own proposal, and for once was enthusiastically received by Auberon. The exhibition's allowed him to contribute to the museum as he's eager to do, through creative ideas, sponsorship, loans from his collection. It's his exhibition, he likes to think, and will show the world that he's not only a man who takes but one who gives. And, of course, he has another major concept, which is very much his own. Today's the day not only to gain formal approval from the board of trustees but to announce his new scheme to the world. He's confident the world will be impressed.

Altogether, today will be a great day for the museum and its chairman, who will be revealed as a leader of London's artistic and academic life. He's never before shown anything from his collection in public, except as a discreet loan from 'Private Collection'. Now, triumphantly, he is lending eight works, each identified in the catalogue as the property of 'Sir Lewis Burslem CBE'. He loves them all: the startlingly fresh Paul Sandby watercolours, the Samuel Scott view of the Thames, the Joseph Wright of Derby depiction of a forge, the portrait of a chambermaid by Ramsay. But one work will be a sensation: his spectacular Gainsborough of *Lady St John as Puck*, the picture he acquired from the excellent Denzil Marten ten years ago and which hasn't been publicly exhibited since 1910. It's going to give so much pleasure when it travels to Japan after the exhibition here, and not just pleasure, either . . . marvellous how pictures can work for one. He's confident that the painting and the exhibition will impress not just the artistic classes but, much more importantly, the royal personage who's attending tonight's dinner. Sir Lewis would not at all object to becoming a peer. In fact, he has been working on the possibility quite hard.

Denzil Marten and Ronnie Smiles, the restorer who works on all his pictures, were very keen that the Gainsborough should not go to the museum until the last possible moment, which was last night — apparently Ronnie had some last-minute work to do on it in the studio, but nothing serious, he said. Longing to see it in situ, *should transform the exhibition . . .*

As the light filters through a crack in the curtains, his head shakes a little, his shoulders move, his forehead contracts, his eyes open. He's fully awake at once, as active and energetic in the morning as in the evening. It's a brilliant day, the sky suffused already with sunshine, a true Midsummer's Day. He surveys his Renoir and for once does not remind himself how much it cost. Today will be busy: he will hardly leave the museum; it will be a day crammed with achievement. Many people will want to congratulate him — and it will be such a pleasure for him, to offer congratulations where they are owed, to one person in particular . . .

And there's his other project, announced today. 'The Nowness of Now . . .' he murmurs proudly, and his chest expands.

Gently he presses his wife's shoulders, as he's done on so many mornings in the past thirty-five years, and murmurs, 'Elizabeth.' She opens her eyes and at once says, 'Darling, it's the big day, isn't it?' as with her left hand she switches on the kettle for their early-morning tea.

TRADESCANT ROAD, SOUTH LAMBETH, SEVEN A.M.

Jane Vaughan is at her desk. She is wearing a dark blue woollen dressing-gown, once her father's, over her striped pyjamas. The dressing-gown has cording round the hem and might have belonged to an old-fashioned schoolboy. In the days of Hamish she wore silk in bed, but since he left for Vancouver she's reverted to the nightclothes of her youth.

Not getting dressed when she wakes up is part of her morning ritual: two early hours in her study before breakfast, dressing and bicycling to BRIT (God, how she hates that idiotic name), where she's Chief Curator and Curator of Art. These two hours are disturbed by nothing: even the cat has to wait for breakfast. Every morning, she slips out of her single bed and goes into the study where her papers and books lie where she left them the night before. Her books remind her that she has a place in the world. They are trusty friends, even on days when waking is bleak.

This morning being this morning, she can't concentrate, as she usually does, on the book she's writing (this is her sixth). In spite of the delicious smiling morning outside, anxieties crowd upon her. What she can do (being perennially anxious about appearing ill-informed) is to study the catalogue for ELEGANCE, to arm herself fully against questions. It is an enormous catalogue, so large it can hardly be held, so heavy it begs to be put down.

Never before has the museum enjoyed so splendid a publication, she reflects once again with raised eyebrows: none of her many exhibitions over twenty years at the museum attracted such opulence. Even her masterpiece, *The Court of George III*, which brought more visitors to the museum than any previous show, was accompanied by the mildest publication, every page communicating through its cheap paper and unimaginative design its ultra-economical production by Her Majesty's Stationery Office. The ELEGANCE catalogue, on the other hand, published by an international university press, has 624 pages, full-colour illustrations, sixteen essays by international scholars, the thickest possible paper. At the front unrolls a symphonically modulated series of acknowledgements, the grades of gratitude indicated by size of typeface, elaboration of cartouche, degree of effusiveness. Page after page lists, in turn, the honorary committee for the exhibition (ninety-two names, none of whom have made the faintest contribution), the executive committee, the trustees, the catalogue contributors, the lenders (headed by Her Majesty the Queen and arranged – the Chairman insisted – by social precedence), the sponsors, the Magna Carta Circle (contributions of £1,000 a year plus), the Merrie England Circle (contributions of £500–1,000, in smaller print) and museum staff (in smaller print still, meant to show how large the staff is, and to compensate for inadequate salaries). Every word has been read by the chairman. Nobody could accuse him of indolence. Naturally, he has never exercised censorship, though at one point he did suggest omitting the information that the wealth of a particular noble family, which has lent generously to the exhibition (and with whom he shoots), derived from slavery. Nobody opposed his suggestion. With his own

27

pictures he has, as the man best acquainted with them, helped the curators to write their entries. He was particularly helpful over the Gainsborough, his prize, which normally hangs in a specially created gallery in his country house.

This enormous catalogue is one of the few objects on Jane's immaculate desk. Civil-Service tradition has taught her to keep a tidy desk, but she allows herself a few keepsakes. The pink marble egg was given to her by Hamish, many years ago, and though she's lost Hamish she has his egg. She bought the Roman glass jug more recently in Sicily, travelling with her friend Rosalind. The Elizabethan silver and ivory pomander is the most expensive ornament she's ever acquired: it reassures her of the moral benefits of occasional luxury. From her window she can survey the neat terraced houses of Tradescant Road, now increasingly expensive and done-up, not at all as they were when she moved in twenty-five years before.

She drinks her tea and rejoices that she does not have to leave her comfortable room for ninety minutes. Reading the catalogue isn't too stimulating since she's read all the entries often and wrote many of them herself, but she enjoys the printed pages. This isn't just her exhibition: it was assembled by a committee of staff and outside experts. The curator in charge of administration was Helen Lawless, one of Jane's assistant curators, a young scholar who's recently emerged from an obstinately avant-garde university on the south coast. Helen is anxious to make a mark and, with this exhibition, is likely to succeed. Jane finds her calculating and pushy, more interested in promotion (as though she were working in a business corporation) than in scholarship or the museum. Being a generous woman, she's tried to dismiss these thoughts, but recently overheard some of her young colleagues expressing themselves energetically on the subject.

Jane is proud that the museum can show such splendid objects, even though in places the exhibition – designed by an imperious interior decorator called Mirabel Thuillier, a friend and *protégée* of the Chairman – looks like a Bond Street furniture dealer's. Rather tiresomely, Mirabel tried to exclude objects from the exhibition because they did not suit her designs, and to include other things (mostly from her stock as an art dealer) because she thought they would look pretty – but Jane (who can be formidable when necessary) squashed her. But over the decoration the Chairman's taste, as interpreted by Mirabel, triumphed. The Chairman's taste runs towards the gilded and in the exhibition gilding rules. She's not sure she likes the Gainsborough portrait, which Sir Lewis has persuaded the Director (who, frankly, knows very little about pictures) to treat as the centrepiece of the display. In fact she's only seen it once, and then only for a few minutes in Sir Lewis's country house, before she was forced to go and have lunch. It's very impressive but there's something about it she finds unsatisfactory. Anyway, the thing's illustrated on the catalogue cover, the posters, the leaflets and the private-view invitations.

'We need good branding, Jane,' young Ben in Press (why are all the men in the museum under thirty called Ben?) explained to her patiently. 'We must use the same image on all the publicity material – and what better than this?'

'We don't want to be branded for life,' she replied, but he never saw the point.

Why doesn't she like the picture? She looks at the full-page illustration of *Lady St John as Puck* again, and at the four pages of enthusiastic exegesis written by Helen. The present catalogue entry differs totally from the first version, in which Helen analysed the painting as an expression of the social and intellectual subjugation of upper-class woman by a male-dominated social order, with the young woman obliged by a structure of power mechanisms to abandon her individual identity in androgynous role-play. Now, she extols its artistic merits as one of Gainsborough's finest achievements, in a remarkable state of preservation (as the attached condition report establishes). Helen, although at first uneasy with the idea of direct contact with a man of wealth, was apparently converted by a succession of one-to-one discussions with the Chairman in his office. Champagne routed Foucault, as her colleagues observed acerbically. Helen seems never to have glimpsed a work of art while at university and was obviously easily persuaded. But what is it about the painting that makes Jane uneasy?

The history seems straightforward. The provenance couldn't be more direct: 'Commissioned by Sir Paul St John, first baronet, 1772; by descent to Sir William St John, sixth baronet; the Marten Gallery, 1989; Sir Lewis Burslem.' A model provenance, only one real change of ownership in more than two centuries. The full-length portrait shows the twenty-four-year-old Lady St John in 1775, shortly after Gainsborough's move from Bath to London. She is seen in a whimsical pose, one arm leaning against a tree, the other beckoning the spectator. The expression on her highly individual, rather pointed features is enticing yet ambiguous: while not exactly beautiful she is highly charged sexually. She wears a shimmering dark costume, half rustic bodice and skirt, half doublet, evidently the costume of Puck from *A Midsummer Night's Dream*. She stands in a forested landscape in the evening light. Around her head fly tiny glow worms – or are they fairies? – and in the distance, among the trees, flickers an almost indistinguishable group of figures possibly engaged in festive activities. Fairies serving Bottom, according to the catalogue. In the bottom left-hand corner of the painting appears, for no very clear reason, a greyhound, rather an individual and English sort of a greyhound. It gazes lovingly at its mistress.

The thought of dogs makes Jane look out of the window to see if her neighbours are out walking their pets and, indeed, that crabby man from over the road is on his way home. She longs for a dog herself, sometimes, but it's hardly sensible to have a dog, which will spend the day shut up in her flat. In retirement, maybe ... She tries not to feel anxious about the day ahead. Is anyone going to like the exhibition? Will they like the Gainsborough, on which so much emphasis is being placed? There are still questions about it. Despite its size and splendour, the picture wasn't exhibited at the Royal Academy (which the artist often found unsympathetic). But why was it apparently never shown elsewhere, at Gainsborough's showroom in Schomberg House or any of the other venues he favoured? It is not mentioned in the artist's correspondence and none of his account books survive. On completion, the picture was presumably transferred from the artist's studio to Bytham Hall, the St Johns' Suffolk house. It was never publicly exhibited until 1885, when the catalogue of the Grosvenor Gallery exhibition of Thomas Gainsborough listed it as 'No. 396, *Lady St John impersonating Puck*, 91 × 58 (inches), St John'. It was fully (not to say fulsomely) described for the first time in *Thomas Gainsborough, The Artist and the Man*, published in 1898 by Mrs Rupert Fountaine. Mrs Fountaine, one of several writers on the artist at this period, apparently studied the painting closely. Her text remarks that 'little is known about the sitter, who was aged 24 at the time of the portrait', but she includes a photograph taken by Messrs Braun, the only early reproduction Jane has seen.

New information has come to light regarding Lady St John. Her husband's family still live in Suffolk, although their old house was destroyed by fire in 1916 and many of their possessions burnt. The present baronet inhabits a farmhouse near by. Jane has not met Sir William St John, but gathers from Helen (who disapproves of him) that he is an idle individual who devotes his time to traditional upper-class pursuits, such as selling off inherited possessions to save himself the trouble of working. The family archives are in the Henry Huntington Library in Pasadena and there Helen found out a little more. A discreetly worded letter from one St John cousin to another written shortly after the picture was executed states that Lady St John has retired from society and moved permanently to Suffolk. A more direct letter was sent by the lady's husband to his steward in the country. Among various instructions over improvements to the family house, it proclaims, in capital letters, 'HER LADYSHIP WILL NEED NO CARRIAGE IN THE COUNTRY – SHE WILL NOT BE GOING ABOUT.' Subsequently nothing was heard of her and she died in childbirth in 1778. There is a mention of her in one of Horace Walpole's letters: he remarks, 'The young Lady St John who lately made so fine an impression in the costume of Puck at the Duchess of Manchester's ball has it seems lost all taste for society and has removed to Suffolk to become a rustic vegetable – it is a pity, since such a fine woman will be quite wasted on country society. Why she has gone, nobody knows.' Nobody knows even now, according to the catalogue entry. The family letter hints that her conjugal behaviour wasn't as dutiful as her much older husband, married for the first time, might have wished.

Jane is still not sure what worries her about the painting. She spends a good deal of time worrying, notably when she's thinking about retirement in two years. She is middling in height and size, not remarkable-looking but not forgotten by the observant. She wears her hair up and when she lets it down – at Christmas or parties – her luxuriant red tresses still amaze her friends. When she laughs her face is transformed from the faintly severe look of her official person into the air of gentle eagerness she must have worn all those years ago, bicycling to lectures at Cambridge. Nowadays she laughs less than she used to, but amusement still bursts forth.

Unlike her desk, her study is untidy. Bookshelves stretch from floor to ceiling, with more books stuffed in wherever there is space. Volumes are piled on the floor or coil across it, as it were organically. Her little Thomas Jones oil sketch of an Italian rooftop is the only picture still visible, now that the books have taken over like a paper fungus. It is her treasure, a present from her father, president of St Magnus College, Oxford, when she took a congratulatory first in Modern History. The carpet is a rich Turkey rug; the walls, where they can be glimpsed behind the books, are painted in French grey. There is an armchair but she never sits in it.

Though Jane (who has been working extremely hard in the past few weeks) is now rather hungry, her rules, which she observes strictly, knowing they avert gloom, forbid her to eat until eight thirty. But why are her thoughts wandering?

She gasps. She's realised something. She gasps a second time, and looks again at the reproduction of Lady St John. Running to her bookshelves, she finds a large handsomely bound book with 'MRS. H. FOUNTAINE – THOMAS GAINSBOROUGH – G. BELL AND SONS' on the spine, pulls it from the shelves with an eagerness it can't have aroused for years, and locates an illustration. She places the book beside the catalogue illustration and stares at them both through her magnifying glass. She sees what she'd never noticed before. Her hands tremble.

'So what does this mean? What does this explain? Or what does it muddle?' she asks herself, staring out at the early-morning sunlight in Tradescant Road. It's going to be a hot day – how on earth will she be spending it?

BRIT,
SEVEN THIRTY A.M.

Today Diana Stanley is wearing her hair short and layered, in a style she's recently adopted, with a long shiny fawn raincoat, which was fashionable last year but still does for early mornings, and high black leather boots, which she dons when she needs to grasp her head of department's attention. She likes to arrive at the museum early on the day of an opening, before anyone else, to make a final check on any exhibition that's about to open. As Deputy Head of Exhibitions, she runs the department, in her own opinion. She sometimes thinks that without her the museum would cease to function. Just under six feet tall and thirty-two years old, with a proud, regular face, straight ash-blond hair to her shoulders, blessedly attractive eyes, and legs that make men tremble, she sometimes adopts an air of haughtiness, her face raised towards the sky, her mouth slightly pursed, a faint tension in her lips. She doesn't want to appear haughty, being a woman of the left, convinced that wholesale change is essential for the development of European society. But she's not too austere in the present circumstances to compromise with the demands of the world, although sometimes she feels she compromises much too much. Although she disapproves of her family background, the expensive public school she left at fifteen, her parents' manor house in Lincolnshire, the connections her early life brought her, she still finds them useful. Nobody would suppose Diana was a victim of social exclusion.

She signs in at the staff entrance and smiles briefly at the security man. What *is* his name? She really ought to remember it. He has a stocky appeal she doesn't altogether discount, she likes the way his thighs fill his trousers, and there's an appealing coltishness to the face . . . She always gives men's physique a quick assessment, even when she knows them well. At university, when the look was very direct, it became known as a 'Diana burner'. The staff entrance is heavily dingy – the dinginess is so unnecessary, she reflects, as she does every morning, but asserts the museum's character as a workplace. Its muddled brownness enhances her radiant, forceful figure as she strides towards Exhibition Suite One. She takes from her wallet the palmtop she uses everywhere (and which the Exhibitions Department identifies as her personal attribute). It is contained in an artist-designed aluminium and silver case commissioned for her in Zurich by a former Swiss admirer. Fortunately, it never reminds her of him.

On occasion at the museum exhibitions are ready several days in advance. This happened in 1976, and again in 1994, when the display contained six objects, all from the museum's collection. That was the only time Diana experienced such punctuality. It's her ambition to make her department as efficient as her beautiful computer. But first, she must get rid of its head.

The museum's exhibition programme has been created by Lucian Bankes over the past ten years. She frowns automatically as she thinks of him. Thinking about him is something she does not only at work but when she's away from the museum, maddeningly but irresistibly. The tall willowy body, the baby face, still handsome (people say, though she's certainly never seen its charm) at thirty-eight, the shock of blond hair (the colour surely enhanced?), the silly first name, all these features of his obsess her, but in a wholly negative way. When she was on holiday last year in Greece, his face would intervene ludicrously between her and a temple front. Most annoying is his inefficiency, his failure to understand that never planning ahead and issuing last-minute contradictory instructions and bullying are intolerable. It is always she who has to soothe chaos, calm insulted lenders, comfort staff he's shouted at.

Maddeningly, it's his ability – oh, hell, the banner to the left of the exhibition entrance isn't quite straight – that's made the exhibition programme so crucial to the museum. He is a historian by training, and his ideas for historical exhibitions have been consistently successful. *Royal Pets* and *Egypt and England* and *The Court of George III* brought crowds from all over the country. The museum's become famous for a style of display that is glamorous and entertaining and at the same time serious. In the past, exhibition titles had to include key words such as 'Treasures', 'Royal' or 'Masterpieces', but this expansive style has been supplanted by single keynote words. *Luxury* was a great success and so was *Garden*, while *Slum* attracted hundreds of thousands. *He has this flair*, she thinks, gripping her palmtop tightly, *even though he's essentially idle and bad-tempered and messed up things with his wife, who was an extremely nice woman, he has this maddening flair for clever ideas and publicity . . . I'm sure I could be equally inventive if only I had the time. If I could manoeuvre him into making a fatal mistake . . . or show he'd been dishonest, or had knowingly exhibited a stolen work . . . or if I could subtly persuade him to mount an exhibition of staggering indecency . . . I could handle the results . . . I could produce an authentic series of my own memos warning against Lucian's proposals . . . I'd be the only person to appoint in his place, and I'd bring in a new style of exhibition, questioning, radical, socially aware, if necessarily subversive but at*

*the same time highly intellectual . . . blast this English intellectual complacency
and lack of adventure out of the water . . .*

She hears a sharp footstep behind her. *Who's this with such a
purposeful step? Whoever it is seems to be catching me up, I don't appreciate
that. Should I be less worried about competition . . .? Turn, get the smile ready,
may want to say hello. Ha! No need to smile and certainly no motivation, it's
Helen Lawless from Art. Don't care for her one bit. Why don't I like her? Do
I dislike too many people? Is this a personality defect? No, on the staff it's only
Lucian and this one I can't take, this efficient, insinuating little number
(actually she's rather tall), hardly a year out of school, consciously clever
clothes, used to claim to be a woman of the left but no sign of that now,
always ingratiating herself with the Director and the trustees, particularly the
Chairman whose special friend she is . . .*

Seeing her turn, Helen tosses her a brisk 'Hello.'

Diana indicates Helen's existence with a nod. 'You look
busy,' she says, and indeed Helen does look busy, carrying three
meticulous files under one arm and a large parcel tied up in
pink ribbon under the other. Diana is struck by the parcel.
'Somebody's birthday?' she asks.

'No,' says Helen coolly. 'I don't do birthdays. It's files and a
leatherbound copy of the catalogue for Mr Kobayashi. He's
arriving today. They like nice parcels in Japan, you know — you
must have had an e-mail from me about making gifts to
Japanese persons, I sent it to all senior staff.'

This is a sensitive point, as Helen well knows. Mr Kobayashi
is the chairman of the company taking ELEGANCE to Japan when
it closes in London. For the organisation of this transfer, Diana,
who would normally have been in charge, has been replaced by
Helen on the special instructions of Lucian (instructed by the
Director who himself seems to have received instructions from
someone above him). She resents such irregularity. Worse, Helen
has been making visits to Japan (often with the chairman of the

trustees and Lucian) and has returned with a lot of irritating chatter about Tokyo restaurants and design, dress and literature. 'Japan,' she has taken to saying, 'really is the coming country . . . we must open ourselves fully to Japan . . .' Some of her colleagues feel Japan would be the ideal place for her to find a new life, rather soon.

'How nice,' says Diana. 'I hope he likes the exhibition.'

'He will, he'll love it. He already thinks it's going to be a wow in Japan. And he loves the catalogue. Thinks it's one of the best he's ever seen.'

'I'm so pleased,' says Diana. It crosses her mind that she must have been rather like this herself when she joined the museum, ten years ago.

'We'll meet,' says Helen, with a curt nod, as though she hopes this will not happen for quite a while, and turns off towards her office.

Diana surveys the exhibition galleries through narrowed eyes. I've not seen them after all for five and a half hours, she thinks wryly. She doesn't like ELEGANCE. The concept's out of date, irrelevant, rich people's baubles. Who on earth's interested in the eighteenth century today – or, at any rate, this view of it? All those piles of gold and silver snuffboxes (in front of mirrors, simulated candles on either side), and gold- and silver-laced court dress, and the swords with their extravagantly decorative handles, and the Canalettos and Reynoldses, and the views of Vauxhall Gardens – irrelevant, completely irrelevant. The only things she likes are the craftsmanship elements, the trade cards and workmen's tools in the re-created Georgian workshop (beautiful work by the museum's technicians), the lace-making and dress-making, the displays of medical equipment and philosophical tomes. And she's proud of her own idea, the video re-creation of the streets of London, the camera travelling through the wealthy squares, the City, the weaving quarters of Spitalfields, the slums – it's fabulous.

And she hates, she really hates *Lady St John*, even though she hardly had time to look at it when it arrived so late last night. Huge self-congratulatory picture, shining in bright new varnish, lady simpering inanely in her theatrical tights as she prances in a glade. She doesn't like the implicit attitude, woman as eroticised semi-human fiction. 'The movement of the body,' its admirers say, 'is so exciting, her outstretched hands are so vivid – what a work of imagination.' Absurd – although it does look startling on the main axis of the third room, against a black background, surrounded by enamel and glass trees, under a subtly stronger light than anything else. Anyway, who were the St Johns, no particular family, London trade one generation back, weren't they?

And she also dislikes the Chairman's ridiculous idea of wheeling the picture into the Great Hall for the dinner.

There are still six object labels missing. There's endless wrangling about these labels. The final versions were only completed the day before following a furious meeting between Melissa in Education ('The labels must all be fully understandable by partially sighted ten-year-olds, it's in the museum's charter') and Helen Lawless ('How the hell do I develop a complex argument in fifty simple words?'). There are other problems. One or two objects have no light on them. The sight lines to the Beau Nash portrait need to be rectified. The miniature from St Petersburg still hasn't arrived but is due at ten.

The display team has left one other mistake. The portraits of a husband and wife have been hung facing away from rather than towards each other, at different heights, and slightly crooked. This is deliberate. On his down-to-earth brass-tacks early-morning visit the Chairman will be steered towards these paintings so that he can point out the error. This will stop him making trouble elsewhere, and put him in a good mood for the day.

Otherwise everything's OK. It's been so marvellous working with my new exhibitions assistant, Hermia Bianchini. What a charming girl she is — can you call her a girl at twenty-five? She is girl-like, so slender, so graceful, with all the loveliest qualities of Italian girlhood. And then she's so enthusiastic, thoughtful, she always knows I'm overstretched and how to calm tiredness away. Close the palm notebook. Pull yourself together, draw in that beautiful stomach. The day ahead won't be fun. But at least my clothes are planned, well, sort of planned, but are they going to be OK and what about my hair and the jewels? Can I really carry them off, am I compromising my principles, should I really be wearing jewels?

She throws her mane of blond hair behind her head and sits for a moment on one of the Robert Adam chairs with her feet up on the matching fauteuil. *It's a relief to flout the regulations occasionally, when no one's looking, all those regulations, and the conservators fussing endlessly about the tiniest detail. Oh, God, will Jonathan enjoy himself? Will I enjoy Jonathan? Will he want me to go back to his flat afterwards, or try to come back to me? Quite a nice body, it's true, not a bad face either, though hardly interesting, but he's so bland, lacking in any real tenderness or understanding, superficial. It's so overrated, sex, once you get down to it. Do I need this kind of attachment, not much more than a fashion accessory? Nicer to spend the evening with somebody really understanding, non-competitive, like . . . like . . . Hermia, for example. If only Hermia was . . . well, a man, really . . . though . . .*

Diana completes her notes for the installation team, who will meet her in half an hour for a final briefing, and sets off to her office. This is located several hundred yards away, since the offices are scattered all over the building. She'll be the person the installation team meet, she thinks with irritated satisfaction — no chance of their seeing Lucian. He'll merely storm in later and order a few things to be shifted, though she may be able to dissuade him. She's found that if she can introduce into a discussion with Lucian the name of a foreign theorist or historian he's heard of but never read, he may retract. Today she has some spicy quotations from Habermas and Derrida in reserve.

What he hates is appearing intellectually deficient, his pig-headed ignorance exposed to the world. There was a glorious moment recently before the *Richard II* exhibition. Lucian insisted on moving the king's portrait from one end of the exhibition to the other. Diana said nothing, anticipating the return of the visiting curator, a choleric German-American scholar. She wasn't disappointed. Dr Weiss shouted in a furious unEnglish way that made Diana tingle with pleasure. Although he tried mumbling about a joint decision, Lucian couldn't deny his responsibility. His mouth puckered as he explained that they (as he put it) had been assessing the visual effect – 'This is not a textbook,' he'd said. Dr Weiss was not pacified. 'Ah, if it is your decision, venerated Mr Head of Exhibitions,' he said, in horridly dulcet tones, 'we must respect it. Your visual sense is infinitely more important than the findings of the Centre for Medieval Studies at Princeton, which has just established the identity of this pair of royal portraits, executed in 1384. Husband and wife are here brought together for the first time since 1399. Now you have separated them! Of course, if Richard II looks charming in his new location then forget historical problems. Please also remove my name from the catalogue and all publicity...' Diana often returns to this moment.

She rounds the corner of the Gallery of Empire. This has recently been reinstalled, no longer as a celebration of empire but as a denunciation of colonial oppression. The world maps covered in pink splodges, the uniforms and relics of Clive of India and Gordon of Khartoum, the portraits of colonial governors and letters from early inhabitants of Australia, the photographs of royal persons cutting ribbons and non-royal persons tapping trees went. In came a ten-foot-high and six-foot-broad sculpture (commissioned by the Projects Department) of a noble black man being buffeted by a nasty small white man in safari kit with a Union Jack on the seat of his shorts; photographs of people working in unpleasant conditions in convict colonies; whips and shackles, illustrating colonial oppression; graphs demonstrating Britain's exploitation of trade with the colonies. As Diana extracts from her briefcase her swipe card, she hears an intensifying sound, of squeaking shoes and rustling clothes and banging bags and finally a shriek of 'Diana! Diana, darling! Save my life! My swipe card is in my office – do let me in or I'll be lost.'

Diana smiles. These sounds emanate from Mary Anne Bowles, Head of Press and Public Relations. Her office is staffed almost entirely by beautiful youths with languishing eyes. As she says, with a Director who needs a publicity department of his own, God bless him, one must have a nice boy or two around to keep one going. Diana once asked Mary Anne whether she minded which schools the young men had attended. Mary Anne looked guilty and admitted she had gone through an Etonian phase but now doesn't really mind as long as they have nice manners and look alarmed when she's cross.

'Diana, you've saved my life,' she says. 'How can I have done anything so idiotic?'

'You do it about three times a week, it must come naturally,' Diana replies.

'Why can't I be wonderfully efficient like you, darling?' cries Mary Anne, who was on the stage in her youth. 'And what a

day! Beastly press conference. Lots of people coming, thank
God, though I wish they weren't so difficult about each having
an individual tour, it's such a job finding the right person to
take them round. Do you know that new man from the *Observer*,
by the way, said he'd do a big piece?'

'Yes, I've met him.' Diana has met everyone.

'What's he like?'

'Nice. Clever. Polite. Gay, I imagine.'

'Oh, good. D'you think he likes hard or soft centres? Shall I
try Luke on him? Or Ben? Or will he want to see Helen? Not
everyone takes to her. Or Jane – though she hates talking to
anyone except the Journal of *Mid-eighteenth Century Studies*?'

'Who's speaking at the press conference, by the way?' Diana
asks.

'Auberon, then the Chairman, so at least we don't need a
sponsor slot.' And, partly to herself, she remarks, 'I suppose he
may want to joke about being both sponsor and Chairman –
I'll have to caution him. You know, darling, I'm a little worried.
Oh, Luke, there you are,' she says, to the shyly dazzling young
man emerging from an office. 'Who wants me from Radio
Three? Oh, *Culture Vultures* – can't you deal with them? Oh, all
right, I won't be a moment. Diana, one or two of the big critics
who've already been seem to find the exhibition irritating. They
don't like the title, they don't like it being eighteenth century,
they don't like the poshness, above all they don't like Sir Lewis
being the sponsor and a major lender as well as Chairman. I've
had one or two nasty questions from the *Guardian*, and even the
others are a bit sceptical. I don't expect the *Guardian* to like it,
they couldn't bring themselves to on principle, but if *The Times*
and the *Telegraph* go the same way . . .'

'Any publicity . . .' says Diana.

'Of course, darling. But not "this is a posh exhibition for

posh people" publicity. And certainly not "this is a self-promotion by the Chairman of a public institution" publicity. I don't know — I just have a hunch . . .'

As they reach the door of her office she says, 'See you in a min, darling,' before hurrying through a door labelled 'Accounts Office'. Though she and her team moved into these rooms six months before, the Works Department has not found time to relabel the doors.

THE ATTENDANTS' MESS ROOM,
EIGHT A.M.

B RIT has just over a hundred attendants. Until recently they were recruited almost exclusively from the armed services. They wear outfits based on police uniform, with dark blue trousers or skirts, and white shirts, black ties and caps with shiny peaks. All but the most recent recruits have been trained to regard security as their prime duty. In the days when admission to the museum was free, tramps who wandered in looking for a warm corner were made highly unwelcome by these custodians of the public good. They would stand beside the intruders, follow them if they strayed, and gaze at them in oppressive disapproval, which soon sent them in search of a public library. The ranks that applied in the museum – warder, senior warder, assistant chief warder, chief warder and head of Security – were rigidly observed, each rank enjoying its own mess room.

Auberon doesn't believe in hierarchy. On arriving at the museum he suggested to the Head of Security that the warders should call him by his first name. He was conscious of the effect of names on the relationships within an organisation, and thought this would be friendlier, more appropriate for a modern museum than the old hierarchical system. This pro-posal met with such contempt (barely concealed) that he didn't pursue it. But he's still keen to change the system. 'I'd like the

warders,' he said to John Winterbotham in early days, 'to be
known by a less institutional name, less reminiscent of a prison,
something warm and welcoming. Maybe "helpers" or "visitor
assistants". What d'you think, John?' he would ask. John did
not voice an opinion, but his expression was vocal enough.
Ignoring him, 'Don't you think,' Auberon went on, 'we should
be in search of a caring environment, where the visitor assistants act as guides to our public? Let's have friendly staff who'll
make "guests" (isn't that a better name than "public"?) really feel
at home. We should drop the uniform, it's military, it's outdated
– shouldn't our staff wear coloured shirts, jeans even, or just
their own clothes? What d'you think?'

'Very interesting, Director,' John would reply.

John doesn't know that the management team has drawn up
a restructuring plan. In five years the ex-services types will have
been phased out in favour of 'befrienders', people half their
age, wearing post-modern red, white and blue outfits and
baseball caps quasi-ironically decorated with reversed-out
images of the Union Jack, and keen to interact excitingly with
'consumers'. The befrienders will share roles with the rest of
the museum staff, act as guides, assess objects brought in for
opinion, welcome the public, do conservation cleaning.
Auberon and the rest of the management team don't envisage
cleaning the galleries themselves – unless a member of the press
is present. Politically, it's perfect: out with authority, in with
sharing. The curators have not been told about these plans yet;
somehow, it seems easier to delay that moment. They may not
be thrilled at the idea of acting as guards.

John's staff are less orderly than he realises, and certainly
than he'd like. He rarely enters the junior warders' mess room. It
is an unattractive place, since an unadorned environment is
thought suitable. The room is situated in the basement, and the

dirty frosted-glass windows below the ceiling admit minimum light and maximum fumes. The neon strip-lights make the occupants look as though they're suffering from a hideous disease. The furniture is transitional. Until the female warders arrived it consisted of mouldy armchairs with missing arms, strange stains on the fabric and in one case only three legs, apparently on release from an institution for defective furniture. The women warders demanded change. Not easy. Providing new furniture for attendant staff, they were told by the perennially unhelpful officers in Admin, fell between budgets – not display, not office equipment, not health and safety. The senior warders resisted because they wanted the junior warders' room to be less comfortable than their own.

This is not a room to linger in. The most comfortable part is the corner for making tea and coffee. Here another drama's been enacted. Until a few years ago, the noticeboard above the sink was adorned with invitations to take redundancy, health-and-safety warnings, startling girlie calendars, a yellowing photograph of a buxom lovely under the headline 'Knock 'em flat, Nigella!' and in due season a picture of the England football team. These have been edged out, apart from the football team. Instead, postcards of the most appealing objects in the museum have fluttered on to the board. A recent shot of the Director (known to the attendants as 'Sunbeam') is always on view. (There's an almost constant supply in the press, since he is very fond of photo opportunities.) In today's photograph the director smiles expansively at a party of schoolchildren who have visited his office as part of the museum's accessibility campaign. A speech bubble ('You're simply revolting, tinies') has been added. The Director will not mind: he has never entered this room.

At eight o'clock the day staff come on duty. Their first job is to clean the public rooms. Most of them hurry to leave coats and bags in their lockers. Only one lingers. He is about twenty-five, tall, slightly undernourished-looking and fair. He looks tense but excited. He holds a carrier-bag with a picture of a flower on the outside. Whenever someone comes into the room he looks up in expectation and blinks when it is not the person he is waiting for.

'Morning, Bill,' they say to him. 'You all right, Bill?' And one or two say, 'Waiting for someone, are you, Bill?' He does not answer, only smiles perfunctorily. When he has looked up and been disappointed thirty or forty times, the door opens and a woman comes in. She is his age, and has startling red hair and pale skin. When she sees him she raises her eyebrows a little and says, 'Hello, Bill — you waiting for someone, then?'

He says, 'Happy birthday, Anna. This is for you,' and he holds out the bag.

She smiles but tucks the smile under control. 'Thank you, Bill,' she says.

He looks at her like a spaniel waiting to be patted but she proceeds briskly towards the locker room. 'Aren't you going to open it?' he says.

In spite of herself, his tone makes her stop. 'All right,' she says. 'What is it?'

'Have a look,' he tells her, rather squeakily.

She puts the bag on the table and opens it. Inside is a parcel, wrapped in thick crackling white paper with a green ribbon round it. *Green's my favourite colour, and this dark green's my favourite shade. Does he know that, somehow? Did I ever tell him?* She unties the ribbon with some care while he offers her a pair of scissors, staring at her meanwhile. *I wish he wouldn't stare; is someone going to come in and find me doing this and jump to conclusions? What can it be? Beautiful paper, good taste — take the paper off carefully, it's pretty nice*

49

too, what on earth . . .? Artist's materials . . . a great box of them. Mm — very high quality, not exactly what I need just now but . . . thoughtful, how sweet of him, he must be serious about me, can't imagine why, I must tell him more about what I actually do as an artist, God, what must they have cost? And he doesn't have any money to spare, giving so much to that awful old mother.

She looks up and his air of anxious expectation is so touching that she puts her arms round his neck and gives him the warmest kiss she has ever given him during their extended complicated friendship. At this point Ros, Neil and Charlie hurry into the room and stop short. Bill blushes deeply and makes to pull away but she finishes the kiss properly as though the others were not there and then turns to them and says, in a friendly sort of way, 'It's my birthday.'

'Happy birthday,' they chorus, and Charlie says, 'Can we all give you a birthday kiss then?' and she says, 'Only if you give me a present first,' and waves the box of artist's materials at them, and then they hurry to leave their things since they're all late, and bustle out of the room. Bill leaves last and before he goes, being a romantic soul and so violently in love he can hardly bear to spend a minute out of Anna's presence, does a little dance in the middle of the floor. 'She liked them,' he says to himself, 'she really liked them. I was right, choosing those artist's materials. Oh,' he allows himself to ruminate, 'I'd do anything . . . Oh, how I love her, how I dote on her . . .'

AT THE MUSEUM,
NINE FIFTEEN A.M.

Fond of routines, Jane has another for beginning her day at the museum. Invariably, when she arrives in her office, she returns to the places where she likes them the wastepaper basket and the tray of biros, which the early-morning cleaners have invariably moved to the positions they favour. She opens the window. She waters the plants. She strikes off another day on the calendar and suffers a pang at the thought of how few remain to her at this beloved museum. She puts on the kettle. She sits at her desk. She opens her mail. She looks as rapidly as possible at the pile of internal memoranda from and about the forty curators who are responsible to her both in her own department and throughout the museum. They have a striking gift for complaining and indeed for being unhappy, which recently has often been justified since their role within the museum has been steadily undermined by the trustees. She puts on the floor (and sometimes straight into the wastepaper basket) the museum management team updates, which supply three inches or so of paper a day. She discards her e-mails.

This morning Jane does none of these things. Instead, she hurls her briefcase on to the floor, wrenches open a filing cabinet labelled 'ELEGANCE' and extracts a bulky file. It tells her almost nothing. On the loan form for *Lady St John* the section headed 'Conservation' notes only, 'Conservation records held by owner. Painting checked on arrival at museum by Mr R. Smiles, picture conservation adviser to owner. Apparently good condition.'

Is it too early to ring Conservation? The head of the department is certainly an ally, if an unpredictable one. This is Friedrich von Schwitzenberg, formerly employed as a picture conservator in Munich and then at the National Gallery in London. Auberon persuaded him to leave the National Gallery a year or two before with the lure of a high salary and a handsome new studio. Jane finds him exciting and excitable, although she knows the National Gallery was not sorry when he left. He wears his grey hair protruding in many directions, and his clothes are unpredictable, ranging from a dapper 1950s Austrian look to something resembling an up-to-date tramp's outfit. (The latter is sported on formal occasions, to irritate the director and trustees.) He clearly enjoys spending the large sums allocated to him by the Director, who wants the best conservation department in the country (a highly prestigious thing to have at the moment).

'Schwitzenberg!' he says, by way of greeting.

'Friedrich, it's Jane.'

'Good morning, Jane. I hope it will be a good morning – one of the great days in the history of civilisation, no?' He chuckles.

'I have a question for you, rather an urgent question. The Gainsborough – have you seen it yet?'

'The *Lady St John* – I examined it last night, *ja*, but only very briefly.'

'It's pronounced "Sinjern", Friedrich, you know that.'

'Oh, so stupid, the English, with all these silly names. Anyway, however it is pronounced, I examined it.'

'But thoroughly? Did you write a report on it?'

'But look, Jane, how could I, last night? Of course I would have wanted to, this interesting picture ... but this man Mr Ronnie Smiles hardly let me look at it, he just assured me everything of Sir Lewis's was in perfect condition and almost pushed me out of the way. He said he had written the condition report, no?' He paused. 'Why do you ask?'

'What do you think of it?'

'Oh, it is a masterpiece. Of course it is a masterpiece. It belongs to Sir Lewis Burslem and it is the *Hauptwerk* of this exhibition. *Ergo*, it must be a masterpiece.'

'But what do you think of it yourself? What is your frank impression?'

'Well, Jane, well ...'

'No, not "well, Jane, well". This is important. What did you think of it?'

'What is so urgent? Why are you so agitated?'

'Please!' she said. 'Please! What is your impression of the picture? I must know.'

'Well, Jane, I have looked at many pictures by this artist and I have to say that even after this very rapid inspection I am a little puzzled with this one, I don't know why, *es ist ein bisschen* ... There is something strange about the surface – I can't understand what ...'

'Did you look at it under ultra-violet or infra-red?'

'No, I was not allowed to. Of course it would be interesting, that to do, since Gainsborough so often changed his compositions, did he not, moved arms, made again hairstyles? But little Mr Ronnie was quite angry when I suggested I might examine it. Strict instructions of the owner, he said ... all nonsense ... But one does not argue with the chairman's adviser, does one, even though he is a silly man who works entirely for the trade, polishing up nasty pictures so they look shiny and expensive? One does not argue with him because the chairman – God alone knows why – listens to everything he says.'

'Suppose we did it now – looked at it under ultra-violet light, and under magnification? Could we do that?'

'My dear Jane, the exhibition opens in a few hours. The place is filled with people, the crew, the press will be here. And there is this strict prohibition . . .'

'I know all that,' she says. 'I wouldn't make the suggestion if I weren't really serious. There's something odd about this picture. Forget the owner's instructions, we need the truth. Friedrich, meet me in Exhibition Gallery C, with your ultra-violet lamp, in exactly ten minutes. I should be able to have the room cleared briefly. I want you to examine *Lady St John* from top to toe, but rapidly. You can do it, can't you?'

'Jane, I have always admired you, you are so serious, but you're usually so English and reserved. I have never known you passionate like this . . .'

'Ten minutes, OK? And speak to nobody about this. Nobody.'

She ponders for a while. She needs help from somebody in the Exhibition Department. Somebody senior. The Exhibition Department – separate from her own curatorial division – is in charge of the exhibition space and Jane cannot do anything there without their permission. Who should she speak to? Lucian? She's not at all sure that Lucian would be helpful: from her observation he's become very friendly with Sir Lewis. One of the juniors? No, none has the authority she needs. It has to be Diana Stanley. She calls her.

'Diana – it's Jane.'

Diana sounds faintly surprised. The two of them are not particularly friendly though they've worked efficiently together on many occasions. 'Yes?' she says. 'We're rather busy – is it a quick call?'

'Diana, I need your help. It's an odd thing I'm asking but it's important. There's a problem over the *Lady St John*. I've asked Friedrich to make a close investigation of the painting on site in ten minutes. I need room C cleared of people, for around fifteen minutes. Can you please arrange it?'

'No, Jane, I can't, not possibly.'

'You can – you must, really you must. This is not a favour, it's a necessity. I'll explain why when we meet. You must be there, too, yourself. Is that settled?'

'But, Jane, no, the place is full of people . . .'

'I am asking you for this particular favour. It's in the interests of the museum, I promise you. We only have eight minutes now. Friedrich and I will be there, nobody else. See you then.'

'I can't do it. You have to explain why.'

Jane plays her trump card. 'Potentially it's a source of great embarrassment to the museum. I want to make sure the person who's embarrassed is not you but Lucian.' She despises herself for playing on Diana's well-known loathing for her head of department, but knows she has to.

'Lucian? How will he be embarrassed?'

'I'll explain. Nine o'clock, then, just for fifteen minutes?'

Diana, who is not used to being dictated to, says, to her own surprise, 'Very well.'

At nine o'clock Friedrich von Schwitzenberg enters the exhibition galleries, carrying his ultra-violet lamp in a long black case. The galleries are filled with people making final adjustments, like an orchestra tuning up. At the end of the second room the double door is guarded by a nervous-looking, tall young man.

'Good morning, Mr Schwitzenberg,' says the young man. 'You're expected. Would you like to go in? I understand nobody else is to be allowed into this room.' He gulps, since he knows this inspection is irregular. In Friedrich goes. He finds Jane, determined-looking and tense, and Diana, impatiently inquisitive.

'Look,' says Jane, and she shows them a photocopy. 'This is the reproduction of the painting from a book published in 1898. Do you see what I mean?'

'No,' says Diana.

'Oh, but yes,' says Friedrich after a moment. 'The dog – its tail – the tail is different. I never saw that.'

'The dog's tail is different?' asks Diana. 'How's it different? Oh, I see . . . You mean – he's got his tail down in the old view, and up in the actual picture. How odd. But, really, is it worth all this fuss?'

'And the dog's eye,' says Jane excitedly. 'Do you see the dog's eye in the painting? Here in the photocopy it is quite normal – but in the painting, the stupid animal seems to be winking.'

'Well, it's only a tiny wink. But it's true, there is a sort of a wink,' says Friedrich.

'How much has it been restored, Friedrich? That's my question,' asks Jane urgently. 'Please, please, will you examine it under your lamp? Can we have the lights out, Diana?'

'I don't think this will tell us much,' complains Friedrich, 'but if you are determined . . .'

Diana gives a rapid command on her mobile and the room becomes dark. Friedrich has extracted a long black tube from its case. He presses a switch and it emits a low mauve light. He puts the tube beside the painting, moving it slowly up and down the surface. It reveals nothing, only the smooth surface of the paint; there are no marks of any restoration.

'Nothing to be seen at all, someone must have applied UV-opaque varnish to the paint surface. This doesn't get us anywhere,' remarks Friedrich.

'Suppose we look at it under your magnification headloop?' asks Jane. 'Diana, will you get them to put on the lights?' As the lights come on again, Friedrich puts over his head a metal band with a magnifying glass attached to it. They edge as close as they can to the painting and peer at it, trying to interpret what they're seeing. He peers at the picture and grunts before handing the band to Jane.

'No sign of anything,' she says, in disappointment. 'It seems to be in perfect condition.'

'Or perfectly restored,' remarks Friedrich crossly. 'The only thing I find surprising when you look closely at this canvas is that the surface is so clean, so smooth, no signs of *pentimenti* here at all — surely Gainsborough was often changing his mind, no?'

'Quick, please be quick,' says Diana, 'we have so little time, we will have to reopen the galleries in only a few moments.'

'It is a very smooth surface,' Jane concurs, 'but there's nothing to worry about on the evidence of this. I don't see where we are, any more than I did before. It just seems odd that the picture is so very perfect, doesn't it?'

Meanwhile Friedrich has been examining the canvas. 'It's very thick, this canvas,' he remarks, 'as though . . . and very tense, like it has been relined more than once . . . There's something about the canvas I don't like but what it is, I really do not know . . .' But as he is speculating the door of the gallery is abruptly thrown open and an alien presence enters their little world.

'What's going on?' shouts a voice. 'What the hell is going on?' A man moves violently towards them and then stops, glaring at them. It is John Winterbotham, Head of Security, in his best uniform, and looking as formidable as an ex-regimental sergeant major in the Welsh Guards can look. In spite of their maturity and seniority, Diana, Jane and Friedrich are assailed by primitive emotions: fear of men, fear of the enemy, fear of authority, and guilt at being caught out like naughty children . . . When he sees who is in the room, Winterbotham hesitates but stays furious.

'Mr Schwitzenberg, Dr Vaughan, Miss Stanley – for God's sake, what are you doing? It's against every rule in the book, extinguishing the lights in a gallery, closing the doors, ejecting the security staff – and when the room is filled with valuable loaned objects, it's unbelievable! We could lose our government indemnity. And tell me why you're looking at that picture – at that picture of all pictures. As you know I have the strictest instructions from Sir Lewis Burslem, no less, from Sir Lewis Burslem himself, that no one can inspect or touch the painting without an OK from him or Mr Smiles.'

'There was a worry about the condition of the painting, I felt I had to inspect it,' says Friedrich lamely. The others shuffle around, horribly embarrassed.

'It was a necessary check,' says Diana, but does not manage to sound convincing.

'Why did you have to turn out the lights and throw everybody out? Why didn't you alert Mr Smiles? Thank God I was in the control room and could respond at once – with luck we won't have to put this in the day book, which means we won't have questions from the indemnity people but . . . The risk! You can explain yourselves to the director and for all I know to the chairman.'

This is not an inviting prospect.

'In the meantime,' continues Mr Winterbotham, drawing

himself up to attention, 'I shall have to position a security guard on permanent supervisory duty next to the picture at any time when there are members of the public in the building – or members of staff who don't understand their responsibilities. That should stop any more . . . any more silliness. And now I must speak to the Director.'

As the three look at one another uneasily, Jane takes the lead. 'If you're going to the Director,' she says, 'I'll come with you. It was my idea to examine the picture, not theirs.'

'As you wish,' John Winterbotham answers.

'I'll see you in a moment,' Jane says to the others. They look at her dumbly and a little reproachfully – it was, after all, at her insistence that they found themselves in this situation. Diana in particular looks resentful – she dislikes being put into this awkward situation. And until now none of them had realised their actions in the building were so strictly monitored. The realisation makes them shudder, rather.

AROUND LONDON,
NINE THIRTY A.M.

Lucian loves driving. It gives him, he realises, a thrill that is almost as good as sex and much more reliable. If possible, he likes to drive fast, his little red convertible thrusting through the traffic before surging up to 80 m.p.h. as he enters an empty road. He even loves doing it in London, especially now that cars in the city arouse such disapproval. It tickles him to drink heavily at dinner and remark to his hosts on leaving that he'll enjoy driving home fast: their reactions are so absurdly confused, their shock repressed by social rules in a way that makes him squirm with amusement. He keeps the hood down in almost any weather and never tires of sitting at the wheel on city streets sporting his goggles and his 1920s motoring hat. The outfit makes him remarkable to the gawking many, and easily recognisable to readers of Sunday magazines, since a goggles photograph is almost always selected for the articles about him in newspapers. He likes best a spread that appeared recently in one of the Sunday magazines and showed him in his neat Armani suit and his favourite green cravat, beside another of him wearing driving clothes. He doesn't care about the clothes but he does like the attention. 'Yin and yang,' he will say agreeably to visitors, 'sun and moon, male and female – rather good, isn't it?' And he waves his hand at the framed photograph on his office wall.

Even today he's not hurrying to work. He started the day as usual — long shower, two almond croissants with apricot jam and four cups of coffee (the Japanese breakfasts he tried for a while after he began to visit Japan became rather depressing on winter mornings, and finding the right tofu was hell). He consumed all this (is he eating too much? he wonders — he thinks something like a paunch is developing, must keep an eye on this unwelcome addition) at the sitting-room window overlooking the communal gardens, before doing the news and arts pages and spending twenty minutes at the piano. His cleaning lady always arrives before he leaves. Since Fanny left him (what a stupid name, he always told her Fanny was a stupid name, period but dicey), he has relied on successive Portuguese ladies to look after his domestic affairs. Such a nuisance, having to look after the house — at least Fanny was effective that way. Big day, yes — everything under control, yes. His team have been trained (by him, of course), although they still need his guidance. Louisa, Joanna, Suzette, each helps the machine run smoothly. 'Teamwork, teamwork,' he'll say, lying on the leather and steel *chaise longue* in his office and gesturing towards the people scurrying about outside, 'that's the secret of a good office.' He's very impressed by their most recent recruit, Hermia, a delightful girl, half Italian, half English, educated at Milan University (which gives her an exotically cosmopolitan quality unlike all those worthy girls in the office from Nottingham University — at least he loves making jokes about Nottingham though he has no idea of where they were actually educated). This Hermia seems to be acting both as his special assistant and, in some curious way he doesn't quite understand, Diana's.

Well, yes, Diana, of course, Diana. He frowns. *A fine woman, many good qualities, hard-working, sensible, conscientious. But, try as she may, she's not brilliant — something's missing. A good second-class brain, that's Diana. No vision, excitement, creativity, the qualities I can claim. Her political ideas, with which she used to keep boring us, were bog-standard New Labour — at least she seems to have calmed down on that one. Efficient to the point of obsessiveness. She believes the position of each object in an exhibition can be planned in advance — whereas I know works of art speak to one another and look different in a new setting beside an unfamiliar neighbour. Just like people in that way — you must seek out the best in them, the unexpected, no point trying to categorise them.*

Diana should be running a laboratory. She adores timetables and spreadsheets and budgets. Of course we have a good working relationship, I have to ensure that. She finds me inspiring, but I wish she were easier, less masculine in a way. And she has so many annoying habits — why must she make a point of being so polite to visitors to the office, whoever they are? There just isn't time to fit in everyone one meets . . . At least she keeps things running smoothly when I'm away, and lately it's true I've been travelling an enormous amount. So tiring, going to Japan every two months — though the Japanese visits have been very interesting lately . . . And he smiles at the thought of his last Tokyo trip.

Lucian swings his car round Hyde Park Corner, pushing his way through a traffic light that has just turned red and waving towards the traffic advancing on him from Piccadilly. ELEGANCE *should be a success. It's full of new display devices inspired by me. The video (again my idea), which takes the visitor through eighteenth-century London, has already been praised in the* London Sentinel, *and the design is brilliant, although I had to spend a lot of time guiding the designers. The Hampton enamel trees look especially glittering although it was disappointing that the conservators wouldn't allow laser beams pointed at them.*

Forced to halt beside Victoria Station, he snorts and considers the morning's press conference. *They still haven't shown me the chairman's speech, my office is disgracefully inefficient sometimes. When will be the moment for my usual brief but essential remarks? And can I be* sure the evening's speeches will mention the members of the department who are doing well, and leave out the lazy ones? And there are all those other things bothering me, though I don't understand why they're allowed to. Why aren't I sheltered from trivial problems? There's my overdraft, for example, so silly and difficult of the bank to refuse to extend it again . . . They just must, it's no good them saying I must realise some assets . . . So tiresome. Of course I'll have lots of money very soon — though paying off Fanny is a bit tricky. I can't leave the London flat, I simply can't, it's all my life in that place. Will Tuscany have to go? Monstrously unfair, particularly when I've made it so beautiful and the garden's just maturing — the framing of the view's sublime.

More red lights in Vauxhall Bridge Road, it's like some sort of game. Auberon's flat is off to the right here. Do I have Auberon worked out? Not really, even now I don't understand him, I don't think he understands himself, he can't make out what he wants in life or at the museum. He's attractive in a way, at least that's how he presents himself, always looking for press attention. He likes to be thought progressive but is oddly inhibited, all sorts of old-fashioned ideas about academic standards . . . It's hard to get him to understand that museums have changed completely nowadays . . .

It's so unfair after all these years of work to have to retrench, and my salary's so meagre, considering what I do. Well, at least I can earn a little from outside. The overdraft will have to wait till tomorrow, or the day after, and then the Cologne cash should come in, and my Hockneys will surely be shifted soon . . . At least the present scheme looks set to work, think we can assume the picture will meet with approval from the buyer, and that'll help a lot . . . Even better if Auberon gets the Bloomsbury Museum, and moves on — Sir Lewis hasn't exactly promised the position but he's made noises . . . eighty thousand a year, and all those possibilities . . . It'll be fun getting one or two people to move on elsewhere, and promoting others, like that little Hermia who could become the director's special assistant, and even — delicious idea — transferring Diana to an access and outreach job in east London, without option . . . She'd certainly resign . . .

The river is grey-green and sparkling as he drives across

Vauxhall Bridge Road and turns left along the Embankment. *In the sunlight — it's going to be boiling today — the office blocks on the South Bank look like a row of Florentine palazzi. I like the South Bank, I think my revival of BRIT has transformed the area south of Waterloo, they're even starting to call it SOWAT. Used to be a dump but it's a centre of cultural life now, a rich slice of London, and the Underground station, too, now called 'British History', that's a bit of a triumph, mosaics of great events from our history, selected to reflect landmarks in women's history, racial oppression and class division. When I remember the moribund place I came to . . . and the moribund director I worked with. His only virtue was that he let me do as I pleased . . .*

Into the car park just before ten. *Hardly any space left, lucky I have my own place. It's important to keep regular hours. This car park, of course, is the site of Nowness. What a great project, it'll transform the museum, allow endless exciting exhibitions, make the place more like an exhibitions hall and less of a site for displaying old jam jars and tattered flags — God, how I hate the permanent displays, can't wait to dismantle them and sack the curators. At least some of them went last year, allowed us to hire some more essential staff in Exhibitions and PR . . . Pity Auberon is a historian, with old-style values . . . Lewis has the right ideas, progress, modernity, newness — and Nowness is the best of them. Of course, a lot of the staff will complain when they hear what's intended. Most of them know nothing at the moment — I was lucky to have such a long talk with Lewis in Japan, very useful it was. I think I persuaded him of my full-fledged support, made him realise how useful I could be as a midwife for the great plan . . .*

I think Auberon and I are the only staff members who call him Lewis . . .

With his eager shuffle, legs slightly curved like a crab's, head and torso projecting forward, Lucian proceeds through the staff entrance. He extends his hand into the security booth for his keys without looking at the man on duty. They all know him here. This morning, though, there's a delay, which interrupts his train of thought. The man behind the desk says, 'Excuse me, sir? What name is it?'

Turning indignantly, Lucian sees a mild-looking unknown. The name 'Bankes' does not produce the usual immediate deference and at least two minutes are wasted while his name is found on the list. 'I'm a busy man, you know,' he says, abstractedly rather than angrily, but he has to be concerned over inefficient bureaucracy.

To which the security man answers, also calmly, 'My orders are to check everybody. I'm new here, sir, and I can't admit anyone without ID.'

'Yes, yes,' says Lucian, and moves on, impatiently clutching his keys.

The exhibition office is housed in rooms originally intended for the library. The first room contains the bulk of the exhibition staff, twelve of them: the catalogue editors, the registrars, the exhibition assistants, the accounts officer. Some have worked for the museum for years and are used to him. Then there are several young enthusiasts who work long hours for little money in the hope of promotion one day. Lucian is amused that some of the nervous ones disappear when he's around (which is not so very often). They sit using the most advanced technology at mahogany desks inherited from the library and now in disrepair. The room is lit by hanging neon tubes, their fixings brutally inserted into the plaster garlands and roses of the neo-William and Mary ceiling. The walls are lined with dark walnut panelling, hardly visible behind the tottering bookshelves, laden with bulging box files from which old faxes and papers seep, with brightly coloured date planners charting exhibition plans for the coming five years, notice-boards labelled URGENT with yellow stickers flapping in the breeze as though waving at passers-by, press cuttings from recent exhibitions and assorted amusing photographs above the desk of Suzette, the fanatically hard-working editorial assistant, the gleaming espresso machine, which is in almost continuous use. Each desk offers a little narrative about its occupant: the steely tidiness of Louisa's work surface, the elegant table occupied by Hermia with its pile of crisp white paper, its sharpened pencils and miniature glass vase containing a single rose, or the cascade of books, page proofs, travel mementoes littering the desk of Suzette. Around this space, sometimes silently absorbed but usually frantic on the telephone ('The Vienna van is stuck at Dover' or 'It's Manchester — they're being difficult about conservation again') or running about emitting brisk instructions to one another, circulates the flock of slender, black-clad workers. As Lucian enters the room they turn simultaneously towards him as though in warm loyalty — this is expected of them. He's late by anybody else's standards but lateness does not apply to Lucian — as he likes to say, the moment he joins a meeting is the moment the meeting begins.

Lucian stands at the door, as though garnering recognition and applause. Then he says, 'Everybody in my office in five minutes.' The babble becomes more concentrated as his staff switch telephones on to voicemail, gather notebooks, subtly adjust themselves to be seen in public. Lucian advances across the room, finding time to smile at the delightful dark-eyed Hermia, who looks up at him — admiringly, he thinks — as he walks past her. Passing Diana's room, he sees her door is open (it usually is, indicating that she is constantly available to her colleagues). Diana is sitting firmly at her desk, as though she has been there for hours, wearing — but really he must not look at this — a pair of knee-high black leather boots of the most interesting sort. She is eating what seems to be a sandwich — a demotic activity to which she is prone (she eats a good deal, in his view). Diana's sandwiches are intended, he believes, to suggest that whereas he is thoroughly self-indulgent, she is so hard-working and down-to-earth that sandwiches are all she has time or inclination for. This particular sandwich has clearly been planned to coincide with his arrival and indicate how long she's been in the office. Not catching her eye, he raises one hand in what is intended to be a neutral gesture but might conceivably, he realises as he does it, look more like a Hitler salute. 'Good morning, Lucian,' she says, in a correct way that clearly is meant to suggest how constantly courteous she is in contrast to him. 'There are sixteen messages on your desk.' Sixteen messages, are there? How helpful of her, how very helpful, to imply once again that urgent business has been accumulating while he neglects it. He does not know she returned to her desk, rather less composed than usual, only a moment before he came in. The sandwich is to calm her nerves.

'Good morning, Lucian,' says Louisa, his secretary. 'I hope you enjoyed the skating last night.' Lucian loves ice-skating and goes skating often. It keeps him trim, makes him feel the years have not affected him. She knows he likes her to chat first thing, so that soon he can show he is in charge and firing on all cylinders by turning the discussion decisively to business. This is what he does now. 'Any messages?' he asks crisply, as though Diana has not spoken.

'Nothing very significant,' says Louisa. 'The *Daily Telegraph* wants a word with you, they'd like to photograph you in the exhibition. Auberon is anxious to talk to you about the press conference. The Chairman is here and has some queries. In the broader picture there is a slight problem about the Australian exhibition, the sponsor for the Australian leg has fallen through and may be sued by Sydney. The figures for the Georgian Agriculture show have come in — the deficit is larger than expected but still under fifty thousand pounds if you look at it in the right spirit. Oh, and Mr Kobayashi rang from Claridges and would like you to call him as soon as possible. Nothing major.'

'Hmm,' says Lucian, who loves receiving calls and not answering them. He moves into his room. This used to be the librarian's office, and was originally designed to look like a seventeenth-century philosopher's cabinet. Lucian, a dedicated modernist, has painted the room white and hung a few Stefano della Bella etchings on the walls. This morning he closes the door immediately, and it stays shut for several minutes. When he presses the buzzer to tell Louisa to reopen it, he is discovered hunched at his desk, which is covered with small white sheets of paper, smirking with what seems to be satisfaction.

His staff advance into the room. Three of them squeeze on to a sofa intended for two, and two perch on each armchair. Hermia Bianchini, slender, graceful, poised as ever in her crisp linen dress, perches on the floor. Helen Lawless, who is cordially loathed by the whole Exhibition Department, whose existence she scarcely recognises since she considers herself as a curator to be a superior person to mere exhibition administrators, occupies the only comfortable chair other than Lucian's. She looks bored, as though this meeting were a tiresome and irrelevant duty. They all gaze expectantly at Lucian, who is yawning slightly and picking at some flaking skin on his chin. Is he in one of his good moods today, they wonder, or did he have a late night, making him liable to be short-tempered? He'll shortly have to move into his public affability mode but may want to be horrid to them in compensation. Of course, if they can persuade him that ELEGANCE is another stunner entirely due to his efforts, life may be OK. Much departmental energy is expended on Lucian's moods.

When everyone has almost stopped chattering in deference to the leader, Diana enters. She carries a chair from her own office, which she places close to the door as though contemplating flight. In one hand she holds her mobile phone, into which she is speaking softly, in the other her palmtop, ready for use. Her arrival soothes the gathering. Lucian again notices, though he tries not to, her long boots. They stop fidgeting.

'Had a marvellous time at the Hammersmith ice rink last night,' says Lucian.

'How long did you spend on the ice?' asks Suzette. His staff couldn't be less interested in ice-skating but they have learnt which questions to ask. One self-promoter was once spotted studying an ice-skating magazine.

'About two hours,' he says, and offers a satisfied grin around the room. One hand rests lightly on his stomach, indicating the improving effect this exercise has on his body.

'And did you meet anyone interesting?' they want to know.

Since the departure of Fanny two years ago roguish questions of this sort are well received by Lucian (and his staff, who love speculating about his personal life). He does not answer, since he is now ringing his hairdresser for an appointment and a little badinage. His staff wait patiently, half smiling in an accommodating way, while he banters with someone at the other end. Then he puts down the receiver, grips his desk and pushes forward his chin.

'All right,' he says, 'no time to waste, are we all set? Everything OK with the exhibition?'

'We need your input on a few problems,' says Diana. It is her prerogative to speak first. 'Perhaps on site? The technicians are keen to talk to you. They're a little anxious, a few things only you can sort out...' Although she dislikes taking this deferential tone, she knows that the thought of being indispensable makes him feel secure. At busy moments this makes life more tolerable.

'OK, OK,' he replies, 'but I can't be everywhere all the time. Everything all right for the press conference? By the way, I don't have a copy of the Chairman's speech. You must remember, Louisa, to give it to me as soon as it arrives. It's vital I'm informed fully on everything,' and his voice moves towards an annoyed crescendo, 'otherwise I can't do my job. Is that clear?'

There is a slight tremor in the office at his menacing tone but Louisa has developed effective control techniques. 'I'm so sorry, Lucian,' she replies, with a concerned, guilty look. Frequent repetition of his name often soothes him, like an incantation to a peevish deity. 'I thought I'd given it to you. My fault. I'll get you a copy now, Lucian.' She gave him a copy four days ago and a revised one the previous day, but does not mention this.

Lucian enjoys these meetings. He loves to sit at his desk, which is broad and deep and piled with serious-looking papers. He seldom looks at these but they give importance to the room. They are removed from time to time by Louisa and replaced with others. He likes to see his staff crammed in front of him, looking at him expectantly, laughing when he laughs, concerned when he is concerned, submissive when he is angry. Generally he is affable, because he is aware of how well he handles these meetings, but at certain key moments he knows how to be firm.

'We know that Mr Kobayashi from Japco will be here today, and is arriving at the museum for the press conference. Has anyone met him – apart from you, of course, Helen?'

'No,' they say. 'Is he gorgeous?'

'Mr Kobayashi is an extremely important person,' Lucian replies gravely, 'and it's crucial that he likes the exhibition. So please, everybody, extra effort there. Helen is his special escort for the day...' There is some covert sniggering at this and he barks, 'Please!' at which the sniggering subsides, more or less. Helen curls her lip.

'Helen, all the export papers are now in order, I imagine?' asks Lucian.

'Yes,' she says, 'and recorded on the confidential file.'

'We know the file is confidential,' remarks Diana, 'though I don't understand why. But wouldn't it be helpful if a copy was available for myself and Jane? Presumably you'll want us to be involved in at least some of the arrangements?'

Helen yawns, very noticeably.

'Thank you, Diana,' replies Lucian, 'for offering. But as we have already discussed in earlier meetings, this exhibition transfer is being handled by Helen. I am sure she will consult you if necessary and use your services when required, but for the time being the Chairman has insisted that anything to do with his property should remain confidential to the nominated staff.'

'It seems a little unusual,' comments Suzette, who has worked in the office for fifteen years and speaks with more freedom than most. 'As though he had something to hide, almost.'

Lucian frowns heavily. 'Let's go to the gallery,' he says. 'Louisa, ring *The Times* – was it *The Times* that wanted me? – and then find out the Chairman and the Director's movements. Tell them I'm tied up for the next fifteen minutes but could talk to them after that. In fact, I must talk to them.' (This is said emphatically. Lucian has a way of asserting things nobody wants to contradict.) 'Fix something, would you? Oh, and we must get the conference right, a few problems might arise there. Is anyone coming from the Chairman's personal office who we have to worry about? I'd like all of you to come to the exhibition, all of you. We can deal with anything else later. Ready, Diana, are we?' he adds, as though speaking to a deaf lady of advanced years. She merely raises her eyebrows.

Followed by his black-clad flock, with Diana striding slowly at the rear as though to indicate she hardly belongs to this procession, he leads the way out of the office. There is nothing more satisfying to Lucian than stalking through the museum with ten or twelve people in attendance.

THE DIRECTOR'S OFFICE,
TEN A.M.

Auberon is sitting in his office and frowning. The cool detachment that he advocates for himself is not at all in evidence this morning.

Why did the Chairman insist on a trustees' meeting on the day of an exhibition opening and a royal visit? The trustees are all here today but that's hardly a reason for filling up the schedule in this absurd way. How can anyone think about policy today? I think the Chairman's plotting, wants to introduce his new idea to the board just when everyone's too busy to think about it properly. If the trustees aren't concentrating they may nod through the first proposals and find at the next meeting that plans are far advanced and the government's been talked round and large sums have been committed to feasibility studies which it would be a shame to waste et cetera, et cetera.

And today we also have to entertain Mr Kobayashi, who's taking the exhibition to Japan. He's inordinately rich and fairly genial, but not exactly entertaining. Great store's set by Mr Kobayashi, however, and being nice to him is a major priority.

The Nowness of Now. Or the Newness of New, or whatever it's called. A dynamic 'Now Centre' to be built on the large empty car park next to the museum, designed in the most advanced materials by a famous British architect — apparently it doesn't matter who the architect is, as long as they're well known.

Wouldn't life be much easier if I weren't burdened with a Chairman and a board who make the major policy decisions? They listen to my advice but don't necessarily follow it, not at all. The Chairman has much more power than I'd like him to have. In any big museum, the balance between the chairman and director is pretty delicate but Sir Lewis overdoes it.

There'll be problems at Bloomsbury, of course, if I do get it. But at least I won't have to deal with such a self-seeking rascal — I really think that's the word — as Sir Lewis Burslem. His main aim in life is his own aggrandisement — oh, and getting a peerage. Whereas the Bloomsbury trustees are famously old-fashioned and amiable and, what's more, honourable.

Auberon stares gloomily out of his office window at the still empty street and the driveway up to the *porte-cochère*. They're putting up the banners for ELEGANCE at this moment, with a lot of shouting and contradictory instructions. Meanwhile the wooden scaffolds for the banks of flowers, which will be installed this evening, are being set out. This is a rare moment for reflection, stolen from the pile of business that threatens him every morning and which, in theory, is made worse by the time analyses that the Department of Cultural Affairs makes him fill in for each day. He has to give an account of how he has spent each fifteen minutes of his working day, whether on management, finance, staff, sponsorship, social inclusion, advice to regional museums and all the rest of it (there's no box, of course, for research or study of the collections). When he started the job he took this duty seriously but now he fills in the boxes fast and at random — or when he's feeling seriously frivolous he does it according to a code of his own, which is reworked every two weeks. No one ever notices that he's doing the same work on Monday the first as on Tuesday the sixteenth — he's confident that nobody at the department ever touches, let alone reads, the piles of paper this system produces. He's supposed to sign his staff's forms but actually his secretary does this for him with a particularly convincing stamp.

He plays with the Japanese toy on his desk, a set of ivory

beads suspended from a frame. It is one of the few non-British items in the room. This is an office which, as Auberon likes to put it, encapsulates the development of material culture in Britain from the early modern period to the present. Even in his predecessor's plain, anti-aesthetic days, it was a fine room. The Edwardian architects, highly conscious of hierarchy, sited it in the middle of the first floor of the entrance front, next to the board room. When he arrived, Auberon contemplated moving to a more modest space. But soon, realising that guests enjoyed it, and seduced by its noble proportions and the parade of anterooms (offices, really, but they feel like a suite of rooms in a Baroque palace) through which the visitor advances to the director's apartment, he decided to stay. He's filled it with objects from the museum's stores: portraits of famous Britons, eighteenth- and nineteenth-century furniture, a rich Turkey carpet, busts of poets and engineers. Among all this splendour hang two small engravings depicting early seventeenth-century London. These are his own, and at oppressive moments they remind him that he is also a writer and historian, and could return to that role. The three windows light one of the handsomest rooms in the city – the only museum director's office which is a favourite of *World of Interiors*. Nobody can accuse Auberon of lacking style.

But at this moment he is taking no pleasure in being stylish, or in the idea that all day he is going to have to kow-tow to his chairman. Instead he worries about the Nowness of Now. Such a depressing concept, he reflects, his lip rising with an academic's disdain. Absurd name, too. Nowness will be a celebration of Britain today, 'reflecting the volcanic dynamism inherent in the twenty-first century'. This breathy tag sometimes runs through his head as he struggles with leaden directives from his paymasters in government. It comes from the Nowness of Now

consultation document produced by a firm of media consultants at the Chairman's personal expense – another example of
his widely lauded generosity, of course. This document was
presented to Auberon only a few days ago, apparently for his
information. His modestly enthusiastic reaction obviously did
not deceive the Chairman, or bother him.

He knows just what will happen if the thing is built. The
old museum will become a sideline, increasingly neglected,
starved of funds and attention, while every available jot of
money or energy will be pushed into keeping the new attraction
running. Did he enter the museum world to create a pile of
modish plastic or collect designer running shoes?

*Nowness, main item for today's board meeting. Lewis must have a reason
for pushing the project on. He hasn't explained what this reason is – can it be
connected with Mr Kobayashi? Is Lewis's idea for Japan really a good one?
Perhaps it's better for me not to know more about it than I have to. It's really
not my business.*

*Is it my fault that the Chairman and I don't agree? I try to be
fair-minded but still I'm sure it's Sir Lewis who's the difficult one. I hate the
way he meddles over exhibitions, purchases, appointments. I hate the way he
keeps saying the museum's a business and should be run like one. However
often I tell him the museum's essentially not a business because its primary
purpose isn't to make money, he just goes on as though I hadn't spoken. Is the
man stupid, or is this an intimidation technique?*

He fills in his time-allocation forms for the next month
and throws them into the out tray. Thwarting the Chairman
isn't listed as an option.

One stratagem, of course, is to deluge the man with papers,
memoranda, reports of meetings, business plans there's no time
to read, so that if he raises an awkward point, he can be
silenced by a reference to a strategy document he hasn't looked
at. But, of course, Burslem is pretty crafty and tough, can

always strike back, use unexpected ploys, demand detailed difficult information – 'immediately, now, I've no time to waste, the board has no time to waste in order to suit your convenience!' – or produce alarming new schemes. To date, Nowness is much the worst. Trouble is, he can block any initiatives that are important to the museum – though it's an awkward technique since he doesn't want to seem wilful. Engagement with the man requires unceasing vigilance. Auberon sighs. He could, he thinks despondently, profitably devote a lot of his energy and time to his career development or his own intellectual life. Whenever is he going to write that book he's been planning for at least four years on the Anglican Church in early Stuart England?

So which of the trustees will be in favour of Nowness? John Percival, glossy retired politician and deputy chairman, supports the Chairman from loyalty, although he's probably out of sympathy with many of Lewis's ideas. If Percival opposed the idea he could probably sink it, strong links with government, expected to enter the House of Lords. But Nowness will certainly appeal to some. Reynolds Brinkman, for example, Chairman of Finance and General Purposes (a nasty little committee set up by Lewis and packed with his supporters), will certainly be in favour. Brinkman's favourite line to the museum is 'Put your stock on view!' He loves saying that because successful retail outlets display 90 per cent of their stock the museum should do so too, or get rid of it. The idea of modernity and appealing to the market will excite him. Amanda Mann, Channel Four executive, is the trustees' link with the media: she's bound to like it. Aged thirty-eight, she's regarded by fellow board members as excitingly young and in touch. Though Auberon has the advantage over her on both counts, youth and popular culture are apparently felt to be her field. Auberon often sees her at parties, and for some reason feels he has to track the woman's movements: it sometimes makes conversation rather hard to concentrate on. If only she weren't so calculatingly spontaneous. Auberon had a lot of trouble with her when she wanted to rebrand the museum: she was the one who suggested calling it 'BRIT' . . .

And Alan Stewart – how will he vote? Professor of Modern British History at a large red-brick university, he's said to be anxious to move to Oxbridge or Ivy League. Very friendly, likes to ask about the progress of Auberon's writing – sadly there's never very much to tell him, must find more time . . . He might well be in favour of expansion. Then there's the ghastly Mrs Hobson, emeritus trustee who's long passed the sell-by date of seventy but stays on the board because the old bag's given so much cash and might give more. She's awful, so thoughtless, rude, self-indulgent . . . those are her pleasanter qualities. She's been a donor to many institutions and likes to make or destroy, preferably the latter: she once insisted that unless the director of a museum was fired she'd withhold a multi-million donation. Auberon has forced himself to remain on outwardly good terms with Mrs H. even though she sometimes talks as though he weren't in the room, but he's become mildly obsessive about her. He keeps a photograph of her in a drawer at home and in moments of frustration thrust the point of a pair of compasses into it, muttering a private imprecation. 'So much aggression, darling, and such primitive fetishism,' Tanya remarked to him, when she discovered the pockmarked photograph and the compasses beside it, 'd'you think it's healthy?' Mrs Hobson will almost certainly support Nowness, most especially if she thinks the staff are against. 'Give them something to do,' she likes to comment. 'None of the staff here do anything at all.'

Auberon takes a sheet of paper from the silver paper-holder on his desk. It is thick creamy paper headed 'From the desk of the Director', one of his few official extravagances. He loves good paper and this is superior to anyone else's. On his sheet he writes 'FOR' and 'AGAINST'. Under 'FOR' he puts Burslem, Brinkman, Mann, Hobson, Stewart (?). Under 'AGAINST' he writes Percival (?) and hesitates.

They won't all be in favour, surely. Sir Robert Pound, for example. Sir Robert is a former civil servant, impeccable in manners, short on ideas, pinstriped in body and mind. 'Sound,' they say about him, in Pall Mall clubs, 'tremendously sound.' They seem to mean that he has no wish to improve anything except his own position but has risen through punctuality, a frank smile widely deployed, an ability to keep to the rules and remember the prejudices of the powerful, and stick to a stock of moderately liberal but adaptable sentiments. He is famous for 'not rocking the boat'. Sir Robert is cautious about money and may dislike the idea of a new building going up with no revenue assured. 'Against?'

Olivia Doncaster — what will she feel? Nice to think about Viscountess Doncaster. How can anyone be as charming, as well-mannered, thoughtful, intuitively intelligent, puckishly humorous as this delicious aristocrat? Although she's so much more than just an aristocrat. She's quite a new board member, Auberon doesn't know her as well as he'd like to but they've already become friendly, almost intimate . . . Tanya is unenthusiastic about her, remarks in her best *Guardian* manner on the outmoded tradition of appointing people to official positions merely because they're titled, though she's happy enough to accept dinner invitations as Auberon's official partner to their house in Connaught Square. Daughter of an ancient noble house, wife to the heir of one of the oldest marquessates in the country, splendid Jacobean house in Yorkshire and collection of Italian Renaissance paintings, every advantage life offers . . . And she's so *charming* and *beautiful*, and so intelligent, astonishingly glamorous, not yet forty. Very keen on developing the party side of the museum, lots and lots of parties are the thing, she says, galvanise the place, make the museum *the* venue that people are *bursting* to come to for a good time . . . and then they'll be hooked and want to come back and give money and be part of the family and you've got them! Such good ideas, really, so sensible in the modern age, and already she's been madly helpful over the dinner and suggested all sorts of exciting people whom even Lady Burslem couldn't really turn down in favour of her boring friends from the City and the counties . . . *Probably she'll be sympathetic to my views — I do hope so — and anyway her manners are so caressing, her hair so long and blond. Pity I've not really had a chance to explain to her what I think about Nowness . . . God, I've got an erection, though only half-way, well, goodness . . . I'll put 'Doncaster' in the Against column.*

Trevor Christiansen — surely against. Trevor's an old-established artist, very fashionable in the 1960s when he was young and ran around with people in Notting Hill Gate and produced atmospheric paintings that explored the magical world of acid. His style has developed since then and his most recent work, obsessive studies of semi-obscure interiors populated by shadowy figures, has restored him to favour at least with traditional critical opinion. His exhibition in St John's Wood the year before called 'Holocurst' in which he expressed his personal anguish about Nazi persecution (one of the finest pieces was a row of unbaked cakes on a baking tray, each labelled with the name of an actual Berlin Jew), showed his ability to wrestle with the toughest contemporary issues. Unlike most artists he enjoys public affairs, and is in great demand.

Nowness of Now is likely to appal him.

Five to four in favour of Nowness, at best. It looks bad, especially since the tenth trustee, Sir John Blow, who's absent today, is an old business friend of Sir Lewis's and certain to be in favour. Six to four, then. But if they do approve the plans, Auberon can always set up working parties and financial reviews and emphasise the museum's difficulties and plant one or two subtly negative press articles – it might be possible to delay progress till Burslem loses interest. On the other hand, the man's determined and well connected and successful at ingratiating himself with government ... and seems completely set on this project ... And the idea could so easily be presented as a way of opening up the collections to a broad audience, as museums are always being urged to do.

His eye falls on his print of Charles I's London and his thoughts are interrupted. *Do I really want to worry about all this stuff?* he asks himself. *Don't I want a more intellectual life, to explore ideas, not donors? Write books, not business plans?*

His buzzer sounds. No more time for reflection. It's his secretary, Emma. Emma is the model of a museum director's secretary: young, charming, humorous, interested in the arts and in people, patient. He is sorry Tanya doesn't share his enthusiasm for her. On the whole Tanya, it has to be said, is not generous about other women. Emma says, 'The Chairman's driver rang to say ten minutes. And Mr Winterbotham has just arrived and needs to speak to you urgently, and he has Jane Vaughan with him. He says it's extremely important – something seems to have happened.'

'Very well,' says Auberon.

Enter John Winterbotham, red-faced, furious, with Jane, palely obstinate, behind him. 'Unfortunately, Director,' he says, 'I have to report an infringement of security regulations by senior staff . . .' He recounts what has happened.

Auberon, surprised, asks Jane for her version. She will only explain her actions in private. 'Thank you, John,' says Auberon. 'You were quite right to inform me at once. But I think we'll keep this confidential for the moment, shall we? No word to anyone?'

Winterbotham looks put out. 'Not even to the Chairman?'

'If you don't mind, I'll discuss it with the Chairman myself.'

'Very well, sir,' says Winterbotham, and leaves reluctantly with a sour look at Jane, remarking that the episode will be entered in the museum's confidential security dossier.

'I only have three minutes,' says Auberon to Jane. 'What on earth have you been up to?'

'I know it must all seem very odd. But I had to do it. The thing is – there's something strange about the big Gainsborough,' she says. 'We had to check the picture this morning, we just had to. After all, it only arrived last night after ten. Though actually we failed to check it properly.'

'What do you think's strange about it? It looks very large and Gainsborough-like to me. A rich man's picture. Prefer the landscapes, myself.'

'Its condition. Friedrich and I are both sure there's a problem, but unless we can examine the picture properly we can't identify what it is. We need to do it today, before the exhibition opens, to prevent possible embarrassment to the museum from a public exposure—'

'Public exposure of what? I wish you'd explain what you're suspicious of.'

'I don't know what we're suspicious of. That's the problem.'

'It's not very helpful, Jane. You know what the Chairman's said—'

'I do indeed. And now Winterbotham's putting a permanent

guard on the picture. Only you could authorise an inspection.'

'Against the Chairman's wishes? He'd be sure to find out. I don't think that's a very good idea.'

The buzzer sounds again. 'Sir Lewis's car has arrived in the car park,' says Emma, one of whose principal duties is to keep her Director informed of his Chairman's activities, including his rather mercurial business fortunes. 'He's looking round the car park,' she continues, 'and talking to a man I don't know. They're consulting some papers, maybe architectural plans.'

'What sort of man?' asks Auberon.

'A smooth-looking man,' she tells him, 'in a not very nice suit, carrying a couple of briefcases. Ah, they're on their way.'

Auberon frowns again. What now? he wonders. It really is too tedious. He turns to his chief curator, who has adopted a denunciatory pose, her breast heaving slightly. 'Thank you, Jane, we must end this talk,' says Auberon. He thinks for a moment. 'A problem with the Gainsborough, eh? Hmm.' A wintry smile briefly agitates his mouth. 'Have you spoken to anyone else?'

'Only Friedrich and Diana. I'll leave this photocopy with you — look at the dog when you have a moment.'

The buzzer sounds again. 'Sir Lewis is just on his way.'

'Thank you, Jane,' says Auberon. 'But for the moment, hold off, would you? We have quite enough problems as it is.'

In the second or two between Jane's departure and Sir Lewis's arrival, he tries to seize his whirring thoughts. *Problem with the Gainsborough? Bad for Sir Lewis — but bad for me, probably, too — terrible for the museum and the exhibition, if anything comes out — can Sir Lewis know the picture is questioned? Can I risk exposing the picture to cause Lewis embarrassment? No, I can't, too many potential complications, particularly for me — if only he didn't know about the museum publication I offered Tanya . . . I never knew it was a breach but apparently . . . grounds for an investigation . . . Hmmm, play this one carefully, Auberon.* He assumes his winning but determined Director's Smile, and opens the door to greet the Chairman.

THE PREMISES OF ANGEL COOKS,
NINE THIRTY A.M.

Angel Cooks occupy non-angelic premises in Battersea. They've been established there for forty years, first under the leadership of old Mr Burnham and now under his son, Mr Rupert Burnham (known as Mr Rupert by his staff and most of his clients, more from affection than deference). They cater for dinners, lunches, drinks parties for private and public clients, indeed clients of every sort (as long as they're rich), and are favoured by the increasing number of people who like to give parties in museums. Mr Rupert, who has run the business for over twenty years, is widely admired for his imperturbability, his blend of deference and firmness, his attention to detail, his imagination in creating alluring settings, his soldierly bearing, his raven hair and chiselled features. He is, people agree, a paragon among caterers. Only occasionally is his smoothness ruffled. If guests are kept waiting for an hors d'oeuvre or a waiter fails to turn up, he'll shout furiously behind the scenes — though nobody front-of-house would know it.

This morning he is sitting in his office with his senior staff: Leonore, personal assistant, Gustavus, Head Chef, and Fred, Head of Operations and second in command. The office is utilitarian, its breeze-block walls painted cream, its floors linoleum, but among the filing cabinets lurk eighteenth-century English tables and Chinese export porcelain, and the walls are decorated with hand-painted prints of English gardens. These pieces, which belong to Mr Rupert, are occasionally lent to his duller clients to liven up their offices. The staff are discussing tonight's dinner for BRIT. The menu is not one any of them would personally have chosen, since they know that dinner for four hundred prepared in a tiny museum space relies on compromises, however grand the host's ambitions and however deep his purse. Most of the food must be prepared in advance, particularly sauces; the main ingredients should be relatively straightforward; it helps if a course or two is cold. Mr Rupert has had some difficulties with Sir Lewis, who has ignored his advice. This is the first time a member of the Royal Family (with the exception of a C-list princess) has visited the museum for almost thirty years, and Sir Lewis proposes to celebrate splendidly. A passionate royalist, he has looked forward to entertaining the Duke of Clarence for months. He wants this to be the best dinner of the year, the decade, and he thinks it will give the occasion additional prestige if as much of the cooking as possible is done on site. There was never any doubt for him that Angel Cooks would be the caterers; the question was what they would serve.

The menu's changed, Mr Rupert reckons, something like sixty times. Sir Lewis's ideas had to be adapted to the tastes of HRH, who as a matter of protocol was sent three sample menus. HRH has pronounced likes and dislikes, which have been conveyed to the museum in an exquisitely courteous letter from his equerry. He likes shellfish (unlike many royal personages who avoid it), allowing lobster to be chosen for the first course. Beef hung on in there for some weeks (it's a favourite of Sir Lewis's), going through four transformations before disappearing in favour of chicken, which gave way to duck, though only briefly since duck soon lost its lead to beef, which finally streaked past the winning post in the form of an extremely complicated dish which for four hundred people poses a formidable challenge. The seasonal vegetables changed twelve times (everything's always seasonal somewhere, after all). Cheese came in, cheese went out, cheese came back, cheese was replaced by a savoury, six savouries were successively accepted and rejected, cheese returned ('But it must be English, Mr Rupert' – 'Yes, of course, Sir Lewis, we have a remarkable supplier...'). Even the pudding went through numerous transformations, since Sir Lewis and his wife – who's acted as an advisory committee – disagree over puddings. A little extra course at the beginning of dinner flitted in and then was knocked on the head, port rose to the surface, port sank again in favour of dessert wine, the news that HRH liked port rescued it, there was much discussion over dessert wine, chocolates looked steady for a long while but HRH does not care for chocolates so *petits fours* came off the benches... From the relatively straightforward menu that Mr Rupert optimistically proposed in March, almost nothing remains. All that has stayed unchanged are the potatoes and the vegetarian choice, which does not interest Sir Lewis.

'This is the final menu. We all know what it is in principle but I want to familiarise you with the names of dishes Sir Lewis has chosen or rather invented. It's possibly the most ambitious dinner we've ever attempted,' says Mr Rupert to his team. 'Ready? Vintage champagne on arrival – yes, after all he is going for vintage in spite of what I told him about how good the alternatives are. Supporting bar for those who can't manage without whisky, but keep it out of view. Canapés: the floured tortilla, the Japanese pancakes, the mini poppadums, the Parmesan shortbread, the mango and rosemary compote tart-lets, the wild mushroom mousseline. Twelve canapés each.'

'Generous,' says Fred. 'Very generous indeed.'

'This is a generous occasion, Fred, you should know that by now. First course, Lobster House of Stuart.'

'What on earth is that?' asks Fred.

'It's Gustavus's brilliant dish, Fred, with spinach laid between the portions of lobster and lobster pâté piped into the claws. By the way, when are the lobsters being delivered?'

'At six p.m. The Head of Security doesn't at all fancy two hundred live lobsters arriving at his precious museum. He's afraid they might escape and run all over the galleries like an invading army, snapping their claws at anyone who tried to stop them, a bit like *The Birds*, I suppose. Could you have a horror film called *The Lobsters*?'

'Thank you, Gustavus, can we stick to the point? Have you got enough staff to crack the claws and decorate the lobsters, and pipe in the lobster pâté?'

'I've got three extra boys, I think it'll be OK,' says Gustavus. 'Time is a bit tight, of course.' For a moment he looks slightly sick.

'Good,' says Mr Rupert. 'Main course, fillet of beef laid on a platter and layered with *foie gras*. Beef Plantagenet, we're calling it.'

'Why Beef Plantagenet?' asks Fred. 'What a silly name. Anyway, I thought this was an eighteenth-century dinner.'

'It's our job to enter into the spirit of the evening and not make difficulties,' replies Mr Rupert. 'As a tribute to His Royal Highness we're going for a royal theme, dynasties of England you know. Sir Lewis didn't like the idea of Beef Hanover, which I suggested, so it's Plantagenet. New potatoes with *foie gras* and red wine *jus* – baby carrots and sautéd spinach, *panaché* of beans with asparagus and baby turnips. No problems there, I think.'

'Awful lot of vegetables,' says Fred.

'Vegetables are the thing just now, as you know. The cheese course is called Queen Victoria's Cheese Platter. We don't know that she liked cheese but it seemed a good way of bringing her in, and there are one or two things on it she might have eaten. With a June salad, a variety of leaves and baby beetroot to give colour. And by the way, no vinegar, absolutely no vinegar in the dressing, please, Gustavus, you know it fights with the wine. All we need is just a touch of walnut oil, that extraordinary oil I brought back from Tuscany last year.'

'I make a wonderful vinaigrette,' says Gustavus sulkily (soon no one will push him around like this, he thinks, he'll be the one who decides everything and whose rages will make headlines). 'People beg me for the recipe. To hell with the wine . . .'

'I must insist, Gustavus.'

'Very well,' says Gustavus, and does a shadow pout. His full pouts bring fear — and to some people, particularly certain sensitive young men and women, desire.

'And the pudding, no problems there, just a choice of berries and other fruit — Berries Tudor Rose. It should be good — apricots, dewberries, purple grapes, green figs and mulberries. And Hanover Puddings, a.k.a. our individual chocolate sponges.'

'It's an absurd menu, with all these stupid names,' says Gustavus. 'No one's going to have a clue what they're eating.'

'Even less after they've tasted it,' remarks Fred jovially.

'It's not the easiest dinner, but I expect we'll cope. And it is wonderfully expensive,' says Mr Rupert. 'So that's the menu, and I'm happy to say it is *not* going to change.' They all laugh. 'His lordship rang me up last night to propose adding celeriac purée to the vegetarian menu, which he thought he'd not given enough attention to. I said no, it could not be done.'

'The whole thing's horribly problematic,' announces

Gustavus, running his hand carelessly through his sensual mane of brown curls. Gustavus is a recent recruit, a fine chef Mr Rupert rescued from a country-house hotel in Wales. Every time Mr Rupert looks at him he wonders how long he can keep him at Angel and off television. Not only is he handsome but he's unashamedly gay in a 'straight-acting, straight-looking' way (as the personal ads put it), an apparently irresistible combination to a large audience of men and women now that chefs have become symbols of sexuality. 'Particularly synchronising the starter and the main course – they're so fiddly. And, of course, the lobster's a nightmare.'

'We can do it,' says Mr Rupert. 'Just as long as the electricity doesn't fail . . .'

'I can't remember a more elaborate menu since I've worked here,' comments Leonore. 'It makes that Turkish dinner in a Thames barge when the barge started leaking look like a tea party.'

Mr Rupert's eyes glint. 'It's a challenge, Leonore,' he says. 'We like challenges here.'

'Yes, Mr Rupert,' says Fred. 'But we don't like starters or main courses being late because they're too complicated, do we?'

'They won't be late,' he answers. 'They're never late and they particularly won't be late tonight.' But they know their boss, and in his smooth manner detect unease. 'Let's go through the programme, shall we? Leonore?'

Time is not wasted at Angel Cooks. 'Job sheets ready?' says Leonore. 'Staff arrival four p.m. Four hundred and three guests at the last count. Access via the staff entrance, all vehicles parked in staff car park. Security clearance via John Winterbotham at the museum, all staff to be cleared on arrival. They must arrive before five p.m. Personal protection officer to HRH is Ted Hoskins.'

'We know him,' says Fred. 'Friendly but very precise.'

She continues: 'Security advance party will have checked the whole museum before we arrive, will recheck Great Hall seven p.m.. Dinner in Great Hall. Cooking facilities in Gallery of Industrial Revolution, in front of the early steam engine. Reception in entrance hall. Serving tables between the statues of Art and Industry, they're all labelled underneath, supplementary tables in Tudor, next to the Dissolution of the Monasteries showcase as usual . . .'

'Will they have the place ready for us?' asks Gustavus. 'Last time they kept us waiting half an hour while they wrapped up a battleship in cellophane to protect it from the canapés. There was a madwoman there from the Conservation Department who screamed at us for hours. The guests started arriving while we were still unpacking . . .'

'Everything will be ready,' she answers. 'Forty butlers in the entrance hall. Fred on duty in the entrance hall, with me. Rupert on duty in the Great Hall.'

'I hope the canapés come out light,' remarks Fred jocularly. 'Usually Gustavus's canapés are so rich they don't want anything else . . .'

'Our canapé chef knows exactly what he's doing. Each canapé will be a work of art,' says Gustavus, who does not always enjoy Fred's teasing, especially on a big day. 'You people in Operations wouldn't understand that.'

'Now then, boys!' interrupts Leonore. 'HRH arrives at seven thirty and meets a small group in the entrance hall before going to the exhibition. He's not attending the reception. No speeches at reception. Flowers by Perfect Plants, delivering six p.m. Sound engineers are Voicebox, we're giving them dinner, Fred?'

'Yes,' he says. 'Outmess for twelve.'

'Equipment details,' she continues. 'Four ovens, three hot cupboards, four urns, three electric rings, six vats for lobsters, all to be set up in Industrial Revolution. Thirty-two tables for dinner, sixty-five waiting staff. Here's the room plan – the royal table is dead centre, with the speaker's podium under the organ.'

'What about the lighting?' asks Fred.

'Set up before we arrive, the Great Hall is closed to the public all day. It's Brightalite – they need a rehearsal with the tables in place. It's an elaborate scheme, meant to evoke the eighteenth century – pretend candelabra, ambient light on wall displays, simulated candles on the tables. We hope guests will sit down at eight forty-five. Speeches at ten fifteen – Chairman, HRH. Then the pageant, which is meant to last fifteen minutes.'

'That may be optimistic,' says Mr Rupert, 'but go on, Leonore.'

'Guests can stay till midnight. We're meant to be out by two, but since it's the Chairman's bash they can't do much about if it we aren't. Is that all clear?'

'All clear,' says Mr Rupert. 'Gustavus, is everything all right at your end?'

'Apart from the nervous breakdown, yes,' says Gustavus. 'Have you ever had a chef drown himself in his own food?'

'By the way,' says Mr Rupert, ignoring him, 'the new royal tablecloths arrived yesterday, with the rose, thistle, leek and harp pattern on ivory damask. Here they are if you haven't seen them, chaps.' They exclaim over one of the rich thick tablecloths woven in Lyon for the occasion. Mr Rupert likes fine furnishings for his dinners. He has a store bursting with damask and velvet tablecloths in aubergine and ivory and lilac, floral-patterned cottons for summer and pure white for contemporary art events, eight varieties of dinner plates, mountains of wine glasses, sixty or so candelabra, approximately Georgian and Victorian and definitely modern Finnish silver, decanters by the dozen and ice buckets and wooden plinths and lengths of silk and velvet, all the apparatus used to make Mr Rupert's dinners seductive. Tonight's decorations will, of course, be Georgian. Mr Rupert will be lending an important service of Georgian silver from his own collection for the royal table, with replicas on the others. At this moment garlands of myrtle and rosemary adorned with violets and lavender, roses and pansies, and interwoven with silk ribbons, all in what Perfect Plants assert is a perfectly Georgian manner, are being arranged around the walls. A choir is to sing airs from Handel, Arne and Boyce from the musicians' gallery. The waiters and waitresses will be in costume . . .

'What about the costumes, Mr Rupert?' asks Gustavus. 'You haven't told us about the costumes.' He evidently finds this amusing.

'Yes,' says Mr Rupert. 'The costumes. They'll be ready for you at the museum. The waiting staff wear Vauxhall Gardens carnival costume. Senior male staff are dressed as eighteenth-century masters of ceremonies and female as ladies-in-waiting. I shall be coming as Beau Nash, of the Bath Assembly Rooms.'

'I'm sure you'll look lovely,' says Leonore.

'Thank you, Leonore. The attendants will be dressed as Georgian wenches and swains.' He pauses. 'I understand they're not altogether happy with the idea.'

Gustavus guffaws. 'I'm sure you'll all look great. I, on the other hand, will be dressed as a twenty-first-century chef. No need to try that outfit on.'

'As a matter of fact, Gustavus,' said Mr Rupert, 'that's not quite the case. The plan is that you should be presented to

HRH after the dinner, so you're due to change into the costume of the great French chef Vatel. We've got the outfit – I do hope you'll like it.'

Gustavus scowls, his handsome, good-humoured face becoming darker and more aggressive than his colleagues are used to. 'Is this a joke?' he asks.

'No, no joke,' Mr Rupert answers briskly, and snapping out, 'Kitchens,' he leads them on a Grand Tour of the premises.

THE DIRECTOR'S OFFICE,
TEN A.M.

Partial to Emma, the Chairman always finds time to toss a smile at her. Being loyal to Auberon, she never smiles back too warmly. Today he allows himself a brief moment of full eye contact as he steams past her desk, waving his companion towards a chair. Then he turns back and says, 'Oh, Emma, Mr Kobayashi will be arriving shortly at the front desk. Go and get him, and bring him to wherever I am, OK? He must be made to feel extremely welcome.'

'Yes, of course, Sir Lewis,' she replies.

He has, she thinks, a faintly alarming walk, his head thrust out with his eyes fixed on the distance as though conquering it, his large strong torso also leaning forward, his legs in their well-cut trousers making long slow strides that cover the ground at speed. He affects a modern cut to his clothes, with narrow trousers, no vents to his jacket, his ties discreetly elegant and indiscreetly expensive. Even to the youthful Emma he is an impressive figure. If pushed, she reflects, someone could do worse than become Lady Burslem – though there's no sign of a vacancy just yet. Pretty tough she is, under that charm. As Lady Burslem one certainly wouldn't need to save for a pension.

Before Sir Lewis reaches the door of the director's office, Auberon emerges. He likes to keep the initiative when Sir Lewis arrives. This is partly because it gives the impression of being polite but also because if the chairman finds him at his desk, he always feels irrationally as though he's being caught pretending to work, like a naughty schoolboy. He likes to greet Sir Lewis at the door of his office, a courtesy that can be faintly threatening. Another reason, Auberon realised recently, is that, unlike anyone else, the Chairman enters his office without knocking or being announced. He made it clear from the moment of his appointment that he was not bothered with such niceties. Auberon found this intrusive, a crude statement of the man's power. But it wasn't the only statement. At their first meeting Sir Lewis sat down without invitation at Auberon's desk, forcing him into another, less significant chair. Auberon now ensures that neither of them sits at the desk by moving his chair into the middle of the room before Burslem arrives. Even Sir Lewis, he thinks, would not shift the furniture round to assert his authority.

On this occasion, both assume the good-humoured air with which they do business in public. Sir Lewis tries to maintain momentum by walking onwards, as it were through Auberon, but Auberon is prepared and stands foursquare. 'Good morning,' they say to each other, before moving into the office, Auberon courteously indicating that as a guest Burslem should precede him.

'How is everything?' asks Sir Lewis. 'How does the exhibition look?'

'Very good, I think,' answers Auberon. 'A few little adjustments still being made, under Diana's supervision. Shall we go and see?'

'I want to talk to you about the agenda for today's meeting,' says the Chairman. This habit of not responding to the Director's remarks but continuing with his own train of thought is a recurring source of annoyance to Auberon. His only recourse is not to reply, in turn. This gives him a temporary edge, at least in his own mind, but he questions whether the man notices, and it rather impedes conversation. He sometimes wonders if Sir Lewis is aware of the symbolic discourse between them, which Auberon, as a historian of court politics, finds objectively fascinating if sometimes alarming.

Sir Lewis is resting his eyes on Auberon in a detached way that the younger man – even though he spends hours persuading himself not to be intimidated by his Chairman – finds seriously unnerving. He tries not to look at Sir Lewis, who pauses before flashing his pure white teeth. 'Now, the Nowness of Now – I think everyone will be supportive, don't you? I know you are, for what that's worth.' This is accompanied by a jocular smile and a flash of the gleaming teeth.

'I'm sure people will want to consider the merits and demerits of the case,' Auberon replies. 'It's certainly very exciting. Of course, your term as Chairman sadly only lasts another two years, Lewis – would you have time to carry the project through? Or would you seek another term?' His tone hints that the Chairman might have to work hard to achieve that. He likes to stress the Chairman's faintly ludicrous first name.

'I've brought some outline plans for the building, which Trusty Owen have just sketched out. You know them, don't you? They've done a lot of work for me, very reliable firm. As a favour, of course, there are no financial implications for the museum at present. They've done an elevation to show how a new building might hold the site, a plan.' And he unrolls two or three large sheets of paper. 'Of course, we'd want to hold a big architectural competition, involve architects from all over the world, exhibit the designs and so forth . . .'

Auberon smiles gamely, fumbling at the sheets. 'Very interesting,' he says. *Am I going to be outmanoeuvred on this one? What's Lewis been up to?* 'They'll need a lot of thought, of course.'

'Yes,' replies Sir Lewis. 'Of course they will. But the process will be much easier if everyone backs the idea in principle. I count on you to involve the staff. After all, you're the ones who'll be doing most of the hard work.' His tone suggests that while their opinions are immaterial to him, the staff, and especially Auberon, will be working on little else for several years. 'As for the trustees, I thought I'd introduce the idea this afternoon at the board meeting and gain their approval. An ultimate decision will depend, of course, on the business plan looking OK and on approval from government.'

'Mm,' remarks Auberon, tested for a sensible response. 'It is, of course, a revolutionary step. I wonder if it ought to be pushed through the board quite so fast. After all, it's hard for people to make up their mind rapidly on such a major issue . . .'

'It's quite clear. Either you think this is a museum about the future, or you don't. Either you are in favour of progress, stimulus, forging ahead, the modern, or you aren't. That's all there is to say.' This is a favourite phrase of his when he does not want to discuss an issue.

Auberon smiles politely and remarks, 'There may be other issues to consider, of course.'

'Undoubtedly there will be other issues,' replies Sir Lewis. 'We'll deal with them as they arise.' He pauses. 'I have your full backing, don't I?'

Difficult one, this. The Director knows the Chairman knows the Director is not happy with the scheme, though how unhappy the Director is the Chairman probably does not realise. On the other hand, the Director needs the general support of the Chairman since without it he can't achieve much. Equally, the Chairman knows that the Director might, if hostile to the scheme, engineer its failure. He in turn needs the Director's support. Within this delicate balance, the Director, who has been learning recently how to impede the Chairman's sillier ideas, must not appear negative. So he says, 'I think it's a very interesting idea indeed – although, of course, I'd want to discuss some points with you.'

'Good, good, and you like the elevations, don't you? Only preliminary thoughts, of course.'

Auberon finds these computer-generated drawings, which ape the Edwardian building, immature and crude. 'Full of ideas,' he ventures. 'Very interesting.'

He wonders if the chairman believes him. It seems so – or at least he's willing to seem persuaded. 'Good,' says Sir Lewis. 'Very good indeed. Shall we go and look at the exhibition? I haven't been in for two days, longing to see progress.'

'I think you'll be pleased,' answers Auberon, as they move towards the door, Auberon standing back to let his Chairman go through first. As he watches the imposing figure walk through the outer office, again with a sidelong glance in Emma's direction, his mind wanders back to the Gainsborough – and the question, whatever it may be, that fascinates Jane.

In the outer office, a man is waiting for them. He wears, as Auberon immediately notices, an unfortunate suit. He eyes it with languid revulsion. Auberon's obsession with clothes is well known among his colleagues – those keen to be on good terms with him know that sartorial effort's essential.

'Mr . . . Mr . . .' says the Chairman.

'Evans,' offers the unknown man. 'George Evans.'

'Oh, yes. This is Auberon Booth, the director of the museum. Important that you should get to know each other.' Only the thinnest veneer of good humour conceals the contempt in this remark. Essentially, Sir Lewis considers that people who are not rich belong to a lower order of humanity. To him, Auberon reflects, what are we but two hirelings?

'Hello,' says Auberon, offering what Tanya, who has studied his personality in some depth and gives him regular and often discouraging analyses of its development, calls his mark-eight smile. It is the least warm and friendly grin in the repertoire, barely more than an upward flicker of the lips and a thinning of the eyes.

'I'm very glad to meet you,' says the man eagerly. 'I hope you liked our outline ideas for Nowness. A wonderful plan – of course, we were only giving the very earliest indications of the way it might develop, on the computer, you know . . .'

'Nothing worse than computer-generated architecture in my view, it's so meretricious. It stops architects from really thinking, irons out the creativity, don't you think?' says Auberon. He has not looked at the man, only observed his ill-fitting brown polyester jacket. He casts his eye in the direction of the man's cheek, not troubling about eye contact with somebody he never wants to see again.

Sir Lewis coughs. Auberon realises he is not being especially polite. Icy superiority, Tanya tells him, comes naturally to him. Unless he watches out, he'll turn into a monster one day. Even Emma has made such remarks as 'You obviously didn't like that person, did you? You made it clear.'

He calls up the charm. 'I'm sure there are lots of good ideas there,' he says, and wonders if this sounds better. 'My mind is rather on this exhibition and today's events, that's all. I shall look forward to it.' He does not specify what he will look forward to.

'Come along with us, Mr . . . eh . . .' says Sir Lewis. They make their way towards the exhibition in silence. At the exhibition entrance, the press staff are arranging their wares on two tables. Their banter drops deferentially as Chairman and director approach. On such days as this, the museum functions like an *ancien régime* court – particularly so today, the apotheosis of Sir Lewis Burslem. As usual on press days, Auberon can hardly recognise the junior press officers. Generally dressed casually (allowable for junior staff, if it's attractive casualness) they assume different personalities in suits.

'You've seen the latest version of the press release, Lewis, haven't you?' he asks the Chairman. '*Lady St John* is to the fore, of course. We've had a lot of interest in her,' and as he says this Auberon feels a curious tingling. The Chairman is inspecting the choice of photographs (which includes everything he owns) and making encouraging noises to the staff. He does it very competently, Auberon has to admit. From the entrance to the exhibition Mary Anne emerges, carrying a pile of papers and looking preternaturally calm. No longer scatty, she has moved into the mood of heightened controlling awareness she adopts for major occasions. Meanwhile, the Chairman is advancing upon them. 'The press pack looks very good, Mary Anne,' he says. 'Excellent. Who's coming to the press conference?'

'Oh, everyone,' she says. 'Not only the arts features people but a lot of the critics, who are coming back because you're here. If you have a moment, Chairman, there are one or two questions that might pop up, perhaps I should warn you . . .' Though the prospect of Sir Lewis's rage is agitating, she knows she just has to pretend not to be frightened. He generally responds well to a show of bright, unafraid competence.

Sir Lewis looks irritated at the thought of the press.

'I think I mentioned to you the other day that there's an aggressive young man called Valentine Green, a freelance journalist, writes for the *Telegraph* and *The Times*, one of those conservative radical types. As I briefed you, when I met him last week he asked at length about the selection of objects and your involvement. I tried to deal with it but he may still want to raise one or two awkward points.'

'Tiresome,' says Sir Lewis. 'Any other silly questions?'

'I've a feeling people may ask about the future direction of the museum, there've been a few rumours about the new building and plans to take the whole of the historical collection off view – d'you want to comment? And perhaps in the Press Office we could have some guidance . . . if you don't mind, Sir Lewis.'

'You'll get some guidelines this morning,' says Sir Lewis. 'I will be speaking on that subject.'

'What, the new building? Do you think that's wise?' asks Auberon, less coolly than usual. After all, the idea of a new building hasn't even been brought before the board. 'Wouldn't announcing plans to the press be a bit premature?'

'I only intend,' his Chairman answers coldly, 'to announce that plans will be considered by the trustees in the very near future.'

'I think that will be great, a lot of fun,' intervenes Mary Anne brightly. There is a silence. The Chairman evidently does not care for the idea of 'a lot of fun'. 'And if the building doesn't go ahead,' she rushes on (how aware is she, Auberon wonders, of the impact made by what she's saying?), 'at least we'll get masses of publicity.'

This is not at all what Sir Lewis wishes to hear. Flushing slightly, he advances into the exhibition. Just inside the door is Helen Lawless. His manner changes. 'Ah, Helen,' he cries, with the warmth used by the great to their favourites to set off their coolness towards others. 'Our brilliant curator! Is everything under control, Helen?'

'I think so, Chairman,' she answers eagerly. Auberon and

Mary Anne, an unwilling entourage, listen closely to the tone of this exchange. 'I do hope you'll like everything. *Lady St John* looks sensational with the new lighting.'

'Let's go and look at her,' he says. As they walk through the exhibition the Chairman, again the pink of urbanity, doles out approval to left and right, to objects and staff, rather as the Sun King might have dispensed kind words to his courtiers on a festive day. He stops to watch the London video tour, nodding at the screen to include it in the circle of satisfaction and remind his listeners that this was his idea. He pauses briefly at each of his own pictures, remarking how different things one knows well look in a new context. This must be true, since he says it several times. Everyone in his entourage, which by now also includes Diana, Jane and Lucian, nods each time as though at a revolutionary insight. Only Auberon maintains the bland half-smile he adopts in moments of tension. Mark-seven, Tanya would say. (Why does he keep thinking of Tanya? He's not at all interested in her, just now.)

Then Sir Lewis spots the error: the misplaced portraits. 'But I don't like this!' he cries. 'What have you done here?' They sigh with relief. And after some scornful remarks and expostulations and directions to the hastily summoned technical staff he sweeps on in high gratification, promising to return shortly to check that his instructions have been followed. Helen, who (alone) doesn't know about this ploy (the others don't trust her), is surprised that her colleagues seem fairly unconcerned. How would she feel, she wonders, if Sir Lewis caught her making such a glaring mistake? Mortified. Struck down. He's such a fascinating man . . .

They arrive at *Lady St John*. It has been artfully lit so that the whole area of the canvas is illuminated without light spilling on to the surroundings. In front of the painting, just for the opening, a wooden trough has been placed. It is painted with *treillage* and filled with sweet peas, lavender and alchemilla, intended — according to Mirabel, who directed the flower theming — to evoke the freshness of the English countryside in June (in contrast to the atmosphere of an old bus station, which the theatre usually evokes). It looks like a stage set, the climax of the exhibition.

They all stop to look at the painting. It is the Chairman who speaks. 'Out of this world,' he says. 'Out of this world.'

As he speaks there is a bustle behind them. Emma appears wearing a look of detached efficiency and leading a large, powerfully built Japanese man in a raincoat. He is already fixing both Sir Lewis and the Gainsborough with an intent stare. 'Mr Kobayashi,' cries Sir Lewis excitedly and loudly, and hurries forward to greet his guest. 'How was your flight? How is your hotel? How do you like the museum?'

'This is the picture?' says Mr Kobayashi.

'This is the picture. What do you think, Mr Kobayashi? Wonderful, isn't it?'

'A very nice lady,' says Mr Kobayashi. 'A very nice lady indeed. Yes, I like her very very much.'

GREAT HALL,
MORNING

The Great Hall has had a splendid history. A large plaque under the minstrels' gallery and above the twenty-foot-high double doors, which lead to the entrance hall, announces that in this room on the twenty-fourth of June 1900 His Royal Highness The Prince of Wales in the presence of Her Royal Highness The Princess of Wales performed the museum's opening ceremony. They were attended by H. B. Truegood Esq., Mayor of Lambeth; The Right Honourable the Viscount Haringey DL KCB; Rupert Vaughan Lanchester Esq. and Edwin Rickards Esq. (architects); and M. D. Molson Esq. (Borough Surveyor). Following the ceremony, newspapers record, Their Royal Highnesses were pleased to favour the museum with their presence at a breakfast of remarkable length and splendour, attended by five hundred guests. The breakfast was provided by Lord Haringey, a fact that was discreetly referred to in the speech of thanks offered by the Prince. Following the banquet, a Pageant of English History was performed on the stage by local children. Given the scale of the repast it is hard to believe the guests benefited much from the re-enactment of the Battle of Hastings by St George's Church of England School, Blackfriars Road.

After that glorious opening day the Great Hall suffered a gradual decline. For most of the sceptical twentieth century it was viewed with as little favour as the entrance hall: bombastic and impractical, too large to be heated, too monumental for any but the most enormous objects. Numerous plans were made (but never carried out) to subdivide it. A Coronation exhibition was staged there in 1911 and again in 1953, but mostly it was seen as a white elephant. The hall was rescued from neglect by corporate entertaining. As museums realised in the 1980s that the best commercial use for places originally con- ceived of as temples of learning was as party venues, the Great Hall became an asset. 'Marvellous, wow,' potential clients would thrill. 'What a space – and it can seat six hundred!' 'Six hundred max,' they would be told, 'but it's more comfortable with five.' And everybody would gasp co-operatively. 'We're afraid,' they were warned, 'the catering facilities are almost non-existent, so you'll have to introduce temporary facilities in the Gallery of the Industrial Revolution, next door.' But ignoring this, 'Wow,' everyone would say again, 'just look at it. It's so amazingly grand!'

The Great Hall lived again. After more meetings than seemed possible to the participants, and the employment of several contradictory experts on historic paint colours, a scheme of redecoration was decided on. In an expensive initiative, which had to be funded by axing the Research Department ('temporarily', the dispossessed scholars were told as they were turned out of their little Eden, but 'temporary' proved an elastic term), the 1950s cocktail bar was removed, the walls were decorated in the historic shades of stone and cream, the doors were stripped to the original mahogany, the carpet was removed to reveal the oak boards, the heraldic achievements were repainted in their early colours, the bronze gasoliers were reinstated, a plywood cover was taken off to reveal the Foundation Day plaque, the two clocks, long silent, were set ticking and chiming once more. Most strikingly, the two monumental murals, very early works by Sir Frank Brangwyn which had been concealed behind wooden screens during the Second World War, were re-exposed. Unfashionable though Brangwyn remains, his vigorous depictions of the youth of William Shakespeare and the defeat of the Spanish Armada (subjects chosen by Lord Haringey to epitomise English history) again make a powerful impact, and stimulate talk whenever social intercourse, steering through the difficult waters of corporate entertainment, hits the rocks.

The room is now in constant use. 'Of course the location isn't absolutely central-central,' Venue Promotions say to clients, 'but it's awfully easy to access, close to Waterloo Station and Victoria Station and very handy from the City – and there's absolutely no problem about parking. Do try it.' And try it they do, merchant banks and insurance companies and legal firms and official bodies, four or five nights a week. Venue rental, as it is known, has become one of the museum's most profitable activities. As the chairman says annually to the board whenever next year's business plan is presented with a note that government financing is once again to be reduced to promote efficiency, 'Thank God for the Great Hall.' He said it more than once when planning this dinner.

This morning the hall is as noisy as usual before a big event. The vanguard of Angel Cooks have deposited large packing cases and piles of tables and chairs behind a barricade in a corner. Mirabel's team are preparing their Georgian decorative scheme. On the stage at one end of the hall, where the Grand Pageant is to be performed, an ominous pile of props has accumulated under a tarpaulin with the occasional golden sword and trumpet peeping out. Melissa, Head of Education, who has devised the pageant, is hurrying to and fro on the stage without apparently achieving anything at all. The Head of Security is making himself disagreeable to the Head of Operations from Angel. Though hampered by the fact that this is an in-house event hosted by the Chairman, he still needs to exercise control. He is assisted by the arrival of the Security advance party, in the form of two policemen and two police dogs, to check the building and particularly the rooms where His Royal Highness will be spending royal time. Their arrival allows John Winterbotham to clear the Great Hall, driving decorators and caterers into the entrance hall with curt commands. Mirabel is not pleased. She is blonde and statuesque and of good family in Shropshire, accustomed to mix with the pink of society, and does not appreciate being ordered out of the room, as her increasingly strangled tones indicate. But out she goes, her pretty band of assistants rustling and shrugging in her wake.

Since the Great Hall's practically unfurnished, the security inspection does not take long. While the police officers guide their hounds round the inbuilt mahogany benches and the throne, and negotiate packages from Angel Cooks, John surveys the space closely. He notes, with surprise, that the security staff on duty are not the ones he'd expect. At one end of the room stands Anna — *OK, she does do the ground floor, and a very nice girl she is too*, he thinks, *wouldn't mind doing a security check on her* — but on duty at the other end is young Bill. *What's he doing here? Goofy lad, one of the new intake, not really suitable, constantly mooning about and looking in the air — shouldn't he be on the first floor?* He approaches Bill, who is staring into the distance with an expression John can't understand — what's the matter with the lad? Nothing unusual to look at unless it's Anna and he's seen her often enough, hasn't he? Anyway he's probably a poof . . .

'What are you doing down here?' he demands of Bill.

Bill gulps. 'I'm on duty, Mr Winterbotham,' he says. 'Jim Baldwin's off sick, so I was transferred here. Mr Burgess sent me down.'

John looks put out. 'I see. It's a bit irregular, having someone from another team working on a floor they're not attached to. You know the security procedures for the Great Hall, do you?'

'Oh, yes, sir,' he says, 'I mean, Mr Winterbotham.'

'You stay at this end of the room throughout your duty, you understand that, don't you?'

'Oh, yes,' he says.

'Carry on,' says John. There's something irregular going on here, he doesn't understand what. He must speak to Ian (who seems to be back early from his break, what's he trying to establish, then?). He leaves to deal with the police officers, who have now finished their check. As he moves away, the look of adoration, which has suffused Bill's face ever since by a blissful coincidence he was transferred to the room where *she* is on duty, returns.

The look is so strong that keen-sighted Anna can see it across the room. She smiles back just as Mirabel and her crew and the people from Angel flock back, followed by Melissa escorting what seems to be several hundred children for a rehearsal of the pageant. The more curious and observant among these many arrivals might witness the unusual sight of a uniformed security guard at each end of the monumental hall, smiling seraphically into the far distance.

PRESS VIEW AND PRESS CONFERENCE, ELEVEN THIRTY A.M.

Mary Anne and her boys adore a press conference. They like the tension, the unpredictability, the struggle to make trivial events appear important, the badinage, the excitement when a speaker enthuses his audience, the danger that somebody might offend an important journalist. They enjoy the beginning of press views when the doors open and early arrivals drift in, ladies in woolly hats from local papers and angular young men from art magazines with no discernible readership. These beginners are followed by a trickle of others – the man who claims to write for a (probably fictitious) journal in the West of England from which no article ever emerges but who comes to all the press views and drinks and eats for four, and the writer for a middle-market daily paper who's weak on opinions but hoovers up other people's, and the ex-museum director edged out of his job who finds journalism *déclassé* and sighs as he surveys the photographs on offer, always asking for something that's not there and pointing out errors of fact or typography. Mary Anne is more interested in the heavyweight critics from the nationals, although many of them prefer to make a personal visit before the press view. She likes the tweedy old-timers, people who have been working as art critics for twenty or thirty years (and can't stop, because the job never leads to anything else): they are generally good-natured and willing to see the best in any exhibition, and only write about one unkind review in four. She finds the younger art critics more professionally disagreeable, but when they arrive, anxious for confrontation, she almost always manages to soothe them. The new style of writer generally produces destructive criticism, since it sells papers, and writes about one kind review in eight. But Mary Anne is not dispirited by a bad notice: as she tells colleagues whose months or years of effort are dismissed in a few callous lines, 'Don't worry, darling – they know nothing. Nobody remembers their actual comments except you – but people do remember the event is on.'

Mary Anne likes to keep an overall view of press events. She circulates slowly round the galleries, ensuring the staff are playing their visitors correctly, neither neglecting the major figures nor being too attentive to the unimportant, and that the exhibition tours laid on by the staff are well attended. She measures the temperature of the event, observing who's making notes, whether the atmosphere's humming or chilly, whether attendance is good. No less than a hundred for a press view is obligatory for any success at all – they had two hundred and fifty for *The Age of Queen Elizabeth* and *The Court of George III*, whereas *Ceres Reborn – The History of Agricultural Implements in Britain*, in spite of its gallant title, only attracted the *Farmers' Weekly* and a couple of dreary craft magazines.

This exhibition's certainly arousing interest. The packs of journalists are dense, the discussions lively as they follow the tours given by Jane and Helen. They love the London video, the mixture of artifacts, the inclusion of objects belonging to people at every level of society. (This last was Helen's idea. It was tricky to persuade the Chairman to accept it till she convinced him that elegance need not be a prerogative of wealth but could appeal to everyone.) The visitors are excited to see the 'unknown' Gainsborough: 'Superb,' they say, 'a hidden masterpiece — what a shame it isn't in a public collection — and who was she?'

Amid this enthusiasm there are only one or two dissenters. Notably Valentine Green.

Valentine Green is a freelance journalist, youngish, ugly, clever and ruthless. He writes for more papers than he'd care to list, on a variety of topics associated with the arts. He is charming until he loses his patience and snaps. A true professional with a nose for anything suspicious, he loves hunting out a new story and sees himself as the scourge of the established order. For Valentine, there is a twist to the most straightforward story. He is a friend of Diana but this does not make him write good-natured articles about the museum.

From the set look on his face, eyes thrusting forward and lips pursed, Mary Anne concludes he's not in a good mood. 'Do you like the exhibition, Valentine?' she asks bravely.

'I find a lot of things about it very interesting,' he replies, and closes his mouth tightly.

Into the throng of almost three hundred Sir Lewis Burslem advances. He wears an air of good humour, though it has an impermanent feel to it. Spotting his approach, Mary Anne, who thinks that an encounter between the two of them at this stage might be disastrous, manoeuvres Valentine out of view behind a large showcase. Sir Lewis is accompanied by a little entourage: his wife, Auberon, his personal assistant from his own office, and Jeannie, the museum's only female press officer. They make a bustle as they advance, and the journalists, turning to look at them, hush and move slightly backwards as though for royalty, perhaps intimidated by the air of conscious condescension that emanates from the Burslems. They advance towards the neighbouring lecture theatre, where the press conference is to be held. Behind the chairman's party swoop the young lady and the young gentlemen of the Press Office, firmly smiling as they propel the press into the theatre.

There is a pause before the Chairman and Director, followed by Lucian, Jane and Helen, mount the stage. From a distance comes the incongruous sound of trumpets and cheering followed by loud chanting. The Chairman places himself in the centre of the long velvet-covered table, Auberon to his right, the others at a tactful distance. Although the lecture theatre is a hideous room in the Utility style of around 1948, the stage has been dressed up. Tall glass cylinder vases of arum lilies stand on Perspex plinths in a 1940s idiom to left and right of the table, and the stage is bathed in a softly flattering light, never seen here before. Behind the speakers' heads looms the image of Lady St John's face, projected to three or four times life size. To some of those beneath her in the hall the image assumes a strangely ambiguous quality, as though her lips were moving, her eyes flickering.

Sir Lewis is less menacing elevated on a platform than he is close to – or so it seems to Mary Anne, observing events from the back of the theatre. He's certainly no good at playing the house. His movements have stiffened, and his air of bonhomie seems perfunctory as he surreptitiously checks his text. No trepidation shows on the face of Auberon, who looks confidently at the auditorium, nodding at acquaintances. He's one of the most polished speakers she knows – she loves listening to him. Auberon moves to the podium and it's curtain up. 'Good morning, and I'm very glad to welcome you all to the museum,' he begins. 'Though the seventeenth century is my own favourite, I'm delighted the eighteenth arouses so much interest in you, as it now does in me. This is a very important day for the museum, the opening of our centenary exhibition. It might

interest you to know that the six hundred and forty-two objects
we've assembled make this exhibition almost twice as large as
The Court of George III, our previous record. We're delighted to
have with us today Mr Kobayashi, chairman of the internationally recognised communications and property firm Japco which
is showing our exhibition in Japan.' (Heavy humming from the
audience – they're obviously impressed by the idea of the
exhibition going to Japan.) 'Most important, of course, is the
chairman of the trustees, Sir Lewis Burslem, who is of course
my boss.' This is said with a throw-away air as though the
concept were faintly humorous, stimulating a ripple of amusement. 'It's to Sir Lewis we owe the exhibition concept and its
realisation. Burslem Properties have generously acted as sponsors – extremely generous sponsors, since the costs have been
huge. Sir Lewis will be speaking shortly and I won't anticipate
what he's about to say – I'll get into trouble.'

There is a further ripple at this point. Auberon can
afford to flirt with his audience. He is much liked by the
press, whom he rewards with pithy original insights when
they ring him. Auberon thanks the staff and the expert
committee and the committee of honour and the minor
sponsors and the Department of Cultural Affairs (which was
about to be renamed Access! when it was realised this might
produce confusion), which has provided indemnity for the
loans. 'But I shall not,' he goes on, 'try to outline our aim in
mounting this exhibition – that's for Sir Lewis to do. We
hope you'll help us make this event as widely appreciated as it
deserves . . .'

He does it so deftly, in Mary Anne's view. Really, he
should have gone on the stage, he'd be a wonderful matinée
idol, transferring to sexy character actor in a bit. Though the
words aren't remarkable, the delivery, the smile, the air of

distinguished youth and self-deprecation, are all so finely contrived. He's been speaking in public since he was at university, after all. He appears to do it so naturally. Only she – who's rehearsed him for so many public appearances – appreciates the hard work behind the charm.

But as for Sir Lewis, now making his way to the podium with hesitant arrogance, what about his public speaking? He's no orator, she knows well, and has received lessons in communication from nobody. Unlike Auberon, who addresses many of his remarks to the most distant corner of the lecture theatre, Sir Lewis confides in the podium. He appears indifferent to his audience – though in reality, as she well knows, he's highly nervous about such events. 'This great exhibition . . . the largest ever mounted by the museum . . . an entirely original approach, analysing the art and industry of eighteenth-century England in the context of contemporary social, financial, political, industrial, intellectual and medical conditions . . . we aim to contrast contemporary constructs of Augustan society with life as it was actually experienced . . .' This bit was surely not written by him, more likely that insinuating little Helen. '. . . mirror to our society . . . we seek to analyse the development of an urban bourgeois culture in relation to traditional aristocratic hegemony,' he stumbles rather over this word, 'but we have not abandoned the consideration of visual imperatives . . . The exhibition studies the aesthetic canon which to this day remains influential within the trope of Englishness . . .'

This is not going down well. The journalists, deferential when he started, are rustling their papers. She finds herself resting her eyes pleasurably on Luke, particularly caressable today in his dark suit and gleaming green tie, which matches his eyes so well . . .

Then the authentic voice of Sir Lewis re-emerges. 'This is

not one of those occasions where the museum's representative forgets the sponsor's name . . .' mild amusement '. . . I am delighted as Chairman to be supporting this exhibition as sponsor . . . an unusual but I hope beneficial relationship . . . Burslem Properties if I may briefly blow my own trumpet . . .'

Auberon looks tense. But there's no alternative to smiling.

'Ours is the second largest property company in the country – including Scotland and Wales, which I'm happy to say don't offer much competition.' This pleasantry evokes muffled protests in the audience, especially from a man who writes for the *Scotsman*. 'We have developments currently under way in fourteen British cities as well as France, Germany, Japan and the United States. We're proud to support this museum since in our humble way we regard ourselves as a part of British history.'

This bit he certainly wrote himself. Then he embarks on a new line: 'I want to take this opportunity to announce another initiative, which will shape the museum's future. At our trustees' meeting today we'll be discussing the possibility of a major new development here.'

What on earth is this about? Entirely unscheduled, surely?

'We're investigating the possibility of a large extension. I can't tell you much except that it will offer a new display concept, based on advanced approaches to audience input and throughput.' He looks at his notes. 'It'll discard the traditional élitist statement of cultural capital in favour of an approach based on maximal social inclusion.' Somebody wrote this bit for him too, Mary Anne thinks, and her eyes swivel back to Helen. She's sitting upright looking cool, but the look of self-satisfaction on her face betrays her.

'It'll be a display by the public, about the public, for the public. It'll deal with life in Britain as it's lived by ordinary women and men, young and old, communicated through all sorts of media — personal possessions, videos of people's daily activities, Internet communication — with views of Britain as it is now shown non-stop within the museum. *Breaking Down the Walls*, that's what we call this programme, and the whole extension will be called the Nowness of Now.'

Mary Anne looks around the room. He's certainly caught them now — and her, too. Lots of press coverage... controversy... sounds a good idea...

'One factor does encourage us. People love the idea — it excites them. We don't know precisely what it will cost but we estimate twenty-four million pounds.' Admiring gasps at the thought of so much money being needed. 'I'm delighted to announce that a donor has already promised ten million pounds. Strictly anonymous, I'm afraid.'

Excited at the thought of so much mysterious generosity, the audience applauds loudly. Glowing with the sensation he's created, Sir Lewis puffs out his cheeks and sits down. Mary Anne is so surprised she can hardly assess the scene but takes control of herself. Auberon is glaring into the distance, face pale, eyebrows raised and tense, hands gripping his chair. Beside him, Lucian looks nonchalant, Jane seems puzzled, little Helen smiles like a pussycat. Meanwhile her boys, standing together in a gaggle, are trying to attract her attention, Ben in particular. She ignores him reluctantly, he is really her favourite at the moment, those melting brown eyes are almost irresistible, if only her rules were not so strict, after all the Loved One would never get to know... Instead she looks straight ahead. There's a peculiar silence until several members of the audience stand up or raise their hands. Auberon moves to the podium.

'Thank you very much, Lewis. Wonderful news — news to me too!' he says. Controlled though he is, he can't avoid sounding annoyed: his rendering of 'Lewis' evokes the French Revolution. 'We'll be happy to take questions – though we must restrict our discussion to the exhibition. The exciting news you've just heard can't be elaborated on at this stage.' Sir Lewis looks faintly disappointed and shrugs his shoulders but does not intervene.

The questions aren't too difficult. Mary Anne is often surprised at how docile arts journalists often are, apart from the little band of nasties. The well-upholstered ladies of a certain age who write in the glossy papers seldom have anything disagreeable to say. But she doesn't allow herself to relax – her eyes are on Valentine Green. He's stationed himself in the aisle, close to a wall light, which heightens the effect of his white face and aquiline nose. There's no doubt he'll speak. Yes, he's waving his hand.

'Valentine?' says Auberon. He seems to relish the idea of some awkwardness.

Valentine Green's delivery, a sneering innuendo shadowing every syllable, provides the perfect vehicle for his famous satirical shafts. He has a way of smiling into the far distance and not looking at the person he's addressing, which can be highly disconcerting. 'It's very impressive to hear about these plans,' he says languidly. 'Congratulations.' Sir Lewis twitches as though being mocked. 'But I've two questions for Sir Lewis.' The knight shifts in his seat. He detests direct questioning from the press unless they are wholly obsequious. 'First, Sir Lewis, are you, personally or through Burslem Properties, producing this enormous sum?'

'That's entirely confidential,' says Sir Lewis, 'but I can state that though the board of Burslem Properties may consider a donation, they're not giving ten million.'

'Thank you. We'll draw our own conclusions,' says Valentine

darkly. 'My other question's about this exhibition. We note that
the picture billed as the centrepiece of the show – visually and
in all the publicity material – is the Gainsborough of *Lady St
John as Puck*. There she is behind you, after all, on a massive scale.
I want to raise another issue, it's a rather delicate one but in
these days of openness I'm sure you'll be glad to discuss it. As
we all know, this picture belongs to you, Sir Lewis. Congratulations, again! A question emerges from all this. You're the
Chairman of this museum. Whatever the picture's merits, one
might question whether an object belonging to a board member
– the Burslem Gainsborough, as it were – should be given such
prominence in their institution. It's as though a new product
were being launched, like a new perfume or car. Isn't there's a
conflict? And before you answer, I have a related question for
the Director. No, I insist, no, I insist! Auberon Booth, did you
personally want to include *Lady St John* in the exhibition? If
you'd said you didn't want it, would you have been listened to?
In short, is this exhibition, generously sponsored by Burslem
Properties, acting as a huge shop window for one business and
one businessman?' Auberon tries to intervene but Valentine
talks over him. 'No, you must let me speak,' he cries, his voice
becoming more squeakily commanding by the minute. 'Isn't it
true that the intellectual integrity of this museum – a public
institution, publicly funded – is being exploited for the benefit
of the person at its head? What do you say to that?' Amid the
rising buzz he lowers his voice and adds emolliently, 'Only an
enquiry, of course, only an enquiry – I expect I'm quite wrong.'

Auberon replies, 'Of course the museum is delighted to be
showing this painting and the other seven works Sir Lewis is
generously lending to this important exhibition . . .' The members of staff on the stage try to look professional, detached,
loyal and enthusiastic all at the same time but succeed only,

Mary Anne thinks, in looking confused.

'Yes yes yes,' says Valentine, 'of course you'd say that, wouldn't you? Of course in theory you're delighted. But let's have an answer, not this boardroom blandness.'

Mary Anne tries not to enjoy these developments. How will Auberon handle this one? And Sir Lewis?

It's Auberon who answers. 'The tone of your remarks, Valentine Green, is entirely unjustified. Sir Lewis is acting in his private capacity as a collector. The pictures belong to him personally, not to his company . . .'

'Yes, but in that case,' interrupts his terrier-like persecutor, 'why aren't the pictures described as belonging to a private collector?'

Sir Lewis is about to speak – explosively, to judge from his bulging eyes and clenched fists – when Auberon forestalls him: 'Why on earth should we disguise the paintings' ownership? Is there anything shameful about the owners of works of art sharing them with the public?'

'So you see no discrepancy between your Chairman's official position and advertising these works in the exhibition? Yes, advertising – *Lady St John*, an unknown work, will become one of the most famous Gainsboroughs in Britain. It's excellent publicity, isn't it, so that if Sir Lewis wants to sell on the picture one day he'll have no trouble? And command a much higher price than he paid.'

This time Sir Lewis does intervene. 'I have no intention of selling the Gainsborough, or any of my pictures,' he expostulates. And then his face twitches and he stops abruptly. Why's he stumbling? Mary Anne wonders.

Valentine is not deterred. Although the microphone has been wrested from his hand, he raises his voice with startling effectiveness. 'Another thing – none of you has persuaded me that this picture has any valid connection with the exhibition. I've heard the party line but it's just expensive wallpaper, isn't it, academic and visual decoration? Isn't this exhibition, and the accompanying nonsense, an exercise in vanity and self-promotion?'

This is going rather far, Mary Anne thinks.

It's Auberon again. 'We can't respond to a question put like that. It's time to—'

But Valentine has more to say. There is an angry look to him: he stares at Sir Lewis Burslem as though he hates him.

Why? Mary Anne wonders. *Why should Valentine so dislike the man? As a symbol of wealth and power? It's not as though Sir Lewis were corrupt, is it? Is this some sort of personal crusade for Valentine?*

'I'd like to know,' he says, 'whether the museum had this exhibition forced on it. It's the chairman's idea, I understand, it contains the chairman's possessions, it's paid for by the chairman, it benefits the chairman. Chairman's bonanza. Shouldn't it be labelled "This is an advertising space"?'

'This is a very serious exhibition with a distinguished academic committee,' replies Auberon. Beside him Sir Lewis becomes redder and angrier, clenching his fists on the table and leaning heavily towards the audience. 'Anyone who's studied the catalogue and the selection of objects will see we're breaking new ground in integrating archival research and recent theoretical consideration of material culture. You should look at the evidence. And I think you've had your say – does anyone else have a question?'

Amid an eruption of chatter, Valentine, apparently satisfied, moves into the shadows. The next questions pose no difficulties. Seeing Sir Lewis reassume his air of a man fully in control of himself and others, Mary Anne reflects uneasily that though they can stop Valentine's talk they can't stop his writing. Since he writes persuasively, and his editors adore controversy, this may be a problem. At least he hasn't been asked to this evening's dinner — that would have been a nightmare.

Stage lights down, house lights up, principals move off-stage, audience out. Mary Anne moves towards her colleagues, who are looking at her expectantly. She is not pleased. She'd thought she'd spiked this line of attack, and that her little lunch with Valentine the previous week had soothed him, but no . . . She assumes her brightest smile as she rejoins her team and says, 'Went very well, don't you think?'

THE SPECIAL EVENTS OFFICE,
TEN THIRTY A.M.

In the Special Events Office they're finalising the seating for the dinner. Or, rather, Lady Burslem, chair of the dinner committee, is finalising and the Head of Special Events is noting. The seating plan has been under discussion for the past three months and has become one of the most important features of the museum's life. As the guests responded, first, to the letter warning them that the event would take place and, second, to the ultra-thick heavily embossed invitation card, accompanied by a fleet of smaller cards outlining the programme for the evening, the list has been revised over and over again.

'Imagine doing this before the days of the word-processor,' Julia, Head of Special Events, remarks crossly from time to time (though not in front of Lady Burslem). Julia hates her job and would like another, possibly as project manager for the Workers' Revolutionary Party. She finds Lady Burslem efficient and amiable as long as she is never crossed and, in her posh way, rather amusing.

In the past few weeks the seating plan has emerged like an unruly quilt. Lady Burslem is famous for her skill in bringing together people who'd like to meet one another. Her husband delegates the seating arrangements to her, confident she'll loyally give him the cream of the guests. At one point, Auberon believed, his Chairman was scheming to impose on him the dullest table possible within the bounds of decency – the most vulgar self-seeking members of the Magna Carta Circle, the ugliest titled lady with the largest overdraft, the most self-opinionated and verbose man of learning. Sir Lewis tried to relegate Auberon to the far corner, telling him some distinguished people must sit on the edges to show that all the tables had equal status – even though he plans to sit dead centre under the speaker's podium. Auberon managed to squash that one but not to prevent one or two seriously boring people from sitting close to him. Sir Lewis and Lady Burslem are, of course, at the same table as His Royal Highness. The selection of the other occupants of that glorious board (twenty-four of them, instead of the usual twelve at other tables) has been discussed *ad infinitum*.

The meetings have been long and numerous, and Auberon has tried to avoid them. 'It's ironic, isn't it,' he remarks to Tanya, 'that a museum director's principal duty these days is doing seating plans?' At each meeting they have reviewed the current guest list, decided whom to include from the B-list as refusals come in, perfected the royal table, tried not to group together the difficult or dull ('You can't put them all on the same table,' Lady Burslem remarked. 'They won't notice,' Auberon replied. 'They don't know we think their table mates are dull, they'll probably get on extremely well'). They have assessed the potential for future financial donations from people they don't know well, moved touchy creatures to better positions, patched up fragmented tables, counted and recounted and yet again counted the numbers. 'It's not the food and drink that make a party,' Lady Burslem likes to remark, 'it's the host and guests.' Wearily, Auberon assents.

One of the issues that has been discussed at length has

been the naming of the tables. They worked on the principle that table numbers would be inappropriate since they imply an order – whereas names create a benign non-hierarchical atmosphere. They settled on the names of thirty great British persons of the eighteenth century, including appropriate women and scientists and representatives of most political leanings, and came up with a curious and varied list, from George III (the royal table) and Queen Charlotte to Pitt and Fox, Gainsborough and Reynolds, Johnson and Delaney, Burney and Goldsmith, Handel and Arne, Vanbrugh and Adam, Herschel and Hume. Thomas Paine was rejected as too radical and with unfortunate digestive connotations. In the end they decided they had done a good representative job.

This morning Lady Burslem, apparently insatiable in her appetite for organising things, is sitting in the Special Events Office. This is their last opportunity to revise. The final lists have to be printed at one o'clock.

'Any more withdrawals this morning?' asks Lady Burslem.

'A few people are ill,' says Julia.

'So inconsiderate,' replies her ladyship. 'Anyone important?'

'The Duchess of Wiltshire . . .'

'Oh, she's practically dead anyway, no loss, but that table – Chatham, isn't it? – becomes rather difficult.' By this time either of them could win a quiz on the evening's table plan. 'Julia, do we have a duchess substitute? We thought she'd do for that dreary businessman who might join the Magna Carta Circle. Has anyone else dropped out?'

'Mr and Mrs T. Sergeant, who are on Hunter. Their daughter's ill.'

'Can't remember who they are . . . Oh, corporate patrons, are they? Who else?'

'Vivian Blow is not coming, the artist, didn't give a reason, just said that she'd decided she had no time for bourgeois festivities.'

'So tiresome, why couldn't the silly girl have thought of that before? . . . Not really a girl, just dresses like one, must be fifty if she's a day . . . But what a nuisance, she's on Hervey, that table's very short of girls.'

A not too aggressive baroness is found to replace the duchess and a member of staff is put in her place; the Sergeants disappear, bringing that table down to ten; the artist . . .

'Is that it?' says her ladyship. 'No late additions? You've put Mr Kobayashi next to me, haven't you? Very important. On my left, with HRH on my right.'

'Yes, yes,' says Julia. 'I suppose I couldn't know a little more about Mr Kobayashi, just in case I have to introduce him to anyone?'

Lady Burslem looks thoughtful. 'Mr Kobayashi is Lewis's opposite number in Japan, chairman of one of the leading property companies. He has been very kind over taking on this exhibition and promoting it in Japan, so that we — that is to say the museum — should make a lot of money out of the event. He's very fond of English painting, and even collects it, I believe, not something many Japanese people do. Is that enough? So, I think we have everybody. Oh, and are all the staff on dinner stand-by alerted?'

'Yes,' says Julia, suddenly resentful again. She is one of the stand-bys herself, condemned to parade all dressed up before dinner in case she has to fill a vacant place instead of being consigned to the outmess table.

'Thank God it's done,' says Lady Burslem. 'I hope never to have to organise a dinner for four hundred again. The things I put up with for my husband! You must feel the same, Julia. Shall we print out the final list?'

The telephone rings. Julia answers. 'Oh, I see,' she says. 'Well, I'm so sorry... Of course we understand. No, no trouble at all. I do hope you have a good holiday. And do come and see the exhibition...'

'Who is it?' asks Lady Burslem.

'Bad, I'm afraid. It's Lord and Lady Pomeroy. They're flying to South Africa tomorrow and can't risk a late evening.'

'Maddening,' says Lady Burslem. 'It's always the grand ones who are most cavalier. And they're on the royal table, too... Well, we'll have to start again. Who do we promote?'

DENZIL MARTEN GALLERIES, ST JAMES'S, LATE MORNING

Yes, Mr Marten can see Jane that morning. Via his secretary (apparently he could not find the energy to speak to her himself, though Jane was sure he was in the same room), he intimated that a few moments could be spared. Could she touch on the reason for their meeting? . . . Ah, it was about the Gainsborough. What was the problem? . . . It seems rather late in the day . . . Well, if she could only tell him in confidence . . . Eleven thirty should be fine, he was surprised she wasn't too busy – it must be urgent . . .

Before she leaves, Jane twitches her clothes and in spite of herself examines herself rapidly in the vanity mirror concealed in her desk. Though she does not care for Denzil Marten, she knows what sharp eyes he has and does not want to feel uneasy under scrutiny.

I can't make out if he's anxious or apprehensive or neither. He must know that the picture's been substantially restored (if that is indeed the case); he probably commissioned the restoration. What am I going to say to him? I need to find out what he knows about the picture's condition . . . about its state when it came into his possession . . . about the restoration. I suppose I'm showing my hand by talking to him, but otherwise I won't make any progress . . .

I'll take a taxi to the gallery. It's against my principles but I've so little time and I don't want to arrive at the luxurious premises of Denzil Marten, art dealer, Bury Street, St James's, in a post-Tube flurry. It would be nice to step lightly from a purring cab looking crisp, worldly, soignée. *I used to be like that, when I was living with Hamish . . .*

On the way she considers her destination, physical and human. Denzil Marten is one of the best-known art dealers in London. He does not belong to the almost-extinct category of condescending old-established firms occupying opulent Bond Street premises, nor sell contemporary art from the pure white premises of Cork Street or Shoreditch. His is a different style. For the past thirty years he has inhabited an externally discreet establishment in Bury Street, St James's. In the window one painting, usually a flower piece but occasionally the portrait of somebody rich, announces his trade, but only the initiated would brave the glass door in its neo-Baroque frame and the lofty young woman making lunch appointments behind a Boulle *bureau plat.* Inside, the atmosphere exudes calm luxury. The Dutch genre paintings and classical landscapes glowing on the dark brown velvet walls beneath discreetly bright lights seduce the trustees of large American museums and the wealthy collectors who buy from Denzil Marten. Nothing indicates overtly that the pictures are for sale or that the place is in any way connected with financial processes.

Generously, he has lent a picture from his stock to ELEGANCE. It is a depiction of a serving wench by Henry Robert Morland. Privately, Jane does not think it is a work of any great quality, and she even doubts the attribution. But Mr Marten was very pressing in his suggestions that the picture would contribute to the exhibition's social themes as well as its artistic qualities, and a note from the Chairman of the trustees to the Director in favour of the loan ensured its inclusion. Well, it looks OK, in Jane's view, but no more than that.

Although not brought up as an English country gentleman, Mr Marten has adopted the style of one. In London he wears pinstripe suits with a stripe slightly too broad for comfort, and a scarlet or orange silk lining. He belongs to a club in St James's Street where he has lunch most days, since it makes him feel he's arrived at the heart of the English upper classes. He's said to have an old rectory in Devonshire, with some acres, where he can indulge his passion for the country clothes he demonstratively sports on Friday mornings in London. He is rumoured to be enormously rich and his passion for the aristocracy amounts almost to a disease. The body within this apparatus is not notably appealing and the face is on the bulbous side, but he has a well-groomed moustache and a mass of smooth black hair, which glistens in the sun.

Jane knows him well, having bought one or two paintings from him for the museum. She feels calm as she negotiates the glass door and says good morning to the lissom Annabel decorating the desk.

From the main gallery a little staircase leads down to the viewing room and then to Mr Marten's office. The office walls are covered in red silk and brilliantly shiny cabinet pictures, which, Jane knows, are likely to be less good than they appear. The proprietor sits behind his desk. He waves at her and points to a chair, but indicates he is in the middle of an exceptionally important conversation that cannot be interrupted. Clearly it concerns sums of money, referred to in a code, which makes them sound mysteriously enormous. From time to time he slips into Italian or French or German, often, mysteriously, in the same sentence. It is an impressive performance but Jane has heard it before and is short of time. After five minutes she looks at her watch.

'I have someone here,' says Mr Marten instantly into the

telephone. '*Ciao, caro.* My dear Jane . . . what a pleasure to see you. Have you seen my little Terborch, very fine, don't you think? Private collection, not been out of the house for two hundred years, wish I could tell you where it came from . . . not your sort of thing, of course . . .' He is fond of secrecy and peppers his conversation with sly references to persons of unimaginable wealth and importance. 'How can I help you with this matter of yours? It must be very pressing – on the day of your big opening, when you're so busy . . .'

'I need to ask you one question,' Jane says.

'Please,' he replies, simultaneously scrutinising a message pad on his desk as though unwilling to waste one second. 'Just one moment.' He presses his intercom. 'Annabel, could you call Lord Woking's office, and say I can't make Brooks's until one fifteen? Oh, and ring Mr S at the London house and check they'll be coming here at three – and they are bringing an additional car for the bodyguards and does it need a *Parkplatz*? Thank you, darling. Yes, Jane?'

Jane tries not to be irritated. 'I'll only be five minutes,' she says. 'Then I'll leave you in peace.'

'But I've all the time in the world for you,' he replies unconvincingly.

'Thank you,' she says. 'The Gainsborough that belongs to Sir Lewis Burslem – you sold it to him, didn't you?'

'Yes, you know that, it's in the exhibition catalogue,' he answers. Does he stiffen slightly?

'I need to ask you about it.'

'Ask whatever you like. I'm an open book. Within limits, of course. By the way, would you like some coffee, a little drinkie?' And before she has time to answer, he presses on, 'Naturally you understand I can't tell you anything that remains in confidence between myself and my clients.'

'Of course. You bought the picture directly from Sir William St John.'

'Yes. That's all in the provenance too.'

'What condition was it in when you bought it?'

'Oh, surprisingly good, really. It needed a little attention, of course — it had been hanging in a cold country house for a long time.'

'I haven't been able to examine the picture in detail,' she says, 'and it looks splendid, of course, but I am a little concerned about its conservation history. I just want to be briefed in case we have any questions from the press — you know how hot they are on over-restoration, even though they understand nothing about it. So — do you have condition reports for the picture while it was in your possession and may I see them?'

Mr Marten no longer looks so friendly. 'I don't see,' he replies coldly, 'why the past condition of the picture is in any way your concern. I'm not prepared to release any documentation. You must know that Sir Lewis has given strict instructions — on our advice, to be honest — that the condition of all the paintings in his collection is a private matter and that they're not to be analysed by any borrowers. People are so ready to make negative judgements. It seems to me you're abusing his generosity.'

Jane sits very upright and stares at the exceptionally glossy painting of two nymphs disporting themselves in a strangely blue glade, which hangs above his head. Then she speaks rather slowly and deliberately: 'You know perfectly well that by show-ing the picture — any picture — in our exhibition we are giving it our stamp of approval, academic validity, if you like.' As she says this, she remembers the questionable Morland he has lent to the exhibition, but she cannot retract at this stage. 'In a sense the picture becomes our responsibility when we give it wall space, and even more so when we engineer so much publicity. It becomes the intellectual property of the community, of all of us, not the personal possession of the legal owner.' Marten sneers, and shrugs his shoulders. What a strong presence he has, Jane remarks to herself. Can it be the remains of his aftershave, or one of those scents that are meant to arouse desire, or sweat, or . . .? 'So – I must be prepared, in case . . .'

'In case what?'

'In case its condition, or its quality, is questioned.'

'Absurd,' and he waves his arm dismissively, 'all this ethical hocus-pocus. It doesn't convince me for a moment. The picture belongs to the legal owner.'

It's odd, she thinks, how he's not allowing himself any eye contact with her. Not a good sign. 'That's how it may seem to you. But you'd be happy to show anything you have for sale here in a museum, wouldn't you – to lend it to an exhibition, for example? You recognise the seal of approval it gives.'

'I don't have time for arguments of this sort,' he says. 'And if you're thinking of the picture I've lent to ELEGANCE, I lent it because I wanted to help the museum.'

'That's as it may be. But museums have their own values, and those are what I want to protect.'

'Museums are the graveyard of art. I shall tell Sir Lewis his instructions have been disobeyed. I'd seriously advise you, Jane, not to cross him in this matter.' He fixes her with a hostile glare. 'Of course the painting was restored after I'd bought it, but no more than many of the pictures in public galleries. It was a highly competent restorer who did the work.'

'Who was that?' she asks.

'I'm not at liberty to tell you. But what I can tell you is that you'd be unwise to spread stories in search of a sensation, if that's what you plan to do. Foolish and damaging, that's what it would be. Sir Lewis owns a very fine painting, bought directly from the original family. He's very happy with it, the details of the restoration are incidental. And now, Miss Vaughan, I know you have a great deal to do . . .'

'I won't keep you,' she says. 'You've been more helpful than you realise.' This remark startles him. He fingers the huge glass and gold paperweight on his desk. 'You're coming tonight, I think, to see your picture and all the rest – and thank you so much for your generous loan,' she concludes insincerely. He nods frostily. 'We'll meet then.'

He does not reply. They do not shake hands. Jane departs.

Back in her office, she looks up Ronald Smiles in the telephone directory. She's known him, too, for years (small place, the art world), since they were both students at the Courtauld Institute of Art, but she seldom speaks to him now. 'Ronald Smiles, Picture Restoration Studio' is how he is described, with an address in Fulham. He's probably at home recovering from a hangover, she thinks to herself, but she'll try the studio.

'Hello,' says a voice. It sounds like him. Perhaps his studio is also his home.

'May I speak to Ronald Smiles?' she enquires.

'I'll see if he's in,' says the voice. 'Who shall I say is calling?'

'Jane Vaughan.' There is a muffled sound at the other end. 'I know that's you, Ronnie,' she goes on. 'I want a word.'

'Oh, yes, it is me,' he says. 'The phone was handed to me by my assistant. What do you want a word about, Jane? It's been absolutely ages. You must have retired by now, darling – are you looking for consultancy work? Don't know if I can help you, really, things aren't good at the moment . . .'

'I want to talk to you about the Gainsborough of Lady St

John,' she says. 'The most prominent picture in our show.'

'Oh, yes,' he says. 'It's rather good, isn't it? Beautiful brushwork, don't you think? The artist at his most refined.'

There is a curious tone to his voice, which is loaded with ambiguity at any time. She must not let him realise that she's trying to find out what has happened to the painting, if it can be avoided. They don't want Sir Lewis to think they might be unhappy about his precious picture. She must be discreet. Being discreet is not easy with Ronnie, whose snake-like mind can usually extract information from anyone he talks to.

'Yes,' she says. 'It's quite remarkable. But I was looking at it yesterday with Friedrich . . .'

'Who is Friedrich?' Ronnie asks. He knows quite well who Friedrich is. 'One of your colleagues?'

'Friedrich von Schwitzenberg, our Head of Conservation.'

'Your Head of Conservation? Really? I've never heard of him. What is his field?'

'Ronnie, don't waste my time.' He makes vague remonstra- tory noises down the line. 'I wanted to ask if you were involved in its conservation, so that we can give the proper credits if we're asked. The picture's arousing so much interest, you see.'

'Oh, yes,' he says, 'I'm so pleased. I did it over ten years ago — that is to say, I worked on a few problems when it came on the market, and cleaned it, of course, remarkable how well it came up after all those years in a dim country house.' And then, more sharply, 'You know you're not allowed to examine it in the museum, don't you? Sir Lewis is strict about that, on my advice I may say. I'm the only person allowed to handle his pictures, we don't want a lot of so-called museum experts crawling over everything . . .'

Ronnie worked briefly at Leicester Museums and Art Galleries in his young days and left hurriedly. He does not like museums at all, and happily is never asked to work for them.

'No,' she says, 'we were just looking at it, in the exhibition. I suppose that's allowed. We were wondering if any areas had had to be repainted.'

There is a pause.

'Not really,' he says, 'not what you would call repainted. I did have to do some work on the edges, the landscape background was a little damaged . . .'

'And the dog?'

There is another pause and a noise like a stifled giggle. 'Oh, yes, the doggie,' he says, 'he's nice, the doggie, isn't he? Well . . .'

'I noticed only this morning that whereas the dog in an old photograph of 1898 has his tail pointing down, in the actual painting his tail is in the air. It seemed a little odd.'

'Well,' he says, as though considering, 'well . . . I did have to do a bit of work there. I realised from the X-ray there was a *pentimento*. It looked as though originally Gainsborough showed the tail in the air. I could see exactly how it had been. And then he, or someone else, shifted the tail downwards, it must have been considered more decorous or something. So I went back to that earlier version, I thought it brightened the picture up, more cheerful, better for the composition.'

'So you removed later paint layers? Don't you think they might have been Gainsborough's?'

'Maybe, yes, but an afterthought, not his original idea. Anyway, I took a snap of the painting. I suppose it was a little irregular but these ethical questions are awfully difficult, aren't they?'

'Indeed they are,' responds Jane, 'though I've never thought they interested you much.' But this is not the moment to antagonise Ronnie, irritating though he is. 'I mean, you're always so original,' she continues emolliently. 'What about the rest of the painting – did you have to do a lot of work on that?'

'Oh, no. Absolutely not. I cleaned it, of course, but it was in beautiful condition, really. Don't you think it looks good?'

'Yes, yes,' she says hastily. 'Unforgettable. Shall we see you at the dinner tonight?'

'Yes, I'm coming,' he replies. 'Looking forward to it. A great day for Sir Lewis, isn't it?'

'A great day indeed,' she affirms, putting down the receiver. And what on earth, she asks herself, does this highly unusual conversation mean?

GREAT HALL,
TWELVE TEN P.M.

There's been a burst of activity in the Great Hall. Garlands and wreaths in the style of Vauxhall Gardens, decorated with gold and scarlet ribbons, have been nailed to the walls by Mirabel's crisp assistants. In the centre of the hall, two marbled plinths have been prepared for allegorical figures, which have not yet arrived. One of these, people have been told, is to be the goddess of True Love, designed by Mirabel from an original idea by Rysbrack. The other figure will be False Love, a beautiful young woman holding a mask, with the legs of a scaly beast protruding from her skirt. On the balcony the technicians from Brightalite are arranging spotlights, while the sound engineers, keen young men in yellow shirts whose mobile telephones have apparently become integrated into their anatomies, are setting up their equipment.

Amid the slow crescendo of preparation, a figure in white and blue stands at each end of the room, following instructions that warders are not to move around the hall but to stay fixed and keep their eyes on everything. At one moment Bill ventured on a tour of inspection, which took him ten feet from Anna. As he moved towards her, he continued to survey the preparations, till he was so close that a glance at her could not be avoided. The sight of her, looking half in his direction and half, nonchalantly, into the air, made him stop, open his eyes wide and twitch his mouth into a tentative half-smile. It seemed tentative, because his heart was filled with conflicting excitements and he was afraid that if he looked at her too long he would lose control. When she saw him coming nearer she tried to look neutral. She was still wondering if she liked him enough to let him think something serious might happen between them, since she is a highly moral person who believes one should only embark on an intimate relationship when truly committed to the other person. Her relationships have been few. She still isn't sure about Bill: she was telling herself he's a kind and nice man, and she'd like to put her arms round him, but wonders if they'd have anything to talk about. He's so keen, it's almost off-putting... As he approached, much closer than he was supposed to, surely, she intended to give him a cool, appraising look. But when she saw his peering eyes and his funny, shy smile she was so touched and amused that she gurgled with laughter, and waved at him in a non-official sort of way. He did not know what this meant and thought she might be teasing and his smile waned so sadly that, unselfconscious for once, she put her fingers to her lips and blew him a kiss. His mouth fell open and he stopped walking, gazing at her speechlessly — until a crash from the far end of the hall forced him to investigate. As he stands again at his post he thinks she is beaming in his direction, though he is not sure of this. Is it a contemptuous smile, perhaps? She is so much better educated than him, how can she be interested in him except as a friend?, maybe that's all he can hope for, like a medieval knight though he does not want a life of chastity, enduring hopeless love for his lady... At one o'clock Ian finds them still standing dutifully at their posts, half a mile it seems away from each other.

'Everything going all right?' he says to Bill. 'I nearly forgot about you two. Any problems?'

No, no problems, really.

'Oh, well,' he says, 'I suggest you both go and have something to eat. I'm sorry everything's so irregular today.'

And yes, he wants them to have a break at the same time, and he will stay in the hall and keep an eye on things, and no, they're not to come back a minute before two, and since it's Anna's birthday (how on earth does he know that? she wonders) why doesn't he take her out somewhere nice? They'll be on duty together all afternoon, and if they want to confer (why does Ian use that word so emphatically? Bill wonders) from time to time, no harm done.

Bill is puzzled. What can Ian mean? His thoughts are always so apparent that Ian smiles. Bill is not particularly thrilled by this. Why do people always smile when they see him?

'Oh, go on, Bill, it's no secret, the whole museum knows.'

What is no secret?

'Go on, off you go.'

But he still hasn't said what isn't a secret and Bill doesn't like to ask and suppose she doesn't want lunch? She might want to go shopping, or have a rest, or go to the chemist . . .

But he asks her all the same and, yes, she would like to have lunch with him. If only she wouldn't laugh so much – he really can't understand what she means by it . . . but, oh, God, the happiness of it, how can one stand being so happy?

THE BOARD ROOM,
TWELVE TWENTY-FIVE P.M.

The board room is one of the museum's most sumptuous apartments. Located over the entrance hall and almost as large, it is lit by a massive Palladian window. This window overlooks a road, which the founder intended as a monumental avenue leading to the river. Only a few houses were constructed and nowadays the processional route dwindles into a traffic-filtering system and a bus station. On the panelled walls of the board room hang portraits of the Queen and the Duke, the museum's founder resplendent in the robes of the Bath, and successive chairmen. At the huge mahogany table (rescued by Auberon from the basement) innumerable committees have debated, candidates for senior jobs have trembled before panels of dignitaries seated kilometres away across the polished board, wealthy applicants for the privilege of making donations to the museum have eyed one another surreptitiously and wondered if it is a bonus to be invited to lunch here in the company of their peers. In rare moments of non-activity, Auberon likes to sit here on his own, enjoying the room's noble proportions, and considering the many things that worry and console him. Above all, he wonders if he is happy here, if he is wasting his talents, whether he should not be back at Oxford and setting some prints on the sands of time by writing real books as he knows he could do . . . He would miss the glitter and the power, but doesn't he realise how insubstantial they are? Is the great world really so great after all?

Today the table's set for a minimal lunch, which would gladden the civil servants who oversee the museum's finances. All these guests will get is sandwiches laid over dispirited lettuce leaves on brittle metallic trays, which bend dangerously when lifted, and own-brand mineral water from one of the dimmer supermarkets.

At twelve twenty-five precisely the room is silent. Sir Lewis Burslem is lounging, as though indifferent to any observers, in the ornate mahogany and leather armchair designed for the chairman. In front of him lie papers which he is studying carelessly, one arm drooping languidly beside his chair. Auberon, resembling a smouldering volcano rather than a man of the world, is rising from his seat on the Chairman's right, perhaps to move towards the principal door, which is opening. Among the muted tones of the half-shadowed rooms, Emma, wearing white linen, crisp and startlingly light, provides a higher accent as she enters the board room through a side door. She carries a pile of papers, apparently architect's drawings. Outside, the warm morning has been growing hotter, and at this moment the sun fills the room with the heady radiance of flaming (but frustrated) June.

Through the door walk three of the trustees, then another, then two more. It is well known that Sir Lewis requires exact punctuality for the meetings he's chairing, with only a moment or two for amiable preliminaries. As they come in, the men all in dark suits, except Trevor in his artistically licensed green corduroy outfit, and the women equally but more competitively sombre, they exude assurance. Auberon greets them at the door, sharing a cheerful remark between two or three to save time, while the Chairman casts off his threatening mood in a burst of controlling good humour. 'Good to see you,' he cries. 'Starvation rations, I'm afraid, but they'll leave space for this evening.'

Auberon and Sir Lewis have been discussing the Nowness of Now. Auberon raised the question of running costs for the new building. Sir Lewis had not thought about this matter but regards it as irrelevant. He does not appreciate the director's apparent determination to diminish his day of achievement. Typical of the modern age, when people won't acknowledge success but insist on quibbling.

'Lunch,' announces Sir Lewis, 'and shall we get started?' As the trustees munch their official sandwiches unenthusiastically, he begins. He hopes they like the exhibition. Yes, they evidently do, judging by their approving hums. He thanks them for their support. The staff are to be congratulated, he continues, especially Helen Lawless the special curator, who has given so much time and expertise. 'And Jane Vaughan,' interjects Auberon, who is less keen on Helen. 'And, of course, Jane Vaughan,' Sir Lewis echoes, with what passes for warmth, 'and the exhibition team and not least the Director.'

'Hear, hear,' the trustees say.

'And let's not forget the sponsorship team for finding a sponsor, not so easy these days,'

They all laugh.

'Tonight,' continues Sir Lewis, 'will be a great event. I don't need to remind the trustees of the need to arrive punctually and act as joint hosts. There's a guest list ready for you all – four hundred and three, at the last count. We expect you to recognise them all!'

They go through the programme: the reception, the distribution of catalogues (all the guests are to have one, but trustees must ensure nobody gets two), the presentations to HRH

('What a shame *she* can't come,' they say), the seating plan. 'This is being finalised as we speak by the chair of the dinner committee,' remarks Sir Auberon. More appreciative chuckles.

What I most dislike about these meetings, thinks Auberon, *is their pretence of good humour. What's the point of this pantomime of cordiality, this deference, when actually the board's almost always split? And it's so galling that the views of board members — who know nothing about museums — are always rated more highly than the staff's. If only the sensible members would say more. Like Olivia Doncaster, for example. She's so sensitive.* At the thought and still more the sight of her — *Surely I can allow myself another glance, I haven't looked in her direction for . . . well, for minutes* — he relaxes and nibbles meditatively at an egg sandwich, his teeth delicately extricating the cress that escapes from the bread like a tendril of hair . . . *She's always so special, and today, in her grey linen jacket, she's delectable. So soft, her arms, a brush of golden down disappearing into the sleeves of her dress, the sleeves are short but not short enough . . . her peachy skin, her faintly vulnerable shoulders, her smooth neck, begging to be caressed . . .*

Talk has stopped and the Chairman is looking at him. They all are. Clearly he's expected to say something, and he tears himself away from studying the bones of her neck. She blushes faintly — has she noticed his contemplation of her? Has anyone else? He is confused by her look and by having no idea of what's being discussed.

'I need notice of that question, Chairman,' he says randomly, but with what he hopes sounds like witty insouciance. They all laugh, even the Chairman, who does not press him. *Obviously this is an OK response — that was a narrow one. I must concentrate. I'm tired, I suppose, after all the recent pressures, but however tired one is, losing one's grip at board meetings is madness. Now they're talking about the press and I must listen but who cares? What I realise is that I no longer care about Tanya, not even a little. Why should I realise this now, at this moment? Tanya's so aggressive, so practical, so angular and strident, so intellectual, always going on about moral values and our obligations, and pointing out my faults, which may be good for me but isn't at all nice . . . unlike . . . Dear God, I can't be in love with Olivia, I hardly know her, this is fantasy . . . but, then, it isn't just lust on my part, it's her character I really like, it's pure feeling on my part, it's her gentleness, her kindness, her natural elegance . . . Oh, God, what are they talking about now? Museum security? To hell with that . . . We've had such delicious talks in her conservatory, stretching in huge deck-chairs in the soft green twilight that inches through the massed plants, talking about business and sometimes other things. She's so attentive, sympathetic, thoughtful — yet perceptive . . . Of course, if we . . . if she left Tony Doncaster she'd never become a marchioness, and would she mind that? And if she remarried she'd have no title at all . . . Isn't this a bit premature on my part? I mean, I've no idea if she even notices me . . . Of course some titled divorcees hang on to their handle whoever they hitch up with . . . I must concentrate but I've heard this stuff a hundred times . . . Maybe she's Lady Olivia in her own right . . . Isn't it time I got married? Really, it's not so cool in your late thirties to be single, people think there must be some reason, they think you're gay, not that I'd mind but it's just not true . . . God, this meeting is boring and it's so hot in here. I wish I were in a green meadow under an apple tree with her . . . It lends cachet to a man, they say, to have a titled wife, absurd shibboleth but persistent . . . Would she be interested in somebody like me from such modest origins, would she like me if she knew me intimately, what on earth am I aspiring to? . . . Am I quite mad?*

'Do you have anything to add, Director?' asks the Chairman. He has nothing to add. *Except that one of the trustees is the most enchanting woman I've ever met and I want to live with her on a desert island and make passionate love the livelong day (with a simple flat in Paris for occasional weekends, and possibly a studio in Venice . . .)* 'No, I think that's all very clear,' he says briskly.

'Shall we have a break from formal business,' concludes the Chairman, 'and resume at two for the real meat of the meeting?'

THE MUSEUM CAFÉ,
ONE P.M.

The museum café is huge and noisy, filled with eager ladies from the Home Counties dressed up for a day in London. It is easily located by the smell of food, which permeates the surrounding galleries. For many years it was apparently designed to evoke a wartime British restaurant, but when Auberon became Director, the interior was about to be reinstalled as a French bistro. He persuaded the board that BRIT should be serving English food in an English setting, and energetic boardroom disputes between the country-pub party and the let's-pretend-we're in-one-of-those-exciting-places-off-Piccadilly school finished with a victory for tradition. There are more important battles to be fought than this one, Auberon (who was of the Piccadilly tendency) felt. In any case the country-pub fit-out might well be interpreted as an ironic post-modernist look, at least by sophisticated visitors. The staff detest it but one of the minor rules of a museum is that the staff always hate the café.

Today there are very few members of staff behind the sign saying 'Private'. When Diana, fraught after this tiring morning, arrives with her tray, she recognises only Terence, the curator of Agricultural History. As usual, he looks mournful, eating soup as though it were the final nourishment of his life. His department, which flourished under the previous Director, has dwindled under urban-minded Auberon, who is bored by plough-shares. Confronted by empty tables, Diana has to join him. She interprets a twitch of his mouth as a greeting. 'How are you?' she says cheerfully.

'Mm,' he replies noncommittally. At least this is better than his previous style of greeting, which was 'I can't remember which department you're in.'

'Things all right in the department?' she perseveres.

'Oh, fine,' he says. 'Absolutely fine. It's marvellous having a post frozen every time someone leaves. We're down to two and a half, compared to nine four years ago. Before the Great Panjandrum arrived.'

Diana thinks it better not to respond directly. After all, her own department has more than doubled in the past four years.

'Ah, well,' she says. 'But at least you have your wonderful collections intact. And you haven't been abolished, like the Instruments of Warfare Department.' This is not very constructive but she must say something. *There's Hermia at the traditional English puddings counter. Oh, Lord, oh, Lord. Why should I be so affected by seeing Hermia? It was only yesterday I noticed how special she is — of course I've always liked her, but in the six months she's been here I've never been so struck by her, not in the way I am now ... In any case, what's Hermia doing here? Is she alone? Is she buying something absolutely delicious and special to take away, or eating her lunch in the café? Hermia is so exceptional — perhaps we could at last get the chance to talk a little now, away from the office. It would be so ... so ... reviving. It's hard to have this dreary curator sitting at the table — surely he's almost finished the stodgy shepherd's pie with carrots and peas he's boringly chosen? But no, he's still talking.*

'Who cares about collections nowadays?' he is saying. 'There's nothing glamorous about collections, it's all exhibitions and P bloody R, begging your pardon, ma'am. Who cares any more here about history or academic achievement? We might as well give up bothering with stupid old objects and turn the museum into a permanent funfair. ELEGANCE – I ask you!'

Diana keeps her positive good-humoured look in repair and says in a warm but noncommittal way, 'Well . . . mmm.' *Hermia's now looking around the café, as people do, to see if there's anyone to avoid. Or perhaps someone she wants to join – who would that be? Who, now? Will she even come over to the staff section?* Diana tries to look encouragingly towards Hermia, while maintaining an air of patient concern towards old Terence.

'It's cuts, cuts, cuts all the time,' he is droning. 'Our dedicated acquisition budget has gone completely, even the trust funds for departmental purchases have been absorbed into the general budget. There's hardly any travel money, no vote even for volunteers' petrol, everything's mouldering away – and meanwhile that bloody Bankes is travelling the world first class in search of another pretentious exhibition.'

I love conversations about Lucian's enormities but I must defend my department. And then – oh, heaven – Hermia is coming in our direction. Say nothing, Diana, just look calm. Smile at her, noncommittally if you can. She's smiling back – warmly, I think. Suppressing irrational joy, she points out to Terence that temporary exhibitions bring in crowds of people, often make a profit and are essential for the museum's financial survival. As she chats she is clearing a space on the table, eagerly but, she hopes, unobtrusively. And Hermia does sit down at their table.

Oh, how I love you! How I dote on you! What am I saying? I'd so enjoy these few moments with you, if only Terence would go away. But he stays, even though there's nothing left on his plate. What will he do now? Is he going to start talking about employment grades in a fantastically dreary way, or how curators are now on a lower salary scale than other departments? He does not know Hermia and she's forced to introduce them.

Though not moved to speak, Terence watches Hermia minutely as she lays out her salad, glass of water and knife and fork on the table. She creates a zone of elegance around her on the pseudo-cottagey table. *But why does Terence stare at her? Can this torpid old thing — in his dusty tweed jacket with leather patches on the elbows and his expression of permanent irritability — be conscious of the ash-blond hair, the high arched eyebrows and the pale olive skin of this young woman, who radiates grace among banality?*

'Have you seen the exhibition yet?' Hermia asks him pleasantly. *There's absolutely no need for her to be pleasant to this old has-been, but how do I tell her that?*

No, he hasn't seen it, not since he installed the agricultural implements — but he tells her this regretfully, not aggressively as he would tell Diana.

'Oh, but you must,' she cries. 'After all, the section you have lent to is of such an interest, it is so central to the narrative — the creation of a folklore around the pastoral ideal and agriculture in the eighteenth century . . .'

He seems to have melted completely, gazing spaniel-like at her as she eats her West Country Farmer's Salad. This is almost unendurable — Hermia will be leaving in a moment and I've hardly spoken to her. Seething, she notices that Lucian — *Oh, God, not him, that really is the limit* — has come into the café and is surveying its occupants. Seeing the group at her table, he frowns, shooting, she is sure, a look of irritated dislike in her direction. Hermia follows her look and waves at the new arrival. 'Ah,' she says, 'I told Lucian I'd be here, he said he might come along too, to talk about progress on the exhibition.'

'I thought he never came here,' says Diana. 'I thought it was beneath him.'

'I don't think he comes very often, in fact I had to give him directions,' replies Hermia mildly, 'but I suppose he's so busy today . . .'

'The department is busy. That doesn't mean he is.' She must not sound disloyal. It must make her seem so unattractive.

'Don't you think Lucian is the busiest of us all? He just has a different way of working . . .' Hermia remarks, innocently as it were. But his arrival brings one advantage. Terence, muttering something bucolic and still gazing at Hermia (if one can be bothered to listen, he seems to be saying he'll pop into the exhibition later though he can't be doing with private views), collects his utensils and hurries away as though terrified of having to share a table with the Head of Exhibitions.

This individual advances upon them, showing no sign of having noticed the agricultural depression. He holds a large tray, decorated with a painting of a picturesque cottage and peasants after George Morland. The tray bears one large espresso (*They'll be serving traditional farmhouse espressos shortly, too ludicrous, this place*). Lucian grips this tray like an offensive weapon, staring forward as though avoiding superfluous eye contact. As he approaches them, his eyes fix on Hermia. Diana recognises this look of Lucian's: she has seen it when he has been in pursuit of an elusive exhibit, ruthless, single-minded, mesmerised by the object he's pursuing and determined to possess it. The intensity of his emotion makes him strangely compelling. Now, though, it's not a work of art he wants . . .

Amid the genteel bustle Hermia remains calm. *She doesn't seem excited by Lucian's arrival. She might well be flattered by his interest, of course — repulsive as he is, he's a magnate of the museum world. But her smooth, untroubled face tells one nothing.*

'Hello, Hermia,' says Lucian anxiously, almost nervously, not at all in his usual confidently abrasive manner. *Ah, he's at that stage. Not sure how to deal with this situation. I want to say, 'Go away, you revolting man, how can you imagine for a moment that this delicious girl' — my God, what am I feeling? — 'could be interested in your bloated power-hungry body or your unpleasant personality? It's impossible, even for a moment.'* As these thoughts run through her mind she offers Lucian, out of politeness, a nod. He responds with a vicious leer, a caricature of courtesy. During this mute exchange, confronted by a man, Diana realises that her feelings for Hermia are wholly new to her. *No man's ever aroused such intensity in me . . . I must be what I now realise I am and not what I thought I was . . .*

In the agitation of this internal strife she leans forward and knocks over her glass. It does not break, merely strikes the table gently and spills its contents over the polished wood. This must be a good omen, or at least not a bad one. All three, two of them at least struggling with pressing thoughts, watch fatalistically as the water slides over the table, absorbing crumbs and fragments of lettuce and carrot before dribbling on to the floor. Then she and Lucian look up and at each other. Each instantly understands the other's state of mind. He seems astonished, as though seeing her for the first time. Meanwhile Hermia, faintly flushed perhaps but otherwise composed, looks conscientiously at her watch as she finishes her salad. Can she be aware, this pure young woman, of the desires surging in their hearts? *Ah, well*, thinks Diana, *the course of true love never did run smooth . . .*

'I'm so sorry,' she says.

There is a pause.

'Worse things can happen,' says Lucian. 'At least the glass didn't break. That's bad luck, breaking glass, you know, old superstition . . .'

'Bad luck for whom?' Diana asks.

'For you, I suppose. Perhaps for all of us,' he says, and for a moment he and Diana study one another, each newly curious about a person they have long known and generally disliked, whom now they see afresh. For the first time in years, she later reflects, she does not feel viscerally hostile towards him, and he seems intrigued by her, not just by her boots . . .

'There's a strange sensation, like excitement, in the museum today. Is it Midsummer's Day madness?' remarks Hermia, for whom the silence at their table, amid the surrounding clatter, must have become uncomfortable. 'Have you noticed it?' As one, they turn to look at her. Each marvels at her grace, the fascinating Anglo-Italian coolness of her warmth, her sophist-ication and yet her naturalness. For a moment neither speaks, and then they turn to look at one another and both in unison say, 'Yes,' and smile. It is unclear whether they are smiling at her or one another or the atmosphere within the museum or the oddity of the human condition.

'How strange you all look, as though you're obsessed by each other,' interrupts a well-bred voice. It is Jane. She speaks humorously but as they turn towards her she realises she may have spoken the truth. She continues, 'May I join you?' but she sounds unconfident that they want her to penetrate their little circle.

'Yes, of course, do,' they answer. Lucian remarks, neutrally, that Diana has poured water all over the table and that Jane must take care.

As she sits down, Jane realises that though she is bursting to ask Diana for more help over the Gainsborough there's little she can say in this company. After a moment Hermia declares she must leave and goes, in spite of their voluble protests. Lucian and Diana both become quiet as soon as she departs, both stare at the table, and frown, and look melancholy. Jane examines them, and does not at all understand their behaviour.

What is it about this girl that makes them so keen for her to stay? Jane asks herself, in the midst of this silence. Is it her looks, her gentle manners, her sympathetic shyness, her willingness to

listen? Is it the mysterious glancing sexuality, which even Jane
thinks she can detect in her? She braces herself for questions
from Lucian about why she was inspecting the Gainsborough
so closely this morning, but no such questions come. Obviously
he does not know about it – or perhaps he has a secret reason
for not asking . . . or perhaps Auberon never told him – and
why should that be?

ANGEL COOKS,
ONE FORTY-FIVE

Angel Cooks is not disorganised today. Of course, Angel Cooks is never disorganised. But compared to the usual strict control, the atmosphere is a trifle tense. Mr Rupert's features betray the flicker of a frown as he restrains himself from breaking one of his cardinal rules, which is to keep out of the kitchen in moments of tension. Instead he is issuing a string of orders to his secretary and tapping angrily at his computer, listing and relisting the evening's order of events. He is not anxious, of course, no, not at all anxious, only concerned about dinner being delayed by the guests not sitting down, or His Royal Highness arriving late, or the lobsters not being acquiescent, all problems that would make the menu even harder to deliver... Much as he admires the Royal Family, he's doubly anxious when they attend one of his events, the potential problems are so much greater. And there's always the possibility of a security alert and everyone being evacuated from the building just as the dinner is reaching its culmination...

Guided by an instinct he can't ignore, he hurries down the passage into the kitchen. Gustavus is not to be seen. In the canapé kitchen, the five thousand canapés for the evening (thank goodness they refused to do that cocktail party for the Lord Mayor tonight) are being assembled as though on a conveyor belt before being placed in the cool room. Six people are working on the vegetables: the *panachés* are beginning to take shape though the turnips are slow today, the new potatoes have been cleaned and are ready to be packed, the *jus* to be poured over them stands in twenty glass containers. The salad is ready to go. Four jeroboams of walnut oil are being packed into cases. As for the beef — well, where is the beef? It should surely be well advanced by now but there's no sign of it at all.

'Where's Gustavus?' asks Mr Rupert, of one of the sous-chefs.

'Oh, he just popped out,' she says, blushing slightly. 'He's been here all morning, he was getting a little tired. It was the beef and *foie gras* that was worrying him — he didn't seem completely happy about the recipe...'

'Not happy about the recipe?' exclaims Mr Rupert, his voice rising steadily as he speaks. 'What right does he have not to be happy, or happy for that matter? It's irrelevant, whether he's happy or not. We've done it at the National Gallery, we've done it at Chatsworth. He's not happy?'

'I meant,' she replies, her hands shaking slightly, 'that he didn't think he was doing it terribly well, he thought his interpretation was wrong. Oh, Mr Rupert, he's trying so hard.'

'Where is he? I don't think he's popped out,' says Mr Rupert. 'I know where he'll be.' And striding towards the back of the huge white kitchen he raises his voice: 'Gustavus! Gustavus!'

Gustavus is in his office. He has taken off his chef's hat and is sitting in front of his desk, his head in his hands. Beside him are an empty wine glass and a plate on which lies a slice of beef, looking as though it's been violently assaulted. He does not turn when Mr Rupert comes in.

Mr Rupert inspects the back of Gustavus's head before

speaking. The situation is not wholly unfamiliar to him, though he has never had any trouble with Gustavus. He speaks gently. 'Gustavus,' he says. 'Gustavus. Are you all right?'

Gustavus turns. His face is crumpled and his eyes are red. 'The beef's no good,' he says. 'I tried it and it's just no good. It's too heavy. I know it's one of your specialities but I can't get it right, it's too rich. I have your recipe but I tried a little experiment, I thought it would be exciting, I shouldn't have done. The way I've done it, it's hopeless.'

Mr Rupert cuts a sliver off the beef.

'Don't eat that,' says Gustavus, in a miserable voice. 'It's disgusting, and cold too. And I did so want to do you credit on this great occasion, and His Royalness, and everyone in the world here and all I do is produce this shit.'

'I can assess beef at any temperature, and I know good beef from bad beef better than anyone in the country,' replies his boss, sliding the meat with its succulent coating of *foie gras* into his mouth. Gustavus looks at him pleadingly. Mr Rupert raises his head towards the ceiling, bites, chews, pushes the meat round his mouth, and considers. Then he looks Gustavus in the eye. 'It's excellent,' he says. 'Better than I've ever made it. What have you added, though?'

Gustavus opens eyes and mouth wide in amazement and gratitude. 'It's a tiny hint of mustard glaze,' he says, 'mustard from Morocco, with a little tarragon and lime in it. Do you really like it? Aren't you just pretending, to make me happy?'

'I really like it. You are very talented. This will be perfect,' says Mr Rupert. 'Now, I have some orders for you. I want you to give your instructions to your chefs for the next hour and then I want you out of here till three. A run round Battersea Park, d'you understand? Definitely not a trip to the pub – you're not to drink any more until the end of the dinner. The more you drink, the less capable you are. And no pick-ups either, just a nice run in the fresh air. And no other substances, either. OK, is that clear?'

Gustavus shudders. 'I just wanted to feel more confident – at least I don't hide it if I drink. That's a good sign, isn't it?'

'That's quite a good sign. Back at three. Run in the park, OK?'

'Yes, Mr Rupert,' says Gustavus, gasping a little. 'You're so kind. And you really like the beef?'

'Yes, Gustavus. The beef will be unforgettable.'

JANE'S OFFICE,
TWO FIFTEEN P.M.

There is a message for Jane, back in her office. Sir William St John would like to speak to her.

Why has he rung back? Has Marten spoken to him? Is he going to tell lies about the state of the painting when it left his possession? Does he imagine he has some sort of a reputation to defend? Will he be as arrogant as most people of his sort (a member of the intellectual aristocracy, Jane despises the territorial variety)? Will this be a *mauvais quart d'heure*?

As it turns out, Sir William is extremely amiable. 'Sorry not to have been in touch sooner,' he says. 'Had to go out with my wife, she insisted on collecting some jewellery from the bank for tonight's bash, awful bore, normally wouldn't let it out of the vaults but I can't stop her having her way, ha ha. She wants to look as glam as possible, after all she is the modern Lady St John you know, doesn't want to be upstaged by the historic one — not sure she's going to dress up as Puck, though. The picture looks glorious on the poster, I must say ... hmm ... Actually I think Delia will look OK in her glad-rags, much younger than me, you know, and quite a looker too, but I can't help teasing her. Anyway, how can I help you — I think we've met, haven't we?'

No, Jane doesn't think they've ever met. She just wants to ask him a question about the Gainsborough. Of course, he'd be happy to tell her anything he can.

What was the condition of the painting when it left his possession? Sir William does not speak for a moment, but laughs. 'Oh, not so bad, really, it needed a clean, of course, wonderful what restorers can do, isn't it? Yes, it had been damaged a bit, there was a fire at the big house long ago. When was the fire? Oh, during the First World War, they never really got to grips with the house again after that, Father sold it in the twenties, just for the building materials — yes, we lost a few things but nearly everything was rescued. The problem with the Gainsborough was, it was so big they had trouble getting it out. It was kept upstairs, yes, upstairs, Father told me, in a cupboard or something, seems odd now, doesn't it? Actually,' he says, 'if you won't think me awfully inquisitive, why d'you need to know all this?' When she reassures him that she's only interested in historical accuracy he remain loquacious but becomes more cautious. Yes, during the nineteenth century the picture was hardly ever shown — it had a bad reputation, was meant to be unlucky according to family tradition, broke up marriages, had a strange effect on people who spent too much time near it, made them lose control of themselves and fall in love with all sorts of unsuitable people. That was the story anyway, lot of bunkum, really. What did it derive from, this story? she asks. But he does not answer. Instead he says, 'I know where we met, we were at Cambridge together, weren't we?' — and as she digests this unfamiliar idea he goes on, 'We acted in *Love's Labour's Lost* together at Girton. You were the Princess, I was Dumaine, one of the lords, as I recall — do you remember? I knew I knew the name and when I heard your voice on the telephone you sounded just as you used to — you wouldn't recognise me now, awfully fat and ugly, but I was OK-looking then, I believe, and you were certainly much more than OK-looking . . . Wasn't your old man a bigwig somewhere?'

Jane is so startled by this development and by the half-lost recollection of a hot summer at Cambridge, and of the beautiful young man who played Dumaine and held her hand whenever possible during rehearsals, that she can hardly speak. But finally, 'Yes,' she says, 'I do remember – but you weren't called William St John then.'

He laughs. 'No, I didn't think it was cool to have a name like that, liked to be known as Bill John. Used to madden my father, that was the point. I turned back into William St John when he died.'

'I seem to remember calling you Billsy.'

'Billsy to my friends – that's me, was me, anyway. Not much Billsy about me nowadays. Anyway, Delia can't stand the name. Well, we'll meet tonight, can't wait.'

'Oh, I'm nothing to look at now,' she says, 'nothing at all. Plain, and dull. Just an old curator.'

'Don't believe you,' he answers. 'There'll be lots to catch up on, won't there? But in the meantime, this picture. Well, Janey – wasn't that what we called you?'

'Yes,' she says. 'In the past.'

'Janey – just to wrap up the story, now that the catalogue's printed, and you can't publish what I say . . .' there's a teasing note to his voice . . . 'the Gainsborough was never shown in the house during the nineteenth century, for the reasons I've given you. And also because that particular Lady St John was thought to be a terrible bad lot and there were stories about her in the family, which no one else was allowed to know. Supposedly she had a great affair with a man in the Life Guards only a few months after she was married, then ditched him because she got bored with him. He killed himself, it was hushed up but the husband got wind of it, he was older than she was, worried about his beautiful wife, worried about whether his little son was really his son, and his heir, you see what I mean... It would have been pretty disastrous, you know, would make all of us into bastards, no right to the title or anything. There's no way of proving it now, of course, but it may well have been true... He forced her to leave London and move to Suffolk where he kept her more or less a prisoner. She died a year or two later, in childbirth, and only the little boy survived her.'

'You've never told anyone all this, have you?' she says. 'There's nothing about it in any of the files.'

Sir William sounded reflective. 'Well, it's a miserable story, it may be exaggerated, I don't know. But you can see why they wanted to keep it quiet. Even now there's still a bit of family property, you know, a few pictures and an acre or two, we don't want our rights questioned, do we?, lots of cousins around... I'm not at all sure they wouldn't sue, the other branch of the family, greedy lot they are. I'm only telling you because you're a scholar and an old friend too, I know I can count on you not to tell anyone. The story was always passed down in the family as a secret, father to son, mother to daughter.'

'And the picture? What did her husband feel about the picture?'

'Her husband didn't like it, not surprising, really. The story is he told the artist to paint the dog in, because he said he'd married a bitch. And he hated the fact she was painted as Puck, thought it was terribly *déclassé*.' There is a silence at the other end of the line and Jane wonders whether to prompt him. But he resumes. 'After her death he put the picture in some out-of-the-way corner, it upset him. When he remarried, the last thing his new wife wanted was a huge portrait of her glamorous predecessor staring at her every morning over the Rice Krispies. It came out again in the son's time and began to acquire this peculiar reputation. It was meant to affect people's emotions if they looked at it. Silly story, of course, but it's true that the son and heir did marry his cook at a young age, she was a very good wife and bore him fourteen healthy children. But marrying the cook wasn't at all what the family had in mind.'

'So when the portrait re-emerged recently,' asks Jane cautiously, 'how did it look? Was it much damaged?'

He does not answer at once. 'Well, as I say,' he responds, a slightly different note in his voice, 'it was not in prime condition. But perfectly all right, just a little . . . eh . . . Funnily enough, the greyhound in the left-hand corner was particularly fresh, I always liked that bit. Well, if that's enough for the moment . . . I've got a few things I should be getting on with . . .'

'Of course,' says Jane, 'me too. I look forward to seeing you tonight.'

There is a pause. 'D'you think we'll recognise each other?' he asks ruminatively.

'Oh, I think so,' she says. 'Look out for the hair, it's not really changed so much, though the rest of me has, unfortunately.'

'Your hair, your beautiful red hair. I remember that. And all you girls wore white, didn't you? It suited you particularly well. What are you wearing tonight?'

'Green actually,' she says. 'I suppose I should be wearing black, to suit my advanced age.'

'I'm wearing black,' he says, and then 'Goodbye,' rather gently.

THE BOARD ROOM,
TWO P.M.

The heads at the boardroom table are not all grey. Though grizzled, the one at the top of the table is compact, clipped and forceful. Two or three are pepper-and-salt and one is hairless, but there's a fine variety of coiffures on parade – a fashionably cut blond male head and a ditto female, one or two short-back-and-sides in tones of black and French grey, a mane of rich curly brown hair arranged with loose elegance on a female support, and even a blue head supporting a diamond net. This is not a fusty board: the Chairman has assembled exuberant youth (relatively speaking) as well as wisdom and gravity. A yard or two from the main proceedings, a short-cropped red head, bent over a laptop set on a little attendant table, hardly looks up.

Nearly all the heads are turned towards the head at the top of the table. It is producing sounds to which the others respond, angling sideways or bending downwards as though thinking deeply. The talking head sometimes looks forward but more often to left and right, driving its gaze up and down one row of attentive listeners, then down and up the other.

A great many words flow from the chairing mouth. 'We're thinking out of the box, looking at a new museum concept, a museum about people, not objects... intensely of today... radical re-evaluation of our society... robust... new...

robust media-inclusive material reflecting life of everyperson. An architectural competition attracting world attention . . . world-class building by internationally known architect . . . make us a totally innovative destination venue . . . a place not for the élite but for all . . . social inclusion's the name of the game . . . showcasing material culture, popular music, sport, shopping . . . globalisation . . . multiracialism . . . humour . . . colour . . . consultants . . .'

At least, thinks Emma, taking the minutes at her little table, *he's reading from a text so there must be a copy somewhere. Sounds quite fun, actually, but Auberon will hate it.*

The blond head to the talker's right is the only one not turned towards the speaker. It surveys the table, while the right hand attached to it takes notes. Only occasionally do its eyes fix on the speaker.

After quite some time the talking mouth closes. The other heads look at one another to see how the rest will react, and shake themselves and bob up and down, and the hands attached to them even clap, discreetly but supportively. Then the talking head announces that a gift of £10 million has been offered towards the project, on condition only that the board is satisfied with the final result. More clapping, followed by a pause and coughs and paper shuffling.

So far so good. Never taken minutes before, I'm already exhausted. What do I do when they all talk at the same time?

'Well?' says the Chairman. 'What do you all think? No progress possible at all, of course, without the board's full approval. Shall we go round the table? John?'

This is John Percival, deputy chairman of the board. Unlike the others, he already knows about the proposals.

How do I write down the names? 'Percival' or 'John' or 'JP'? How do I record what they say? Wish I could do shorthand like Mum — must concentrate

— hard to catch what some of them are saying . . .

Self-assured, patrician, John Percival compliments the Chairman on his foresight, energy, ability to raise enormous sums of money apparently without effort . . . He wonders about the impact of the new building on the existing museum, which is already almost more than they can manage . . . Running costs are a problem . . . In the past year or two they've had to lose so many curators, close the Research Department . . . Shouldn't they commission a feasibility study before making further commitments?

'. . . JP expressed his general approval of the scheme and admiration for energy and enterp. of Ch.' That should do it . . . *'approved of the idea in princ. but we have to look at overall implics.'*

The chairman draws these comments firmly into his grasp. These are important considerations, he agrees, but housekeeping mustn't halt exciting initiatives . . . Museums must adapt to a new audience and new technology . . . Nowness should offer a reflection of modern Britain's financial and business achievement . . . infinitely extended access, making heritage part of now . . .

How much of this do I have to put down? Some of it's just hot air . . . I can give him a draft and a sexy smile, that should do the trick.

Doris Hobson, to John Percival's right, is enthusiastic, her blue-rinsed curls darting, bowing and jerking as she speaks. 'A wonderful idea . . . we must show the best of contemporary design and prove how dull and old-fashioned other museums are. Much of our museum is out of date and could be closed without loss, and look at the opportunities for corporate lettings this new building will give us, and it will create close links with exciting aspects of the modern world – and the staff here don't have enough to do' (this is said with a jerk of the head towards the Director). *I certainly won't minute that. How dare she, the old harridan? The sooner she dies the better but let's get some more cash out of her first.* She'll see if her trust can find some money — she has an idea there might be some funds uncommitted over the next three years, would that be helpful? *'DH said a further contrib. might be available . . . Isn't that the right sort of note? The polish comes later, thank goodness some of these people are so verbose you don't have to write down everything . . . and* OH NO, *now they're all talking about minuting, will I have to say something? . . .* PANIC . . .

'May we minute that?' says the Chairman, with a conniving laugh.

'Certainly,' says Mrs Hobson, 'but please keep the amount open. A substantial sum, you might say at least three million pounds . . . Do you understand that, young woman?'

That must be me — the old cow . . .

Appreciative gasps erupt around the table and the Chairman beams expansively. Even Auberon beams, in Pavlovian reflex. 'Yes, Emma, will you minute that with great care?' says the Chairman jovially. 'Maybe in capitals.' Everybody laughs.

'A contrib. of at least three mill. would be made available from her trust . . .' Big deal — it's easy to be generous if you're rich . . . and it allows you to be courted all the time and be horrible to people who work for you . . . Auberon hates her, quite right . . .

The master head bobs almost uncontrollably at this announcement and if possible harder yet when Amanda Mann (who actually has to dash, in a few moments, to a frightfully crucial meeting at Channel Four, so sorry, but simply must say something before going) intervenes: 'What I find terribly exciting,' Emma thinks she's saying, 'is the opportunity to mix media. There's no need to stick to the conventional museum. Here's a chance to combine film, photography, video art, the most sophisticated contemporary communication with the stuff that goes on in an old-style museum. We can use Nowness to analyse and celebrate – yes, I mean it, celebrate,' and her glowing contralto glows even more richly, 'things from the home, things people can relate to from their everyday experience, bring them into the stuffy museum context – put a VCR beside a vestment, a Ryvita next to a Rembrandt! This is one of the most thrilling moments of my life. Well done, Chairman!' she concludes, the warm emphatic contralto that has energised so many executives at Channel Four meetings resounding like an organ.

What an idiot . . . hate her makeup, pretending to be so funky when she's not that young . . . 'AM said this was the most thrilling moment of her life' . . . ??? . . . What kind of a life d'you have, darling?

The temperature in the board room is rising, both physically (the room, lofty as it is, is absorbing the growing heat of the day) and mentally. The heads are leaning inward eagerly, eyes flashing to and fro as they assess others' reactions, mouths opening and closing as each seeks to make a dynamic contribution.

As Amanda gathers her papers into her black and silver attaché case and prepares to leave, it's Sir Robert Pound's turn. He, too, is swept into the current: Auberon's projections, he realises, were quite wrong. Bold scheme, says Sir Robert, will cost a lot of money but we can't reject such an idea and the amount of money already raised is astonishing . . . Can we afford to turn down such a possibility?

And Lady Doncaster likes the idea too, so up to date, and can it involve the young?, so important to get them interested in museums and the countryside and traditional things; sometimes they seem to have no knowledge of their roots, it's so sad when our heritage is so rich (*What's she on about? Doesn't she realise this thing is about Nowness not stately homes? She's really not so bright though Auberon seems to think so, ho hum*) as well as our future . . . 'I wish,' Lady D goes on, 'I wish I could contribute seriously financially as so many of you have promised to do' – *Typical of the aristocracy, they all say they've no money however rich they may be, just mean, that's what they are* – 'but perhaps I can do something about organising a ball or a fund-raising dinner . . .' *'Lady D offered to organise a ball or a FR dinner' . . . Please not, please not, balls are the pits, I'll end up doing most of it and there's so much work and so little profit at the end of it . . .*

There's vigorous assent at the end of the table. 'Yes, young people are crucially important,' says the Chairman. 'They have a vital role in all of this,' and the heads nod again like porcelain Chinamen's. *Clearly there's full agreement about this fascinating insight of Lady D's – though actually no one's likely to say young people are irrelevant.*

Reynolds Brinkman, captain of finance, a man with such a reputation for fierceness that those who meet him are captivated to find him relatively polite, welcomes the proposal too. Links with industry and the City could be immensely fulfilling . . . He could get six men round a table for lunch to discuss this scheme and by coffee time the museum would be richer by six million pounds . . . ongoing support, too, almost guaranteed . . . Brinkman UK should be able to make a contribution and is there any chance of one of the rooms being named for us? Not on the same scale as some of the figures mentioned but would something around five hundred grand be any use? Are you accepting small donations, ha ha? . . . Nowness will create a shop window for the UK, sorry, I mean Britain or do I mean England? . . . It's a pity we can't rebrand again – a Museum of Europe would be fabulous, branches all over Europe, Brussels, Berlin, Paris . . . HQ, of course, here in London . . . business opportunities, trade openings would be incredible, with this place as the centre of an international empire . . . We should really be pushing the envelope on this one . . . *Even more money – this is extraordinary.*

Do I have to minute that stuff about Britain not really being relevant? Actually RB is quite sexy, though Viv in his office says he can be really foul . . . What is this, am I fixated on older men? Auberon's looking tense, obviously not enjoying this orgy of generosity. Will any of them say no?

Trevor Christiansen, Auberon's old friend Trevor, even Trevor is carried away. This is vibrant, exciting talk, he thinks, just what is needed . . . He asks about contemporary artists and whether they will be represented in Nowness. It will be a showcase for the best of contemporary British art, he hopes. (*Why do they all talk about 'will' instead of 'would'?*) Of course, he's assured, contemporary artists will be well represented, there are wonderful opportunities here for patronage, lots of exciting site-specific commissions are envisaged illustrating British art at its best but reflecting contemporary British life and culture and particularly the lives of ordinary people . . . Trevor purrs.

'Alan?' says the Chairman cautiously. 'What do you feel?' He can't rely on Professor Stewart. He is a large man, both physically and intellectually impressive, and when he speaks he has a way – which can be annoying to those who don't agree with him – of filling the space. In the ensuing pause the heads calm themselves, no longer glancing to left and right but concentrating on the professor's polished and pleasant dome, the curly brown hair that clusters around it still vigorously youthful.

'I've listened to this discussion,' he says, 'with the greatest interest, and I congratulate the Chairman on his bold proposals. But I do have a few reservations, if I may?'

'But of course,' says the Chairman.

Unlike anyone else in the room, Professor Stewart allows himself a moment's consideration before he speaks. His voice is mellifluous and measured, authoritative but humane. He is not, the others instinctively feel, a man who is easily intimidated.

'This is what I'm worried about,' he says. 'Practical problems about this new extension have already been voiced, notably how we pay for the running costs of this new building once it's up. As we all know, the government in its wisdom reduces its grant-in-aid every year, whatever we do. Like John, I'd remind fellow trustees that recently this has led to serious cuts in staffing and conservation and care of the collection – which we tend to forget on a day like this, when everything's so positive and cheerful.'

The heads are now looking not at him but at the table or the ceiling or even out of the window. Only Auberon revives like a flower plunged into water (though he tries to disguise this). The professor goes on: 'I think this museum is doing wonderful things. But I don't subscribe to the view that curators are redundant or that scholarship has no place here. They represent what is really important, and they're at risk here now, as they have been for years. They are the people who understand what we possess, they hold the keys to all the objects we look after.' Mrs Hobson sneers at this, and Lady Doncaster looks politely surprised. 'In my view it would be completely unacceptable to cut expenditure on the main museum to run this extension. We don't want all icing and no cake, do we?' *How does that go in? 'AS stated that the museum should not be all icing and no cake . . .' God, it's hot in here, I wish they'd stop.*

'Many thanks, Alan, these are crucial issues,' says the Chairman equably, 'and ones I've given a lot of thought to, as we all have. I see Nowness as self-supporting, with an admission charge. Contributions to the endowment fund are built into all donations . . . There are major possibilities for fund-raising events . . . Hopefully it will make a profit, which will support the loss-making main museum . . .'

Stewart listens impassively. 'Well, I don't want to be a bore,' he says, 'or to go against the general mood, but I think I must put my point of view. When I sit round this table and other similar tables, and listen to talk about cultural institutions, and how they need to be renewed and the importance of visitor figures and marketing policies and accessibility and new buildings, I sometimes wonder if we're forgetting their ultimate purpose.'

'I don't think that's true, Alan – through you, Chairman,' says Reynolds Brinkman. 'We know very well what museums are about.'

'What *are* they about, then?' asks the professor, turning enquiringly towards his colleague.

Brinkman looks firm for a moment, and then uncertain. 'As far as I'm concerned the point of a museum is ... is ... to be a welcoming, well-run, efficient centre of activity where the public feel at home and can have a really good day out ...'

The tension's rising, no doubt about it. How about 'There was some general discussion over the role of museums'?

Professor Stewart surveys his colleague with narrowed eyes. 'Well, yes. With respect, your definition of a museum's more appropriate for a shopping mall. Men like Tradescant or Denon or Eastlake or Bode, the men who created the great museums, would have been astonished. I know the world's changed, but I still see no fundamental reason to abandon their ideals. What I've heard so far about the Nowness of Now doesn't convince me it would add anything substantial to what the outstanding museum in our care already offers. I don't want to be aggressive but is this idea truly what we're about? Can't other organisations do it better?'

Brinkman does not relish these remarks. 'There's no point in being rude ...' he begins, but Stewart overrides him. 'I'm sorry to be a bore, Chairman, but give me one more minute.

The original purpose of a museum is to collect, preserve, display and interpret objects. Those are still the essential purposes – the other activities that have emerged recently are just subsidiary. Scholarship is what's crucial in a museum, knowledge, conserving and understanding the past and study- ing the present – not just presenting it in a jazzed-up form without comment. I'm sorry to be so dogmatic but we do tend to forget these objectives. The only thing that makes museums special is their collections. If we forget it, our museums will turn into theme parks, probably not very good ones. They're the guardians of our past. We need our past, and if we're going to understand the past we need to work at it.' He laughs. 'I'm sorry,' he says, 'I'm used to lecturing to large groups of dozing undergraduates. But I hope you see what I mean.'

Oh-oh-oh, how do I minute this?

The sun beats more hotly than ever through the board- room windows. The heads waver uncertainly, unsure whether they should respond to this speech (which most of them have found hectoring) or seek guidance from the leading head. One grey pate, overcome by the hot afternoon, nods at its chest before jerking unhappily upward. The leading head seems briefly nonplussed. But it has met more aggressive opposition in board rooms, and at rallies.

'We all agree with you,' it asserts. 'Of course, our core purpose here is looking after our collections. But we can't sit about and hope for the best. The days of dusty old museums filled with arrowheads are past. We must animate our museums – they must contribute to today's debates.' Most of the heads nod and emit a consenting hum. 'As I see it, the Nowness of Now will be full of contemporary objects – not just works of art but advertisements, cosmetics, cars, cleaning equipment, bicycles, commercial products, film, photography. It's just that they won't be historic objects, they'll be about today, for today. Must a museum only be about the past? Don't we all spend too much time looking backwards?'

Professor Stewart stares into the distance. 'You've put your point of view, Chairman, and I've put mine,' he says. 'On a practical level, I do think we need to know more about how the Nowness of Now is going to work. It's one thing to build an extension, another to keep it going. I'd like to know too what the staff feel. They'll have to do the work, after all.'

No problems about that bit . . .

The Chairman looks briefly uneasy. 'Of course it's important that the staff should be involved. They're completely behind these proposals.'

'Perhaps I could say a word,' says Auberon tentatively. The Chairman turns towards Auberon, who avoids his eye, but instead fixes on Sir Lewis's large, white, sharp teeth.

'I should make one point clear. It would not be accurate to say the staff are happy.' He pauses in an unconsciously dramatic way, and blushes. The faces show faint surprise. This is not the cool Auberon they're used to. 'They're not happy with this idea because most of them don't know anything about it. It's never been explained to them and they've played no part in developing it. This should be understood by members of this board.'

Quite so, but this is bold and even bald. I'll have to get Auberon to write this bit out.

The Chairman assumes a new look, this time of patience, as if he is dealing with an able but somewhat unruly child.

'I might have consulted further,' he says, 'but I wanted to clear the idea at the highest level before taking it to the workers, as it were. I really couldn't clear the proposal with the staff before speaking to the board. What I'm looking for now is the board's approval for a feasibility study. All costs will be met from the promised donation, that's been sanctioned. Leaving aside what the director thinks just for the moment, do I have the board's approval in principle?'

Clever. Puts Auberon in his place, makes him look like a fusspot. And once they've committed themselves to spending money, nobody's going to want to waste that money, even though it's only a fraction of what'll be spent in the end.

The heads look around and nod at one another and at the chairman. All except Professor Stewart.

'How do we express reservations?' he asks. 'Are we voting formally?'

'I prefer to avoid votes,' says the Chairman, 'but if you want one . . . I suppose I hoped approval would be unanimous,' he ruminates, as though suggesting disloyalty. 'Those in favour?'

Six hands are raised.

'Those against?'

Up goes Stewart's hand.

'And I'm an abstainer, for what it's worth — but I'd like my abstention recorded,' says Percival.

'We're all abstainers until we know more,' replies the Chairman smoothly. 'Thank you all for a most interesting discussion, and thank you all for your support, in all sorts of ways. At the next meeting we'll report further — won't we, Director?'

The meeting is at an end.

'The meeting concluded at 3.48 p.m. All present congrat. the Chairman on the proposal he had put forward. Working group set up . . .' Oh, Auberon, poor Auberon . . . he looks so upset . . . none of that sparkle . . .

THE EXHIBITIONS OFFICE,
THREE THIRTY P.M.

The Exhibitions Office is empty, its usual inhabitants whirring round the exhibition. Two ceiling fans hum above the unoccupied desks, setting the piles of paper rustling. In the swelling heat, more indolently powerful by the minute, the potted plants droop as though wanting refuge in their roots. The windows are scarcely ever opened here because of the traffic noise, but when the blinds are left open, as they have been today, the afternoon sun assaults the room.

Into the stuffy emptiness steps a figure in a soft cream cotton dress. She moves to the windows, opens a little casement and pulls down the blinds. The room is calmed at once as Hermia, cool amid the heat, walks to her desk and sits down. She shifts one or two papers that lie in front of her but hardly pretends to work. It's too hot today. She looks reflectively into the distance. No expression appears on her face.

This lassitude is not unusual in Hermia, when she's alone. She blooms in the company of other people, changes according to their characters, reflects unconsciously what they want her to reflect. It's very easy to fall in love with her, not only because of her looks but because she can so readily be transformed by lovers into the person they're looking for. When her office reaches its high points of frenzy (several times a day, on the whole) she becomes as animated as the rest of them, but alone she finds it pleasanter to remain quiet – and contemplative, no doubt, though no one knows what she contemplates.

Her thoughts are interrupted by a red-faced, impatient noise. It is Lucian, desperate for a telephone call. For Lucian telephone calls are like the call of nature for other men. He tears across the room to his office but as he passes her desk he notices her, stops, and gasps. 'Oh, Hermia,' he says, and blushes.

She smiles, just a little, and raises her eyebrows. 'Can I do anything to help?' she asks. 'I have some work for Diana. But Diana is not here.'

'Oh, yes, I have something that needs to be done urgently,' he says. 'If you could . . . if you could . . . if you could help me with my speech for this evening.'

The telephone stops ringing and he jumps nervously. The door opens again, admitting Diana. She walks into the room slowly, looking at the two of them, and advances towards Hermia's desk. She stops. There is a silence. This is broken by the telephone ringing again. Lucian jerks as though to answer it but, pulled by some force he cannot analyse and which surprises him by its strength, he stays where he is. The two standing figures both gaze at the young seated woman. She looks questioningly from one to the other but does not speak.

'Hermia,' says Diana, 'you were going to help me with those faulty labels – but perhaps you have other things to do for Lucian . . .'

'No, no,' says Lucian politely, and then, 'or, rather, yes, I have got things that need doing. Can you help me?'

'Of course,' says Hermia. 'You are the head of the department, so if you need me you must take the precedence.'

'Take the precedence?' Lucian repeats the words as though this foreign-sounding phrase conveyed no meaning to him.

'In matters of work, you must take the precedence,' she says.

What does this remark mean? Diana and Lucian ask themselves. What is she thinking? Is this peculiar triangle apparent only to two of the people involved? She seems so innocent, so unaware . . .

Diana cannot endure this situation. She is sure Hermia means more to her than she does to Lucian – oh, to hell with what Lucian is feeling, anyway. Recklessly, she asks a question that has to be answered, one way or another.

'Lucian is clearly senior in every respect,' she says, 'but if you had the choice, which of us would you sooner help?'

Hermia looks perplexed, but not Lucian, staring as he is at her lips, her firm, curving lips.

'What do you mean? How can I answer that?' she asks, and laughs. 'Working here is not a matter for gratifying oneself.'

They still regard her silently. *Is she right?* Lucian wonders. Can working in a museum – or anywhere – ever truly offer pleasure or self-fulfilment? Has he been deceiving himself all these years?

'But it is true,' she continues, 'that Diana did ask me to help her with the labels some time ago, and that does seem to be quite urgent. So unless Lucian has something very important, perhaps he will forgive me . . .'

How charmingly, they both think, how modestly, with what thoughtful deference, she makes this enquiry. How can Lucian insist on anything in such company? They look at one another instinctively, as though sympathising with the other's admiration for this perfect girl.

'No,' he says, 'nothing so essential, or that it . . . that . . .'

What he intends to say is never known. The telephone rings and this time Lucian answers it in his own office. After a moment he closes the door.

Diana continues to stare at her young colleague. *What does her answer mean? Can it be a statement of love? Can I hope?* 'I ... I ...' she says, and chokes.

Hermia smiles. Warmly, Diana thinks. 'So, shall I help you with the labels? she asks. *Oh, yes, you certainly can, sweetness. Oh, how vulnerable I feel — I, Diana, sophisticated, good-looking, fashionable, clever, politically committed — I could be a teenage girl, I feel so unsure of myself ...*

GALLERY OF MODERN TECHNOLOGY,
FOUR P.M. ONWARDS

Bill and Anna are on duty in the Gallery of Modern Technology. It is situated at the top of the main staircase, overlooking the stairwell. The wall opposite the stairs is interrupted by two large official-looking doors, one leading to the board room and the other to the director's suite. It is a thoroughfare for the public and staff, who hardly notice the highly improving displays (sponsored by an IT firm which, by coincidence, has been invited to provide at least half the exhibits).

For the warders, excluded from the museum's official business and kept rigidly in their place, this is a favourite duty point. It lets one glimpse goings-on at the top, if only by guesswork. Who's in favour, who's out, who's rising or waning can be assessed from the way people walk, their expressions, the weight of the files they carry. Some passers-by forget they're being overheard, and speak much too freely – forgetting that their words will be scrutinised by the junior attendants' staff room minutes later.

The room is little visited today by the public. A few people enter, gaze without enthusiasm at the instructive diagrams and flashing screens, and enquire where the toilets are. On this bright afternoon the museum looks dispirited, its exhibits tired and uninviting. Even the traffic on the Trafalgar Road and the tinkle of the ice-cream van are more appealing than anything indoors.

Internal staff activity, on the other hand, offers lots of distractions today, enough to interest even Bill and Anna, who are now on duty there and who, after all, have many other things to think about. They had a successful lunch, they both think, their first ever. She talked to him about her art – another first – and explained why she works on making models of human torsos out of newspaper and mud sprayed with paint even though she actually prefers painting recognisable land-scapes. He reacted more intelligently than she expected – indeed, he appeared to know quite a lot about contemporary art. She realised that she'd expected him to be ignorant on the subject, she'd seen him as a museum attendant with very limited interests, while she was an artist who made a living working in a museum. Class prejudice, in fact. She shuddered at herself. Now they approach the afternoon expectantly, unsure where it will lead them but confident they'll like it. The heat makes them languidly amorous.

But they're not left long to enjoy this mood. Almost as soon as they are on duty, the door of the board room opens and out come the board members. At the sight of these remote, august figures, powerful, mysterious in their actions and faintly absurd, Bill stands unconsciously at attention, the unruly curl at the back of his head standing up in sympathy. Anna adopts a pose intended to express simultaneously politeness, efficiency, artistic integrity and the rebelliousness aroused in her by authority. In any case, none of the trustees notices them. The little group at the front talk excitedly in a hum of approval: 'Marvellous,' they say, and 'It must be Lewis who's giving the money, mustn't it?' and 'Sssh,' and 'We must move the place forward, no good just sitting on what we have.' They make for the stairs. They are followed by two men who look less filled with enthusiasm. One is Mr Percival, Bill and Anna recognise: he looks up as he passes them and nods. 'I'm very concerned,' the other one is saying, and 'Will it bring the whole place down? The figures look so very bad, and the department's being so impossible . . . ?'

After a while the door to the Director's office opens, and the Director and Chairman emerge. They seem tense and glare at one another, as they stop in what they think is a solitary space. Instinctively, Bill and Anna have hidden behind a showcase.

'There's no evidence for what you say,' says the Chairman, 'or, at any rate, your account's greatly exaggerated. The picture wasn't in perfect shape when it was put on the market but fundamentally it was in fine condition. Without any doubt, it's a key Gainsborough. I have certificates, three in fact, from important scholars, to prove it. I think you're trying to embarrass me.'

'I'm not trying to embarrass you,' replies the Director. 'I'm just warning you that doubts have been expressed about its condition and questions may be asked.'

'In which case,' Sir Lewis goes on, in a hectoring tone, 'I expect you to defend the picture absolutely. Any doubts cast on it publicly would be calamitous – not for me, I'm just its owner, but for the museum. You'd look the biggest fool, Auberon. It was you who sanctioned the publicity material.'

'Under pressure from you.'

'You had the chance to say no, you said nothing. I'm not responsible for your lack of courage, am I? Remember what I say. And don't forget, any negative publicity will look bad for all of us. It certainly won't help you. D'you have a date for your interview at the Bloomsbury Museum, by the way?'

'Yes,' says Auberon fretfully. 'A week today.'

'The Bloomsbury board will be here in force tonight, won't they? Better make sure your collar's clean.' He sounds sneeringly dismissive.

You can see, Bill and Anna think, why people are said not to like him.

And on they walk.

Bill and Anna emerge a little flushed from their hiding-place as Auberon returns to his office. As he approaches his door, a voice calls him. It is that airy-fairy expensively dressed trustee, Lady Doncaster, who keeps featuring in photo magazines you see in the dentist's waiting room. She hurries along the gallery towards him, eagerly expectant. 'Auberon!' she calls. 'Auberon!' His frowning face lightens. He turns and strides towards her and they meet in the very centre of the room, between Bill and Anna who are standing by the walls. As the Director and the lady meet, they clasp hands and gaze into each other's eyes. Then they realise they're being watched. For a loaded moment, the emotions linking the two couples crackle in the stuffy room among the unconsulted computers. Auberon and Olivia, bound up in one another, become aware for the first time of the two motionless figures to either side of them. Then Auberon says, 'Shall we speak in my office?' They disappear through the great mysterious door (through which neither Bill nor Anna has ever gone), as though these other lovers did not exist.

Bill and Anna gape at one another. There's so much to talk about, but they can hardly say anything when they're supposed to be patrolling the gallery (and then they'll be under observation from the security cameras). How strange it is, Anna reflects, to stand so close to someone you think you're falling in love with, yet not speak to him. And he thinks, *If I'm going to be worthy of her* (in fact he first thinks, *If I'm to be a worthy husband,* and dismisses this term as absurdly optimistic) — *if I am going to be a worthy partner, I'll have to give up this futile job where all I do is stand and stare, and never get anywhere . . .*

They're not alone for long. An anxiously eager lady from Education who is organising a session called Finding Yourself in Yesterday appears with her class, which consists of one small and faintly tearful child. He is her sole pupil and she is not letting go of him. More bustle at the end of the room, and a string of people comes in: *Mr Bankes from Exhibitions, and that bossy Diana, the man from Early Modern, isn't it?, the sweetly smiling lady from Education who likes everything done exactly as she wants it and nearly always gets it and a couple of curators we hardly know and Mary Anne from Press, oh, and Miss Vaughan from Art . . .* They march towards the Director's office, preoccupied and determined. As they reach the door, it opens and Lady Doncaster emerges, slightly flurried and hot-looking. She smiles at them distractedly and hurries down the corridor, tweaking at her skirt.

'Isn't she called Lady Bonkaster?' Anna offers, and they giggle.

Silence resumes. Only for a moment. A group of neatly suited ladies wander through, bright-eyed, drinking in the knowledge imparted by their voluntary guide — though Bill, who's read the labels several times, knows that almost everything she says is inaccurate. Then the torpor resumes, and in the afternoon quietness, broken only by the noise of traffic, they are too hot and sleepy to talk to one another. They do not have to wait long for the next development. The Director's door opens again and this time the staff tumble out, chattering like little birds.

'You can't think it's a good idea, Lucian,' says Jane, in resonant tones. 'You simply can't. It's so crude. The Nowness of Now — it's embarrassing!'

Lucian looks away from her. 'Not to me, it isn't,' he says. 'It's contemporary, it's exciting — we have to embrace the here and now.'

'Oh, come on, Lucian,' she urges. 'You can't believe in this stuff. Where's the Lucian I know, the man who made the museum's exhibitions the best in Britain?'

'We could have a series of themed events,' suggests a woman, Bill and Anna think she's the Head of Press, 'like a Dutch picture exhibition, *The Downess of Dou.*'

They seem to be amused by this.

'Or an agricultural exhibition, *The Cowness of Cow.*'

'Or one on etiquette, *The Bowness of Bow.*'

'Or a prisoners-of-war installation, *The Powness of PoW.*'

'And how about a pussy-cat happening — *The Miaowness of Miaow?*'

Lucian alone does not smile. Following his sternly forward-looking figure, they giggle their way down the corridor and disappear from view, meeting on the way John Winterbotham. He glares at Anna and Bill as he passes towards the Director's door. They return his look in what they hope is a keen but deferential way, and peer around the gallery as though it might contain something for them to be watching out for. They hope the next passer-by will offer them yet more entertainment. And as Mr Winterbotham disappears through the Director's door, Bill mouths something to Anna, who laughs, and they clasp hands, and together they do a silent waltz along the sunny parquet.

GALLERY OF INDUSTRIAL REVOLUTION
AND GREAT HALL, FOUR P.M.

The Gallery of the Industrial Revolution is one of the 'unimproved' galleries, as Auberon puts it. Laid out in the late 1940s, it contains a replica of the original Spinning Jenny, paintings of Manchester in the early nineteenth century, cases of complex machinery, and in the centre a steam engine. But displays about Britain's past industrial prowess are no longer acceptable to most senior curators, who think it hopelessly old-fashioned to present any picture of Britain's success as an industrial nation or its technological advances, and consider that the portrayal of social otherness in early industrial Britain is of much greater importance. Unfortunately, reinstalling the gallery, and removing the huge pieces of machinery that crowd it, is financially impossible. To save the public from inappropriate messages, which might be interpreted as nationalistic self-congratulation, the room is frequently closed, particularly since it is now used to prepare events next door in the Great Hall. On such occasions, and particularly when the dinner is large and magnificent, the room is closed for days and many of the exhibits are wrapped in thick plastic, filling the room with white-sheeted, indecipherable forms. These have excited a number of conceptual artists interested in the decline of industrialism, and have, indeed, sometimes been mistaken for works of art in themselves.

This daunting space has been invaded by a group of formidably efficient people led by Fred, Angel's Head of Operations. They carry an arsenal of heavy metal objects, curiously appropriate to the room in their way. 'Urns over there, under the picture with the smoke,' says Fred, 'and the ovens next to them, yes, it's four ovens today, which means we can't do the usual, just put them below the case with all those shiny things in it, would you? No, Nick, you idiot, not so close – hold on, it's my mobile – oh, hello, darling, hold on a moment, would you, I'll ring you back – yes, immediately – yes, Mr Rupert, everything's cool – hot cupboards under that model thing, the factory or whatever it is – yes, close to the power points, obviously – do we have the spare generator ready? – hello, Jim, have you checked the power again? No, there should be no problem in a big place like this – what? They haven't rewired this side of the room? – I think it'll be all right – cool, then, cool – two more electric rings, yes, there should be room for them under the steam engine.' The metal objects are disposed around the room and the delivery team goes. Fred's mobile rings again. 'Hello, oh Sam, yes, hello,' She says, 'not a great moment, actually – look, darling, we're just setting up, absolutely crucial time, just got into the venue – I know we said we could go out properly on Saturday but I have to do this event, I just have to, I'd be letting Mr Rupert down – he has to be away – no, it's not always me who ends up doing all the work, Mr Rupert works all the time, he's amazing, it's just – No, it's not silly calling him Mr Rupert, it's just what we call him – No, I am not a toady – Yes, I know your sister's going to be in London, I know, dearest, but look, petal, maybe I can join you after the dinner, it should be over by eleven, we could go out clubbing or something – Yes, I know I fell asleep in the club last time but I'll take it easy before we go, I mean the night before – OK, if I have to work I'll get up late – look, Sam, I love you, yes, I do, but I have a job – oh, fuck fuck fuck . . .' and as he utters these words the team come back saying, 'Where were you, then, Fred, we missed you?' and Fred says, 'Canapé table in Regency, yes, Regency, that one through there, yes, two tables, and the dessert table in that room over there, Early Georgian, yes, we can use as much space as we like, it's the Chairman's do, two dessert tables, yes, and the lobster unit,' at which they all giggle, 'the lobster unit, keep it clean, Nick, on its own in Late Georgian . . . Main preparation table here in Industrial – no, Jim, this is Industrial, that's Early Georgian, look, it's got a steam engine, Industrial, get it? Can we have the tablecloths ready—' and as the rooms take on their new guise as a temporary kitchen his mobile rings again and he answers it desperately, 'Samantha, hello, darling, great to hear you, yes, we're still very busy,' with a clenched smile. 'No, our relation- ship is not on the rocks but I really can't talk about our relationship now, I've got a huge reception starting in two hours – No, receptions don't matter more to me than relationships – Of course I love you, look, we're going to the Cayman Islands, aren't we, next month? Well, of course that's got everything to do with our relationship, we'll laze about and love each other and – No, I will not stuff my face with food all the time,' and then he loses his temper and shouts down the phone, 'Oh, get stuffed yourself, it's better than being a fucking anorexic,' and turns shaking but still compe- tent to his team, who have returned with more metal objects and are looking at him quizzically, and says, 'I'm a bit worried about the electricity, we don't usually have this amount of machinery, it's having so much on the go, can we get Harry to come and do a check for us?' And as Harry is summoned Fred nods to the team and says, 'OK, we'll set up the reception next, please, all the stuff into Early Georgian for the moment ready to move into the entrance hall at five o'clock. After that, tables for Great Hall, please.' And they disappear. The mobile phone rings and he switches it off, then switches it on thinking this may be work rather than wife, changes his mind and turns it off.

'Check the Great Hall,' he says to himself, and moves into it. What he sees does not delight him. Instead of the empty space he'd expected, ready for forty round tables and four hundred chairs, he finds the hall filled with tiny children. Some are dancing in a ring round a peculiar pole in the corner covered with ribbons and flowers while dozens more are lying on the floor cutting coloured paper into small pieces.

'What the hell . . .?' he asks himself, and of one of the children, 'Is anyone in charge here?' She points out a tall lady with a seraphic expression and a bleached linen smock, who is smiling gently and making cooing noises to the children around her as she moves around the room. 'Can you tell me . . .?' he begins to ask her.

'My name is Melissa,' she says. 'I'm the Head of Education and Community Outreach. Can I help you?'

And when he tells her that he has to set up for a large dinner that evening, she says, with untroubled calmness, 'I know about the dinner, to which I am coming, and I'm sure if you have everything organised it will all be fine. In the meantime my team of young helpers are working together on the pageant. That's the maypole over there.'

'Is that thing staying there all evening?' groans Fred. 'Nobody said anything to me about it. It's just where we need to put two of our serving tables.'

'Yes, it's staying, it's the maypole for the pre-pageant

dancing,' she replies calmly. (Does she ever stop being calm? Fred wonders. It's extremely irritating.)

'You see,' says Fred, 'the maypole is right between several of the tables and I'm afraid the dancing tots will collide with the guests, which may not be very popular particularly if the tots get trampled on . . .'

'Oh . . .' she says, less serenely, and blushes and Fred sees she isn't as bad as he'd thought and gives her one of his twinkles, which makes her blush.

'We do have to set up, you know,' he says. 'Any chance . . .'

'Yes, really it's time they went home anyway and the coaches will be waiting – but we do have a pageant rehearsal on the stage later. Will that get in the way?'

And in a few moments, as though in the dramatic finale of a grand opera, the paper-cutting children are removed, the doors are thrown open and forty round table tops are rolled through, followed by trolleys bearing hundreds of little gold chairs, six-foot-tall flower arrangements in Rococo vases appear through a distant door, the Head of Security bustles in with his clipboard and informs Fred he shouldn't have started work without authorisation, and is told in return that he's failed to give Fred any warning about the maypole, so they reach a not very cordial truce which includes the maypole being moved into a corner. A sound engineer repeatedly intones, 'One two three four one two three four,' from the stage, the lighting engineers experiment with an extended range of effects. Through all this activity, order is maintained, narrowly. Only the children rehearsing on the stage, endlessly singing a ditty to the effect that 'Elizabeth's our queen, Elizabeth's our queen, Yours is One, Ours is Two, Elizabeth's our queen,' make Fred grind his teeth, as does the certainty that his mobile, switched off though it is, is trying to get him . . . At least, he reflects, this event is more of a strain for Gustavus than it is for him. How is Gustavus? he wonders. He hasn't seen him for a while. But when he goes back to Industrial Revolution he finds Gustavus, subdued but in control, conferring with his team of twelve chefs.

'Oh, Fred,' he says thankfully. 'Fred, collecting the lobsters is Operations, isn't it? What time are they being delivered?'

'Six on the dot,' says Fred, 'by the staff entrance. I'm taking charge of them personally. I'll deliver them to Industrial Revolution, shall I?'

'Yup. I'm not sure exactly where we're setting up – at least the beef is done, sort of, apart from the garnish. I'm still not quite happy with it . . . The lobster, that's what makes me anxious . . . I just hope the spinach is ready in time for all this layering we're doing.'

Fred smiles at him reassuringly. 'Of course it will be OK,' he says, in a warm, encouraging way. 'Angel's dinners are always OK, and a lot more than OK.'

'There's always a first time . . .' replies Gustavus lugubri-ously, and his chef's conference continues.

GALLERY OF MODERN TECHNOLOGY, FOUR P.M.

Bill and Anna have not been bored at all this afternoon. Although there have been few visitors to look at or talk to, the movement into and out of the Director's office has been most interesting. After his staff had left, the Director emerged from his office with John Winterbotham, both carrying clipboards. They were discussing the details of the royal arrival this evening, particularly the security arrangements. 'Can we do this walk-through pretty quickly?' said the Director. 'I have to get home and change.'

'No problem,' said Winterbotham.

Once again Bill and Anna looked brisk and assumed efficiently self-deprecatory smiles as the pair passed.

A moment or two later, a new group arrived up the stairs. It was the Chairman of the Trustees, and that rude Lucian man again, and a large Japanese man, and that tall nasty girl, Helen, who everyone knows is having it off with Sir Lewis. Helen was carrying a bottle, for some reason, looked like champagne. As they passed, Sir Lewis talked about an export licence – 'all sorted out, Lucian, no worries there, the minister was completely understanding, special exemption against Waverley, the chairman of the Export Licence Reviewing Committee raised a bit of trouble but a few cases of Château Something, his favourite, dealt with that one … He said if we could prove the picture had been shown abroad in the recent past...' They disappeared into the office. A few moments later Emma, the Director's personal assistant, came out, looking seriously annoyed. She carried her briefcase as though going home but did not seem happy about it. 'Bloody rude,' she said to herself, as she hurried past them, not even saying, 'Goodnight,' as she normally would.

Anna and Bill thought it unwise to talk to each other, as they would normally do. Not only were there the cameras, but the door might open again and the Chairman emerge. Though Sir Lewis never bothers to acknowledge the staff's existence, he's very observant when any detail is not exactly right. They merely moved a little closer to the great door, just to keep an eye on things, as it were. But of course they could hear nothing, since behind that door was the secretaries' office, and then the personal assistant's office, and only after that the Director's office where the meeting – whatever it might be – must have been taking place.

A little while later the door opened and the group came out again. They were laughing, and seemed triumphant. Bill and Anna had anticipated this moment, and were almost concealed once again, this time behind particularly large interactive displays. 'I am so pleased,' said the big Japanese man. 'It is a wonderful arrangement. You get what you need – I get what I need: a lot of Gainsborough! It's a good exchange, I think!' Then they all shook hands. 'Keep that document safe, Mr Bankes – it's valuable!' They all laughed heartily.

Somebody must have looked enquiringly at Lucian, since a moment or two later he said, 'In the control room, with Winterbotham, it'll be as safe as a document could be any- where.' Then they all went.

When they have all gone, Bill and Anna emerge from their

retreat and look at each other. What on earth does this mean? Should they tell anyone? 'It's not our job to interfere,' she says, 'we're only the slaves round here.'

'Something very odd is happening, that's clear,' says he.

'Yes, but what can we do about it?' she wants to know.

'We can tell someone who'll know whether to take it up,' he insists.

'But it's not our job,' she repeats, 'and all we've done is overhear a conversation we weren't meant to overhear, just because we're under-persons and they don't think we're worth bothering about.'

'I don't care about that,' he says, 'I know something's wrong, and they ought to know.'

'They?' she asks. 'What sort of they?' She is impressed by his determination.

'Here's Ian, we'll tell him,' he says, with relief, as the deputy head of Security comes round the corner.

'How are you two doing?' he asks genially. 'Had a nice afternoon?'

'We've had a very interesting afternoon,' says Bill, 'and we think we ought to tell you about it.'

CONTROL ROOM,
FIVE P.M.

John Winterbotham sits in his control room and growls at the screens. The day's been chaotic and makes him wish he only had to supervise the daily routine without these special events. *Staff all over the place all day, two of them behaving in the oddest way, staring at one another all the time like maniacs and even dancing in the galleries at one point, senior staff shouting at each other, Director in a rage, and then three of them turning off the lights and trying to examine that painting . . . and when I take them off to the Director nothing happens. After all, the instructions from the Chairman were very strict and that Mr Smiles keeps going on about it too, and Sir Lewis has shown how strong his feelings are financially (very useful it's been, too) as well as threatening major trouble if anything goes wrong — funny, actually, you wouldn't think a bit of old canvas was worth so much worry . . . Very friendly Sir Lewis was, when he left a short time ago, but it seemed best not to mention the incident in the exhibition gallery this morning since the man has a temper . . . And this evening there'll be hundreds of strangers in the building and the catering staff are full of actors and dancers and unreliable people of one sort or another and there's the delivery of lobsters, which I don't like at all . . . It's my job to keep the place in order and what does anyone do to help? All they do is make trouble and resent me when I try to sort it out.*

There's Diana leaving from the staff entrance, funny one that but at least she's organised . . . and that young girl from Art, well, I could tell a story or two about her and someone who shouldn't be mentioned — why on earth they had to do it in History of Women's Freedom after a private view . . . Don't they know I can see everything that goes on in the galleries, even in the dark? . . . Girls going home no doubt to put on their frocks . . . Odd, those two don't seem to be speaking to each other . . . Lucian going off as well, he seems to be OK, at least Sir Lewis thinks he's a good thing — though I've hardly had the courtesy of a good-morning from him in seven years until this evening when he arrives in my office with an envelope, says it's high security, would I put it in the museum safe, wonder what that's about . . . attendants leaving for the evening, some of them back in an hour, have to allow the buggers out for a bit — pity I don't get a break myself, not that I'd want it really . . .

He looks at the entrance-hall screen. Final visitors are out promptly, as usual. He loves the organised way the museum empties every evening: first warning 1645 hours, second 1655, final one at 1659, but by then the building's always clear. Hardly any public in today, weather too sunny and hot, it's been stifling, and there's no big exhibition open but they expect crowds and crowds when ELEGANCE opens the day after tomorrow, he may have to take on temporary staff. At least the Lodge will help him find reliable types again.

The temporary exhibition galleries are empty, as per instructions. Only one attendant in there, standing beside *Lady St John*. No one, but no one, to go in until six fifteen.

As for the Great Hall, they've finished fussing around on the stage making all that din with the kids, damn nuisance in my view. The tables are laid. The flower arrangements, some huge, some small for the tables, have been delivered. God knows how much they must have cost but probably it's all necessary, like regimental dinners — at least in the Army everything's done in the same way each year and you don't have to worry too much about temperamental women the way you do here . . . I wonder what's going on in Industrial Revolution, I sometimes almost prefer not to know, but it seems to be in good order, that man Rupert has it all under control, good man that, amazing the way they can start with a table with hundreds of empty plates on it and within an hour every plate is all set up with its fancy starter in place, twelve different items sometimes on each plate . . . There seems to be a bit of agitation in there just now but Mr Rupert is dealing with it . . . Ah, well, only eight more hours . . . and I have to be all over the museum during that time, making sure every detail is in order, no good just staying watching the screens, they don't tell you everything . . . at least I'll get some dinner, looking forward to that . . .

He'll be on duty here for another hour or so, then let Ian take over for a while when the Royal Guest is due to arrive.

It's good to be able to keep an eye on things . . .

ALL OVER LONDON,
FIVE THIRTY P.M. ONWARDS

In two hundred or so houses and offices, people are embarking on strenuous preparations for dinner at BRIT: in official residences, in mahogany and chrome offices in the City, where slipping into evening dress is a regular activity, in handsome flats overlooking Eaton Square and Regent's Park, in the discreetly expensive hotels masquerading as private houses round Sloane Square in which BRIT puts its foreign guests, in gentlemen's clubs in St James's Street, where members find it handy to change in the loo, in Fulham and Wapping, Dulwich and Hampstead, men are squeezing themselves into tail coats rented for the occasion and protesting vigorously ('Cheaper to take you out to dinner, darling, somewhere really nice, than go through all this palaver'), and women are willing the children to shut up and worrying about their hair and whether somebody else will be wearing the same dress. Instructions have been strict: guests must be at the museum by seven fifteen, before a Certain Person arrives. The prospect of venturing across the Thames (even if only four hundred yards) is so alarming to many of them that dozens of emergency plans have been made. Diaries have been wiped clean, fleets of cabs commandeered, babysitters bribed heavily to stay from six till one, jewels removed from bank vaults by the treasuryful. An invitation from Sir Lewis Burslem is not to be ignored.

This is, after all, one of the most heavily publicised social events of the year. The exhibition has been generously previewed in the *Sunday Times* and elsewhere; interviews with the director and others have appeared as extended features that morning, along with the usual shots of technicians pretending to put finishing touches to exhibits that were actually in place days before; the Duke of Clarence is one of the most popular members of the Royal Family, and known to be a good speaker; the guest list is said to be glittering, if traditional; and gastronomically the dinner (already gossiped about by the diary of a well-known evening newspaper, which succeeded in being wrong about every single detail except the name of the chef, who was profiled under the headline 'The Great Gustavus' as the culinary star of the coming decade) will clearly be memorable.

Police Sergeant Ted Hoskins MVO (he's proud of his membership of the Royal Victorian Order) of Metropolitan Police Royalty Protection, who is driving in from Surrey, has reached Wandsworth. He concentrates on the road conditions: traffic flow pretty fair, density fair to middling, weather excellent (he can hardly remember a more beautiful evening, it would have been nice to stay at home and play cricket with the boys). Has to be at the boss's place by 1830 hours, ready for departure for venue at 1930. This evening should be pretty straightforward, at least it's all in one place, no public access other than the strictly controlled lists of guests, museum and catering staff. The latter can be a problem since caterers tend to draft in dubious extras at the last moment but this outfit won't do that. Ted Hoskins is a fine figure of a man, all blond six foot two of him, and the old-established tailors behind Burlington House who make the evening dress and the morning dress, the dinner jackets (winter and summer varieties), the pinstripe suits, the tweed jackets and the sporting outfits he needs for official duties, contemplate the results of their tailoring with satisfaction. A devoted but not uncritical royalist, he is proud to be considered a friend by the Duke and Duchess (whom he's known for a decade and sees on more than half the days in a year). At public engagements he manages, like his colleagues, to be both invisible and highly present, never noticeable until trouble arises. To his wife and his friends he claims to feel detached about the celebrities, the parties, the visits to places all over Britain and the world – 'All in the day's work,' he tends to say – but in fact they still fascinate him. Only occasionally does he want to offer his own point of view as an individual rather than a reassuring shadow. But he expresses forceful views at home.

Ted, used to wearing black and even white tie two or three nights a week, has had much less trouble organising himself than some of the other participants. Lucian is in wild disorder, can't find his collar studs, finds it hard to tie his tie (Fanny always did it), has lost a crucial part of the white waistcoat's internal mechanism, has a taxi waiting outside, will have to set out half dressed and create his armour *en route*. He is excited and apprehensive about the evening. It's crucial to his future, he thinks, as he pushes his face into the little boxes on his bedroom table and casts their contents on the floor and wrenches open drawers in search of his gold cufflinks (he really can't wear the flashing Mickey Mouse ones tonight). *Thank God everything looks promising, this afternoon's meeting with Mr Kobayashi went well – at last the paper's signed and safe in the museum, export licence sorted out, things moving on nicely. As for one's own career, let's just hope the evening is a huge success and dazzles those old fools at the Bloomsbury Museum into thinking Auberon is the brightest star in the museum constellation so that we get rid of him. The competition for Bloomsbury — one gathers — is pretty dim.* He smiles as he thinks of Sir Lewis wringing his hands at a recent private view and remarking unctuously to Lord Willins of Plympton (Chairman of the Trustees at Bloomsbury) how much he'd miss young Auberon but 'gosh — he's able!' *And Hermia — how delightful she was this afternoon, and she'll be at my table this evening. But I mustn't be too attentive to Hermia, I must be seen being extra-nice to Helen. Helen — hm — need to take a lot of trouble over her. If everything goes according to plan how am I going to promote her? My job, Head of Exhibitions? Is she up to it yet? Better to think about Hermia — what a dream she is, I thinks she likes me, too, I thinks maybe she likes me very much — Is there any chance . . . tonight . . . a bit soon? Funny about Diana, she really does seem to have made the leap . . . actually I find her in the role of a dominating dyke rather exciting, can imagine her in enormous thigh-length boots, I've always liked her in boots, only thing I do like about her really, must be something about her Germanness . . . Must concentrate . . . Who invented these fucking collar studs? Impossible to squeeze them through these stiff white holes.* And he dashes out of the door.

Naturally, Diana is much more organised. Her hairdresser and friend, Imogen, has come round to check her hair and arrange the silver comb with a spray of egrets which she's bought for the occasion (rather cheaply, she was pleased to find). Diana has decided not to wear black — she hates grand parties that look like funeral wakes, men in black and white, women in black and black. She doesn't approve of spending large sums of money on clothes, and felt it was loyal to her principles to choose her dress in a second-hand design boutique — although even there the price she had to pay was a shock to her principles, and her purse. She has to admit she's pleased with the dress she found, grey and silver layered organdie, over cream silk, shimmering almost to the ground. From the low neck, her creamy shoulders and arms (she never tans) emerge like the necks of two swans.

All day her thoughts were darting back to her outfit. Everything looked OK when she did a dress rehearsal for her very critical friends Susanna and Dolly, but how will it be this evening, at the real thing? And is she even going to have time to enjoy herself, or will Jane keep her running around the museum in search of clues? Just before she steps out of her bedroom into her sitting room to try the effect on Imogen, she seizes a silver organza wrap (given to her years ago by some man or other), which for some reason she pulled out of a drawer days ago and dropped on to her bedroom chair. She's been vowing not to wear it, but now, intoxicated by the moment, she throws it round her shoulders. She doesn't look at herself before she goes out of the room, she's too full of nerves – does she look too commanding, or too tall, or as though she's trying too hard or . . .? Imogen says nothing for a moment and Diana peers at her nervously at which Imogen says, 'Darling, you look *astounding!*' So Diana turns to inspect herself in the mirror, and in the soft light of the sitting room, more flattering than the one in her bedroom, realises that, yes, well, she does look quite striking . . . 'You look like a princess, a Scandinavian princess!'

'Do I look like an ice queen?' asks Diana nervously.

'No,' says Imogen, 'you look like your namesake, the goddess.'

'Not over the top?' says Diana.

'Totally, darling, but it's magnificent. And we haven't done the diamonds yet!'

'D'you think I need to wear diamonds, with all this silk and stuff, couldn't I just wear . . .?' asks Diana.

'You absolutely must,' cries Imogen. 'If you're ever in doubt about diamonds, say yes.'

'But it's not correct, according to my principles, to wear so much jewellery,' cries Diana. 'I mean a diamond and pearl sunburst necklace, and diamond and pearl earrings – they're not very comradely, are they?'

'Oh, darling,' says Imogen, 'don't take life so hard.'

'Do I take life so hard?' asks Diana in surprise.

Just as Diana is coming to terms with wearing jewellery and whether she takes life hard, the telephone rings. 'Shall I leave it?' she asks Imogen.

'It might be important,' says Imogen. 'It might be Jonathan.'

'Oh, to hell with Jonathan,' says Diana, but she picks up the receiver. It's Jane. *Oh, no, not Jane*, says Diana to herself, *at this moment I do not want to have to think about Jane and her mad schemes, really I do not want to be involved in this peculiar Gainsborough business at all, it's too much for me just now, I want to think about myself and her . . . her . . . Hermia*. 'I'm so sorry to bother you,' says Jane, 'are you struggling with your jewels? I have to tell you something. There's some strange sinister scheme afoot here, I don't really understand the details, but Ian Burgess, the security man, rang me and told me that two of the attendants overheard the chairman talking about some secret arrangement over the Gainsborough, it wasn't quite clear what. Some crucial document has been put in the Security control room, Ian's going to try to get hold of it for me . . . Yes, I know it sounds bizarre but museums are bizarre places . . . Diana, I know this is asking a lot of you' – *It certainly is*, thinks Diana – 'but I want you to ring your friend Valentine Green and insist he comes to the dinner, he has to drop everything, he must be there, he's exactly the sort of trouble-maker we need. I can't ring him, I don't know him, but you and he are great friends, aren't you?'

'Yes,' says Diana rather grudgingly, 'I suppose so. What do I tell him?'

'Tell him everything you know but not quite everything so that he's intrigued and needs to know more — yes?'

'All right,' she says, 'I'll try.' All she really wants to think about at this moment is her clothes.

'And there's another thing — I want you to arrange for us to inspect the picture... The Gainsborough, of course, Diana, which picture d'you think? As soon as HRH is out of the exhibition and before it comes into the Great Hall... No, it's a loan, it comes under you and Lucian, not me, I can't do anything about it... Diana, I know I'm being impossible but it's very important. And what is emerging is that Lucian...' She pauses.

'Lucian?' asks Diana, rather more interested.

'That Lucian is deeply implicated in all these plans. My feeling is that if and when the whole story comes out, Lucian will be a goner as far as this museum is concerned. His position will be untenable, and not just untenable here.' She pauses again.

Diana hesitates too. *Lucian? His career destroyed? Forced maybe to leave the country? Of course he's a remarkable man... I owe a lot to him... one should not be vindictive... but then it's only the truth we're trying to reveal, he's obviously behaved badly... Just imagine, Lucian out of the museum, oh, bliss, and probably out of Hermia's life too...*

'I'll do whatever you ask, Jane.' She feels horrible as she says it, and she also feels triumphant.

'Wonderful,' says Jane, and rings off.

God, she's so bossy, this Jane, Diana tells herself. *And I always thought of her as a bit of a mouse. Still, I can't let her down.* 'I have to make a call,' she says, 'persuade someone to come to this stupid dinner at short notice.'

'You look as though you could persuade anyone in the world,' says Imogen.

Lady Burslem is wearing diamonds too. Her husband found them for her at Tiffany's a few years before, when he was ending a longish affair and as usual in these circumstances felt guilty towards his wife. (She has a great many jewels.) On that occasion he gave her a tiara, a necklace, a brooch, pendant earrings, and a diamond and ruby bracelet. Privately she feels that all this jewellery *en masse* is rather overpowering, and she knows wearing a tiara for this sort of occasion isn't right, but since Lewis is so keen on it and (she suspects) insisted on white tie for the event so that she could wear the blessed thing, she has invested herself in the full array. Her outfit has been made for the occasion by her dressmaker in the country, a reliable woman whom she's persuaded Lewis to approve of (though he'd much prefer her to buy a famous label). It's a black velvet dress over which, since she no longer trusts her arms, she's wearing a soft, loose *devoré* jacket in very dark blue — she thinks the contrast with the black is rather successful. Reluctantly she agreed to buy a new pair of black velvet shoes for the evening (she has several pairs already, but Lewis insisted that they had to be new). She thinks her favourite place in Mayfair have done a beautiful job with her hair — though it was disconcerting when she went there this afternoon to meet two friends who'll also be at the dinner having their hair done in the neighbouring seats in exactly the same style. She thinks she looks OK and she does hope Lewis will approve — he can be so outspoken if he doesn't like something. As she meets her husband, who's assumed his tails with ruthless speed, they smile at each other warmly.

'My God, those jewels,' he says. 'I certainly did you proud with that lot!'

'And do you like the dress?' she asks.

He looks at it and does a thumbs-up. 'Fabulous,' he says.

'Best of British!' she says. 'Such an important day for you, darling.'

'Speaking of which,' he replies, 'one never has time for a drink at those dos. Shall we have a quickie before we go?'

'Why not? We've got ten minutes,' she says. 'I'm sure Mrs Sterling will have it all ready.' And indeed Mrs Sterling has laid out a tray in the pantry with two glasses and a linen napkin, and in the fridge are two half-bottles of champagne.

Auberon is not drinking champagne but glass after glass of water. He is perspiring with anxiety. There's a leaden feeling in his stomach. He cannot understand precisely what's going on in the museum, whether Jane is exaggerating over *Lady St John*, what on earth they were all doing in his office this afternoon when he was elsewhere, whether Sir Lewis supports his candidacy for Bloomsbury or not, what the critics will say about ELEGANCE, whether he likes ELEGANCE himself, whether his clever friends will sneer (one caustic piece in an influential weekly can set swathes of less courageous people mocking). He feels quite sick at the thought of the Nowness of Now, and having to smile and look enthusiastic when plans are announced, especially after this afternoon's board meeting. There are so many complications . . . oh, and can he put the cost of hiring the tails on expenses? Tanya reacted badly — he might have been a bit abrupt, suddenly he can hardly bear to speak to her — when he said they'd meet at the museum because he hadn't time to collect her.

'How low key d'you want me to be this evening, sweetest?' she'd said aggressively.

'As low key as comes naturally,' he'd replied.

What's crucial is to keep the show going, make sure the guests enjoy themselves (especially the guests from the Bloomsbury Museum), and see the exhibition gets good reviews soonest. I will not have the staff manufacturing difficulties . . . They must remember this event is a public performance . . . like a court masque, with comparable financial, social and political implications. Then there's their own pageant . . . oh, Lord, the pageant . . .

He glances at himself in the mirror. He looks awful, eyes almost glued together and bloodshot, tired, slightly red in the face, bags under the eyes, faint air of dementia – he should have given himself time for some meditation. No doubt when the party starts he'll revive. He always does.

In the taxi to the museum he peers at the evening paper. Nothing much in it. The private lives of assorted manufactured celebrities have taken surprising turns – one has to be aware, at least, of this brand of futile popular culture. He turns to the City Dweller's Log Book on page seven and his whole body jerks. The lead story is about the directorship of the Bloomsbury Museum. Prospective candidates are listed . . .

Oh, NO, we're just arriving at BRIT . . . What's the fare? Surely not so much . . . Why bother with this kind of article? It's always inaccurate . . . Can't read it now but I must, won't be able to concentrate on the party if I don't . . . Did I give the driver too much? The flowers outside look fabulous . . . What does this article say? 'Professor Alan Stewart . . . highly admired, a very strong candidate . . .' Alan Stewart – my trustee? Is he applying, for God's sake? How do they know? He'd certainly be a strong candidate, much too strong . . .

Auberon pretends not to notice the Head of Security approaching with his usual officious air as he hovers behind a column scanning this idiotic article . . .

'Liz Birley, Keeper of Urban History at Bloomsbury . . . well respected, a lively, feisty woman . . .' Rubbish, she's got no chance at all, sheer

tokenism, but then maybe she has connections I don't know about . . . Aren't I in here? Ah — 'Auberon Booth, the clever and high-profile Director of the Museum of English History (now oddly rebranded as "BRIT"), is admired for his highly developed social skills and his unrelenting pursuit of a stylishness or "elegance" (the awful title of his new exhibition at the museum), which some think he never quite achieves' — Ooh, nasty, who wrote this? Could it be that horrid little journalist I told to wait the other day because I had no time? 'He is considered aloof and superior, slightly surprising from a graduate of Bradford Grammar School and Southampton University. He has not made much impact during his brief period at the museum . . .' Intolerable, what makes them say that? '. . . he is thought to be too young for the Bloomsbury Museum job and could wait till next time round, especially if he achieves more at BRIT . . .' Will anyone read this stuff, will anyone serious be influenced by it? No, surely not. A heavy scowl at John Winterbotham, who retreats. *'A dark-horse candidate is Ranald Stewart, Director of the South London Museum . . .'* Aha, little Ranald, goblin-like, humorous, heart-of-gold, look-at-me-caring-for-the-socially-excluded little Ranald, what do they have to say about him? *'He has attracted attention for his lively and innovative approach to accessibility . . .'* Exactly, he must be good at something. *'His flamboyant manner conceals highly developed managerial and fund-raising skills.'* Huh, why so nice about little Ranald, twit of twits, never stops boasting about his working-class background? But on it goes . . . *'The trustees may want to show their interest in the regions by appointing a non-London figure in the form of the only non-metropolitan-based shortlisted applicant, Susan Higgins, director of Manchester and Region Art Galleries and Museums. A plain-speaking former opera singer famous for her sense of fun'* — Where does all this drivel come from? She's as lively as a wet Sunday in Oldham — *'she has done a superb job, experts feel, in solving the problems of the area's numerous under-funded museums . . . If appointed, she would be the Bloomsbury Museum's first woman director and her appointment would show the way the trustees want to steer the museum . . .'*

He drops the paper behind the pillar, realises this is not helpful, picks it up again and greets John Winterbotham, who is lurking at a discreet distance (and no doubt has read the article too). 'Just a few points I wanted to clear with you, Director,' says John.

Auberon sighs. 'I don't have long, you know.'

Upstairs in the museum, Jane is making her *toilette*. As the curators' corridor outside her office fills with noisy steps and slamming doors and loud goodnights, she opens her cupboard and extracts a plastic dry-cleaning bag. Inside is a green satin evening dress bought at Christian Dior by her mother in a moment of uncharacteristic abandon in the 1950s. It was stunning when new and still looks pretty good. She thinks it will be OK this evening – and it fits pretty well, she knows from experience, and doesn't look too young for her, even now. She hopes it won't look eccentric with the jewellery she's chosen, an amber and silver necklace she bought as a girl travelling in Syria, and silver hoop earrings from a trip to India. Hardly a self-conscious woman, she knows that in a museum – nowadays more a party venue than a house of learning – people in her position are obliged to be reasonably well dressed, if subtly less elegant than the genuinely rich. It takes her ninety seconds to arrange her hair in the mirror inside her cupboard door, and around three minutes to put on the dress. She smiles to think how long some of the other guests will be spending on dressing, and her thoughts drift back a long way to how pleasant it used to be, in those days of sweet intimacy, to chat to the man one was going out with as one changed one's clothes. She smiles again, more sadly. Is it the loss of such intimacy that makes her so aggressive over things like the Gainsborough? No, she thinks that sort of tiresome integrity was born in her, though sometimes she worries about her own fierceness.

But Jane has things to attend to, and wants this dressing business finished. And once she's changed her clothes her personality should alter just a little, too.

She can't resist one look at herself full-length and hurries along the corridor to the ladies'. *Green always suited me, at Cambridge I had a beautiful floaty dress I'd wear to May balls – perhaps at one's advanced age one should bow to the years and just wear black . . .* She passes one of the attendants: his eyes widen as he presses himself against the wall. In the ladies' she turns off all but one light, and stands in front of the mirror. *Faint moment of dread. Must do something about my hair. But the dress? It looks OK, I really do think it looks OK.*

There are more important things to worry about this evening than clothes. Such as meeting Ian from Security in Early Georgian, which we chose because if the meeting's observed in the control room and arouses suspicion I can say that as chief curator I wanted to check the catering arrangements from a curatorial point of view. I'm sure my movements are being monitored, maybe my telephone's being tapped.

Early Georgian is surprisingly quiet and orderly. On an enormous trestle table four hundred plates are laid out, each with a minimal garnish – these must be the plates awaiting lobsters. Beside the table stands another table, covered in sealed boxes, some marked 'Spinach', others 'Lobster Pâté', and rows of huge metal vats, filled with water and plugged into sockets on the wall. Her precious Rysbracks have disappeared under wooden boxes, the Haymans are swathed in thick plastic sheeting, the ship models encased in protective wooden cases so heavy they are hardly removed even on the rare days when the room is open to visitors. There is Ian, looking amiable and anxious. They pretend to look around the room and gesticulate now and again at the cooking equipment, just in case they are being watched. 'It's my turn to take over in the control room,' says Ian. 'The boss is busy with the royal arrival. I think the papers we want are in the control-room safe, I'll get Bill or Anna to come over and collect them, make a copy, we'll sort it out somehow.' Eight fifteen is clearly the crucial moment for their plan, after the crowds have left the exhibition and while the Duke's making his way towards the Great Hall. Ian knows who'll be in the control room at eight fifteen — no problem there, it's one of his own men, Ralph, he won't say anything to John. He'll make sure that Bill and Anna are on duty in the exhibition room beside the Gainsborough . . . they already know a bit about what's going on, they're the ones who overheard the conversation about the document . . . They don't like Winterbotham, won't report anything to him. Jane should have six minutes clear, but not a second more, the inspection absolutely must be done in that time . . .

As they conclude their plans, they hear flustered bustle from the direction of the staff entrance. A procession enters the room. At its head walks John Winterbotham, looking stern. Behind him, wheeled by Angel's junior chefs and manual team, trundle four large metal containers, each labelled 'FRAGILE — DO NOT TOUCH'. On either side of the containers walks a file of attendants, most of them grinning. It is an impressive, if mystifying, sight.

'What on earth . . .?'

'It's the lobsters,' replies Ian, 'arriving for dinner. Your dinner, not theirs.'

'The lobsters?' breathes Jane.

And indeed it is the lobsters, and already the water in the waiting vats is being warmed, and sixteen chefs and sous-chefs under the leadership of a devilishly handsome young man with a flushed face are waiting to embark on lobster preparation. Four people to a vat, it seems. Jane and Ian abandon their discussion to watch the containers being opened and the live black lobsters, clenching and flailing, being pulled out and thrown into the now boiling water. Recalling herself, Jane remarks, 'It's awfully improper, I'm sure lobster preparation is not allowed here . . .' to which Ian replies, 'Chairman's orders, you know, HRH and all that, loves lobsters . . .'

As they confer, a tall urbane man, evidently in charge, appears and bows slightly. 'Is everything OK?' he asks. 'I'm Rupert Burnham, the managing director of Angel Cooks. I think it's Miss Vaughan, isn't it? We had the pleasure of meeting on the occasion of the Chaucer private view. Ian, how are you? Is everything all right from your point of view? The lobsters are a bit demanding but lobsters always are, we can cope . . . They're going to be stuffed with spinach, you see, and lobster pâté, I think it'll be delicious.'

'It looks very organised,' says Jane. 'If it weren't you and your team doing it I should be rather nervous,' and so she is, but not as nervous as she is about her other activities.

'Can I offer you a glass of champagne?' asks Mr Rupert agreeably. 'Then I'll leave you to the lobsters.'

ENTRANCE HALL,
SIX FIFTEEN P.M.

The preparations are perfect. When Sir Lewis and his lady emerge from the Jaguar and give a gracious wave towards the well-mannered group of spectators being held back strenuously by a line of policemen, they can allow themselves to glow with satisfaction. The enormous blue and gold banner proclaiming 'ELEGANCE' (no sub-titles, it was decided, no dates, just the one word) has been hoisted above the main entrance. Even though it's a golden evening and extremely warm, blue and yellow gas flames are shooting from the Edwardian gasoliers on either side of the main steps.

On each step, left and right, bewigged footmen in eighteenth-century livery hold flaming torches. A red carpet of huge width and depth runs from the pavement under the *porte-cochère* up to the front door, which is flanked by a bevy of Georgian country wenches. There were wench-recruitment difficulties among the staff since some buxom potentials refused to oblige on principle while less promising ones pressed their services, but now the ranks of wenches look very fine in their white dimity dresses sprinkled with flowers and their pink sashes and their poke bonnets, poised to bestow programmes and beams on the arriving guests. The appearance of the Chairman stimulates an electric shock through the senior staff waiting at the door. Auberon, again in his courtier-like mode, emerges from the museum precisely as the Burslems step out of the car.

'Good evening, Auberon,' says Sir Lewis. They co-operate well on an occasion like this, when both are being watched by many eyes.

'Good evening, Auberon,' says Lady Burslem. 'It all looks marvellous, doesn't it?'

'It certainly does, thanks to Mirabel,' says Auberon diplomatically. Praise for Mirabel always pleases. At the moment he needs to please the Chairman.

Sweeping up the steps, the Burslems nod graciously at the wenches, who curtsy in ragged deference. *The curtsies aren't quite right yet*, notes Auberon, *oh, well, it's a bit late now*. 'Those curtsies are a bit rustic,' remarks Lady Burslem, and laughs. 'Shall I give them a lesson? My mother taught me. Look, girls, this is how you curtsy.' And to her husband's embarrassment she demonstrates, until he pulls impatiently at her hand.

As they walk into the entrance hall, the Burslems stop short and she puts out a hand to clutch his arm. The windows have been blacked out for the evening and the room is transformed. It's not only the vast array of delphiniums, peonies, larkspur, all white (the flowers for the evening are rumoured to have cost more than £100,000) twisted around ten wicker columns, or the lighting from dozens of tiny electronic candles twinkling on gilt candelabra supported by carved Moorish pages, not only the practically naked full-sized statues of classical deities on plinths or the army of footmen extending silver and glass trays with the whispered enquiry, 'Vintage champagne, madam?', not only the costumed chamber orchestra on the balcony playing Handel's *Water Music* with amplified enthusiasm or the scented clouds of vapour pumped by half-naked children from little silver bellows. It is the gloriously harmonised combination of all these elements, brought together this evening like the instruments in an orchestra, which makes the museum feel like the antechamber to Paradise. The Burslems exchange a tiny nod, and Sir Lewis almost beams.

'Very good,' says Sir Lewis. 'Immaculate.'

'Marvellous,' says Lady Burslem. 'It's all perfect. What time did you close the museum today, Auberon?'

'Five o'clock, as usual,' he replies, trying not to sound smug. 'Teamwork, you know.' Meanwhile he's wondering if his warning to Jane and Diana will be listened to. He caught the two of them whispering to each other just before the Burslems arrived and penned them in a corner behind the largest candelabrum. 'What are you plotting?' he asked them.

'Oh, nothing,' they replied.

He didn't believe them. They were to say and do nothing about the Gainsborough, he told them — no doubts were to be cast on the picture's condition. Diana lowered her eyes. Jane looked inscrutable. This was not helpful. He went further. Any improper conduct would lead to dismissal, he told them. At this their heads jerked upwards and they fixed him with what he saw as nervous but resolute defiance, Jane in particular. Something's certainly up.

Meanwhile Sir Lewis is greeting the staff, who are grouped in readiness (and order of precedence) for his encouraging words. They have certainly tried their best with their clothes, he notes with satisfaction, and for museum curators on pathetic salaries they really look quite creditable. That woman Diana, for example, is stunning tonight, in silver and grey. Helen's all in black, very nice little number that dress, just to the knee, showing her arms and lots of the rest of her. He probably paid for it, he thinks, with a slight stiffening of the groin, and her toes look very sexy painted red in those little sandals, wonder what the shoes cost, they can't have been cheap either, well, no doubt they were paid for by him too. In fact he seems to have paid for everything on her except her body . . . and in a sense, well . . . what a naughty girl she is . . . worth every penny he's spent on her, though. He winks slightly at Lucian, smiting him on the arm with a muttered word of congratulation, kisses the hand of Diana (good-looking she certainly is, but there's something a bit chilly about the woman, can't say what), shakes the hand of Jane but then realises he'll have to kiss her if he's not going to look too conspicuous kissing the next one in line, who is Helen. So he embraces Jane, who looks startled and faintly resentful, and then with much more enthusiasm takes Helen, who's wearing a minxish look, into his arms. She wriggles seductively at his touch, a movement observed by everyone except Lady Burslem who's looking in the opposite direction.

An enormous man dressed as an eighteenth-century night watchman advances, asserting himself by occupying a great deal of space.

'Sir Lewis, this is Sergeant Major Jenkins of the Corps of Commissionaires, who will be announcing the guests,' says Auberon.

'Ah, Mr Jenkins, a very good evening to you,' remarks Sir Lewis genially. He is good at shows of geniality. Pretty shallow shows, thinks Auberon sourly.

'Good evening, sir,' says Mr Jenkins. 'I just had one question for you and your lady, sir, if I might.'

'Yes?' asks Sir Lewis.

'Where would you be proposing to stand, sir, to receive your guests? I would suggest just here, so that those in the line can be indoors. And do you wish the guests to be announced by their full names and titles in every case, or may I abbreviate as and when, sir? It does save time.'

A rustic wench hurries up to them, rosy and squeaky. 'The first guest is arriving, Sir Lewis!' she cries, looking as though she's about to faint at the excitement.

'Time to get into position,' says Sir Lewis. 'Come along, Elizabeth, come along, Auberon,' and into position they go. 'Who can it be?'

'Baroness Shawe and Mr William Shawe,' booms Commissionaire Jenkins as a commanding female with a modest husband in tow approaches the hosts for the usual rapid exchange of civilities. *God, what a dreary beginning,* thinks Auberon, *the bossiest sort of right-wing life peeress, always wanting to improve the nation's morals and knowing best.* She passes on, husband behind her, and there's a pause.

'I always wonder on these occasions,' says Lady Burslem, 'if anyone at all is going to turn up. Maybe this will be the evening when nobody does.'

'D'you think we could make a go of it on the basis just of Baroness Shawe?' wonders Auberon.

'It might be a bit sticky,' she replies.

'Think of all the food she'd have to eat, though I dare say she'd make a good job of it.'

'Where are all the trustees?' grumbles Sir Lewis. 'I told them to be here in good time.'

As he speaks, they arrive. 'Sir Robert and Lady Pound!' announces the commissionaire. Auberon is not thrilled to see them either. *Lady Pound is one of those constantly thrilled, insincere upper-class types, and Sir Robert is looking more of an old bore than ever, continuously stroking the medal round his neck as a bride might stroke her bouquet.* 'Viscount and Viscountess Doncaster!' *Better. Olivia's wearing a tight-fitting scarlet dress, Versace, I should think, her arms are tanned and beautiful, her face smiling and soft, her lips like kissing cherries, her hair particularly soft and flowing, a choker there's hardly time to admire is sparkling round her neck ... Have to say hello to her beastly husband, why must he slap me on the shoulder?* They move on. 'Mrs Hobson!' *and here's the old cat, nose pursed, in something much too young for her, looking around venomously to see how the room compares to the Moorish tent she organised for her own seventieth birthday, and hardly bothering to greet me.* 'Mr Kobayashi, Mr Shimuzu, Mr Tanaka.' *Our Japanese friend with his two henchmen, to whom the chairman's again being unctuously polite. Ah, there are Lady Pound and Lady Doncaster, like social commandos primed for the task, swooping on the Japanese guests and smothering them with kindnesses.* 'The Bishop of London, Mr and Mrs William Beckley-Smith, Miss Amanda Mann and Mr James Mantling ...' 'So glad you could come, so glad you could come, so glad you could come, isn't the hall looking good, all done in seventy-five minutes, yes, it was Mirabel, isn't she clever?' prattles Auberon. *Is there an alternative to 'So glad you could come'? Lucian and Mr Kobayashi, over there, conferring together — what's going on?* 'Professor Hilary and Professor Gabriel Ironside.' *Ah, the Ironsides, my role models, so successful, so serious, he took her name when they married, such an effective move. Brilliant, the way they combine academic weight with big popular reputations, their recent books (particularly his* Crunching the Apple: Culturing Consumption in Augustan England, *which has been hardly less admired than her outstandingly original* Identifying Identities: Signifiers for a Post-Industrial Age) *are constantly in the learned journals and on television ...* 'Amanda, darling,' Hilary cries, and the Bishop turns sharply towards him *(Why on earth? Can 'Amanda' be his nocturnal name?)* as they embrace effusively. 'James, how nice to see you,' he asserts, though he can't stand Amanda's husband, 'd'you know the Bishop of London?' *It's amusing to introduce people who've not one thing in common. Wish those cameras would stop or perhaps it's glamorous, is it? And who's this with Trevor Christiansen, this woman like a mobile duvet?* 'Trevor!' he says, less warmly than usual.

217

Trevor has been pretty annoying about Nowness and has the presumption to say, 'Marvellous about Nowness, Auberon.'

'Marvellous to see you,' intones Auberon, and then 'I did enjoy the latest, many congratulations' to Gregory Noble. *Noble's a peculiarly successful novelist — I've never managed to read more than a few pages of any of his books but have to pretend, he can sometimes be flattered into making passable donations to the museum, wasn't it five thousand last time? God, why are Englishwomen so badly dressed, even for a big occasion like this — the men look terrific in their tails and decorations but honestly, the women, how do they do it? The inexact cut, the lack of colour sense, the grazing bosom, the careless shoes . . . This one looks OK and somehow familiar — oh, Lord, it's Tanya, heavily made-up and hard-looking tonight. Screws up her face when I kiss her cheek. Red around the eyes, not good. Has she been crying — oh, no, surely not? For heaven's sake . . .* 'Sir William and Lady St John.' *Further flutter. More flashing of teeth and jewels. Sir William's tall, red-faced, broad-shouldered, she has a blond boiled, posh look.* 'Marvellous you could come,' says Auberon, 'actually we're longing to have a photograph of you beside the other Lady St John, is that really OK, and you, too, Sir William?' and as he speaks the mildly blushing Lady St John is swept off to be photographed.

'Professor and Mrs Alan Stewart.' The Professor and Sir Lewis exude antipathy as they exchange cordial handshakes. Obviously unaware of the *London Sentinel* article, Stewart greets Auberon warmly and says, 'God, what a meeting that was this afternoon, I felt for you.' *Decent of him.* 'Very difficult situation . . . well, at least you may not be forced to do battle . . .' and he gives Auberon one of his rare but charming smiles.

His lawyer wife merely jerks her head towards the festivities. 'The Sacrifice of Athena to Mammon, I suppose,' she remarks.

The guests are pouring in. 'Sir Richard and Lady Frazier,' proclaims Jenkins proudly, 'Sir Thomas and Lady Frazier.' *The Frazier brothers, in their sixties, owners of the family business, unfailingly generous patrons of the arts. The country's studded with mementoes of their generosity. 'Where would we be without them?' people often ask. Much jollity as they greet Sir Lewis. Not that they like each other, but members of the wealth club must appear to be on good terms.*

Behind them treads Lord Willins of Plympton, life peer, Chairman of the Bloomsbury Trustees for quite a while. Large bushy moustache, thrusts it into people's faces, staring eyes, quite alarming. 'Ah, Noël,' says Sir Lewis. No doubt Lewis envies him his title and the Bloomsbury Museum, definitely a notch above BRIT. Their director always gets a knighthood; the director here's lucky to get a CB. 'Nice of you to find your way here,' says Sir Lewis.

'Enormous contribution you've made, Lewis,' remarks Lord Willins, in an only faintly patronising way, 'splendid event, looking forward to it hugely . . .' He embraces Lady Burslem.

'You know Auberon, don't you?' she asks.

'Of course,' replies Lord Willins, and nods at Auberon with a half-smile. 'Looking forward to seeing what you've been up to in the exhibition, was looking at your displays the other day actually . . .' *Is he teasing? Stomach churning, I really do want that Bloomsbury job, don't I? They say Lord Willins is decisive, brisk with his charm, controlling, shrewd in detecting talent (or its lack).*

Each time Auberon glances to his left he gives a little gasp. Over half of the guests have arrived and the entrance hall has become a place of celebration, the noise convivial yet not too loud, the festive music still audible, the flash of cameras enlivening, the candle-type light showing soft and haggard cheeks to advantage, the liveried footmen (apparently selected for their looks and fine calves, and much handsomer than most of the male guests) moving dextrously from group to group. Thank goodness he's been able to invite some of his own friends, so not everyone's a frowsty friend of the chairman. Tim and Vanessa (performance artists who fit in anywhere) look

particularly decorative this evening, Tim in his wittily deconstructed tail coat, one tail red, the other white with a slash
down the back, Vanessa delicious in full male evening dress, the
dark trousers hugging the thighs that once Auberon knew so
well . . .

'Mr and Mrs Denzil Marten . . .' *Why does he have to be here, little
creep? Nobody really wanted that picture of his.*

'So glad you could come,' Auberon remarks, looking
beyond them at the next guest . . .

'Mr Valentine Green.' No friendly greeting from the
Chairman, who looks appalled to see him. And what on earth
is Valentine doing here? His name certainly wasn't on the guest
list. 'Nice of you to make it,' Auberon says coolly (but he
hopes not too rudely, this is an influential man in his way).
Valentine smirks at him. Auberon looks quizzically at his
black shirt and white bow-tie outfit, remarking, 'Reversing out?
That's rather clever.'

'Mr and Mrs Ranald Stewart,' enunciates Jenkins rotundly,
though not with the rotundity he applies to a title. There's a
certain flatness now in his announcement of any mere Mr
and Mrs, though only those who've heard him delivering
several hundred names at the top of his voice (almost always
accurately) would be aware of it. What he loves is introducing a titled person: when a duke or duchess appears he
becomes almost ecstatic, as though announcing the arrival of
a divine being.

*Hm — Ranald. A rival. Pity he had to be asked. Ranald will be aware
of the impression he's making and, no doubt, will find himself talking to Lord
Willins. He's a snappy dresser in a flip way and is wearing an enormous
silver bow-tie, which rotates — he's demonstrating it to Lady Burslem. This
stuff is considered amusing by the great, like having a court jester. Ranald's
managed to make his little museum, which has nothing in it, into one of the*

most visited places in London. He's created this personal cult, it's hard not to be irritated. His choice of his favourite socks and tie of the month fascinates the press, there's even a special display case to show the rubbish in the museum hall. He's still cooing at Lady B, won't he move on? Well, no doubt he'll want this job if I move on to Bloomsbury — BRIT's a big step up from south London . . .

Ranald and Auberon greet one another as though presenting swords before a duel.

'Nice to see you,' says Auberon coolly.

'Lovely to see you. You must have been so busy,' replies Ranald, 'what with the exhibition, and I hear you have an extension planned — oh, it was on the news, didn't you hear it? Too busy reading the papers, I suppose — and then there's next week, of course.'

'Next week?' enquires Auberon, as though surprised. 'What d'you mean?'

'Little museum job, isn't there?' says Ranald archly. 'Tiny interview. Darling, you know Auberon, don't you? He's just about to be appointed Director of the Bloomsbury Museum.'

'What makes you think I'm applying?' asks Auberon, with a pretence of calm though he knows other guests are pressing to speak to him.

'Little bird.'

'Aren't you applying, Ranald?'

'Me? Oh, no, it's all nonsense that stuff in the *London Sentinel*. I'm not grand enough, am I? I just scrabble around in my little museum dealing with my local public . . .' *All this is said archly, suggests he can't be telling the truth. Oh, God, that draining stomach again. Now, social inclusion, crucial issue these days, we haven't really grappled with that yet at the museum. It's an omission, especially given the views of the person who's arriving now. And, of course, Ranald's wife's a teacher and he'll know all the current education jargon for the interviews . . .*

haven't had time to do any proper preparation on that, will they ask me about it in the interview? OH, SHIT . . .

'Ms Margaret Mills, Minister of State at the Department of Cultural Affairs,' announces Mr Jenkins, and the hosts stand up straighter and smile harder, knowing that this plain woman in an unidentifiable but faintly ethnic costume will shortly be deciding their financial fate for next year. She moves rapidly past the Burslems and stops at Auberon. 'We expect a lot from your exhibition. I gather it's very innovative,' she says to him. 'Is there any chance of a little pre-tour from one of the experts?'

'Certainly, we've arranged it,' he replies, and there indeed is Jane, looking competent but slightly flustered.

The names go crashing on, countesses and MPs and business people and chairs of trusts and historians and the rich and the great and the good and media people and the merely fashionable and dozens of owners of objects shown in the exhibition, and all the people who – how wearisome it all is, he finds sometimes – keep the whole commercial and public relations and glitter operation rolling along. But he goes on smiling and chuckling and exclaiming and kissing and repeating his mantra. Finally there's a slackening in the arrivals, and an extended pause, only briefly interrupted, and a longer break, and Lewis says, 'Well, I think that's about it, don't you? We can go and wander in the crowd.' The arrival of Friedrich von Schwitzenberg wearing a dinner jacket seriously too small for him and green with age encourages the Burslems to wander. The noise level is rising. The party is a success.

For Angel Cooks, everything is going well too, front of house at least. The dinner-waiting staff have been cleared by Security and have piled up their crash helmets and handbags in Early Georgian and slipped discreetly into their Georgian footman's or maid's costumes behind the showcases. The tables are all laid, the knives and forks and the five glasses are gleaming in ordered lines, the name cards are in place (though a certain noble lord has left his wife behind, pressing the reluctant Julia into guest duty). In the entrance hall, the forty butlers are pouring rivers of champagne (mutteringly identifying the vintage, as instructed) and dispensing the fascinating canapés arranged on replica Royal Worcester and Chelsea serving dishes, each with a little porcelain Chinese person in the centre playfully pointing to the food.

Mr Rupert is ready. He's allocated all the staff to their tables (the girls to hand the plates, the boys to serve the main dish, the girls to follow with sauces and vegetables). He's delivered his talk explaining the name and nature of each course, the wines, the timing, the directions for visitors. He's quelled the resting actress who claimed she'd been promised the chance to serve HRH with her own hands. Salt and pepper are being poured into eight hundred tiny silver pots, two for each guest. The places of vegetarian guests have been identified. Now the waiters and waitresses are sitting on the guests' chairs, gossiping mildly and admiring one another's variations on blue liveries and white dresses, hoping Mr Rupert will not reappear to propel them into activity.

Returning to Industrial Revolution from the Great Hall, Mr Rupert senses more than ever that everything's not quite right. He does not know that Gustavus has just seen a name on the guest list that means nothing to anybody else (and certainly not to Mr Rupert, who on no account must be allowed to guess): the director of a leading television company is coming to the dinner. This is the man Gustavus has been talking to about a television series, his own series, his very first — he's due to see him again tomorrow. From time to time he sips his glass of water. Although there are sixteen people working on stuffing the lobsters, this turns out to be even less easy than they expected. Four hundred lobsters are needed (although, of course, there are some veggies among the guests) and fewer than half have been finished and stuffing these obstreperous creatures is taking the chefs away from everything else. The beef is almost ready but not quite since a few touches have to be made at the last moment, not least heating the stuff. At least the vegetarian *compote frappée de légumes italiens* is done, and the salad dressing is pretty reliable. It would not be quite true to say that Mr Rupert is nervous . . . but he's had better evenings . . . if only HRH were not coming . . . and to calm his spirits he throws himself into stuffing lobsters too.

Stripped of their champagne (which they relinquish protestingly at the exhibition entrance), the guests involve themselves in ELEGANCE. The completed effect is triumphant. Sir Lewis and his party parade complacently around the rooms. 'How clever you are,' the guests say to Sir Lewis, 'what a marvellous show, it will be such a success.' Some of the guests move past the material about the working classes with raised eyebrows, but the silks and the swords, the portraits and the country-house views, the busts of kings and poets, the virtual London, have them cooing and glowing. Since so many of them try at home to pretend the eighteenth century is going strong, it's not surprising they are thrilled.

The owners of objects stand obliquely close to their possessions, enchanted if people say, 'Darling, I know who that one belongs to!' pointing to something labelled 'Private Collection'.

To this the owner replies, 'Well we have to say Private Collection, you know, the insurers insist, absurd, isn't it?' or 'I never thought there was anything to it but the curators seemed to like it,' or 'Henry was awfully against lending it, such a hole on the drawing-room wall, but I persuaded him – isn't it gorgeous?' 'Gorgeous' seems to be the word for the evening.

Surveying the scene but wondering what is going on behind it, Diana wanders through the exhibition. Her sleeve is pulled – or not exactly pulled but touched, urgently. She turns to see one of the women attendants whom she recognises vaguely – pretty girl, startling pale face, odd how she's never really looked at her before. The girl says to her, 'Miss Stanley, there's an envelope for you, top secret. Ian Burgess asked me to give it to you, but please would you not let anyone except yourself and Miss Vaughan look at it?'

Diana stares at her and abruptly realises what this means. Where on earth is she to put this envelope? She has no handbag, being at home as it were . . . but as she struggles with this problem she is accosted by the Hon. Mrs Ferdinand Hill. This lady is one of the more difficult lenders, who has had to be asked to lunch or dinner and stroked at least once for each of the loans she eventually agreed to make and endlessly fussed over loan conditions and government indemnity. 'Where is the exhibition, then?' says Mrs Hill loudly, oblivious of the large notices pointing to it and the hordes of people moving in its direction.

'I'll show you,' says Diana. 'You'll see how splendid your objects look.'

And out they go towards the exhibition room, meeting Jane on the way. She has a harassed air and rolls her eyes at Diana. 'Can I have a word?' she asks. 'I mean, when you're ready.'

'Do, do,' says Mrs Hill, unexpectedly affable after a glass or two of champagne, 'catch me up, will you, Miss um . . . eh . . . and show me where my little things are – oh, there's Rodney, how nice to see him, what fun this party is, all one's favourite people,' and she yells, with surprising vigour, 'RODNEY!'

Heading towards Jane, Diana encounters Jonathan, and reminds herself that he's supposed to be her partner. He is looking smooth and slightly disconsolate.

'Hello, darling,' he says. 'Wow – you look fantastic, what an outfit! And those diamonds – they're just brilliant.'

'Thank you,' she answers, making herself accept a kiss. 'I'm afraid I'm rather on duty. Will you be OK? Lots of people from the City here – you'll know masses of them.'

'Aren't you going to speak to me, then?'

'Yes, later, at dinner. Enjoy the exhibition. See you!' and she hurries away, suppressing a hint of guilt.

Jane is nearby, and anxious. 'I think I'm being watched. And followed. Don't you think you are, too?'

'No,' says Diana, 'I don't.' She looks at Jane in concern. Is the pressure affecting her? 'But I have something to tell you...'

As they speak, John Winterbotham passes them. He does not greet them, as he normally would. He merely turns his gaze towards them for a moment, impassively, and walks on. When he reaches the entrance to the exhibition room, he stops and turns back towards them. He is speaking into his mobile.

'You see, look at that,' says Jane. 'Someone wants me to know I'm under surveillance. I suppose I'm being watched from that control room, too – but with all these people the control room probably can't follow me. I find it horrible... Anyway, we don't want them to think you're involved in all this, go away, don't talk to me.'

'But I must tell you about this document...'

Helen passes them. She looks determined, as though on a mission. She conveys subtly that she's noticed them but doesn't need to acknowledge their existence.

'Dear little thing,' says Jane.

'You should have seen her ogling the Chairman,' remarks Diana, with distaste.

'I suppose it's true . . .'

'Oh, I think undoubtedly. What are you doing now?'

'I'm progressing,' says Jane. 'Eight fifteen. It's all set up. But I don't know what we're going to do if we find real problems with the Gainsborough.'

'Quite,' says Diana. 'Auberon was very severe.'

'He can be as severe as he likes. Do you think Auberon is part of this conspiracy?'

'Conspiracy?'

'Obviously there's a conspiracy,' says Jane, 'but personally I doubt he's part of it. If we can get hold of that document . . . or will you, in the ladies' or something?'

She looks so anxious that Diana can't help smiling. *I do admire her, she's so passionate, so determined, so unlike me in her resolution and courage, her assurance of what's right, and as for me, I don't even know that I believe in anything, even my political convictions, they're pretty lightweight, aren't they?, all conveniently set aside on an occasion like this — but at least I seem to be doing the right thing by helping Jane over this peculiar business. And now Jane's off again and talking to one of the guests.*

'Oh, good evening, Professor Ironside,' she is saying, 'are you on your way to the exhibition? I do hope you'll think our interpretation of the role of the canals in the industrial economy of late eighteenth-century England is reasonably lucid, within the confines, of course, of the imposed discourse . . .'

Back in the 'kitchen', there's been more tension. 'No more lobster pâté in the lobsters, they'll do fine without, we'll just have to make sure the top tables get the full works,' Mr Rupert has decreed.

'What?' says Gustavus. 'We've only got about a hundred more to do.'

'No time even for twenty,' says Mr Rupert, 'you'll be lucky to get the spinach into them.'

'Who's the chef round here?' cries Gustavus angrily. 'Me or you?'

'You,' answers Mr Rupert, still calm, 'but ultimately I'm the boss. Do as I say. Six of you finish spinaching the lobsters, the rest on the beef.'

'But what will they say,' wails Gustavus, 'all the people who don't get any pâté in their lobster? They'll be furious.'

'They'll be fine,' he is told. 'If we give them enough to drink, they won't even notice.'

Gustavus obeys scowlingly. 'Put the proper lobsters on to that table,' he orders, 'and keep them well away from the unstuffed ones. And carry on with just the spinach.' As he moves into the other room to deal with the beef he wonders how life will be if he does become a television chef. Can't go on working for a caterer, unless they triple his salary. He'll need a better showcase than this kind of event, but he'll miss Mr Rupert and the sense of excitement . . . and he'll miss some of the chefs, too . . .

Fred is showing some strain. His mobile rings at intervals and he hustles into a corner of the room from which he emerges looking flushed, and swearing. 'All the ovens functioning?' says Gustavus.

'No problem,' replies Fred. There is a strange humming sound, a click, a flickering of the lights, and darkness.

'Christ,' says Gustavus. 'Power failure.' And he starts to laugh, softly and then less softly and then so unsoftly that his cackles sound around the room, which is suddenly hugely threatening in the dim emergency lights.

'Steady!' says Fred. 'Get Mr Rupert, will you?' he says, to an underling. 'And ring Security. Gus, it'll be all right, old man. A power failure's par for the course, power for the course if you know what I — We'll get it fixed in a jiffy.'

'It's a hot night,' says Gustavus, 'why worry? Let's serve the beef cold . . . After all, His Royal Bloody Highness is due any moment, isn't he?' He laughs again in a stagey way, which makes the chefs look at one another anxiously.

There's been much agitation about the royal arrival. Sir Lewis wanted His Royal Highness to be received at the main entrance by a bevy of petal-throwing wenches and a row of trumpeters. The Duke's detective felt this might lead to complications, and suggested the royal guest should enter by the staff entrance. Sir Lewis was distressed by this proposal, which would have had him greeting the Duke among unmovable sandbags and fuse boxes. They compromised: HRH is to arrive quietly at the front entrance at 1940 hours, and will then move along a prepared route through the crowd to the Gallery of Early English History, which will lead him circuitously and secretly to the exhibition by 1953 hours. On his way he will shake some waiting hands and in the exhibition meet the curatorial team, plus three visiting scholars, plus the managing director of Burslem Properties, plus Mr Kobayashi, plus the entire board of trustees. The tour of the exhibition will conclude at 2025 hours when HRH proceeds to the Great Hall for dinner, where he is due at 2030 hours. By that time the entire cast of guests will be ready for the royal entrance, to be announced by a fanfare of trumpets from the minstrels' gallery. This programme has been discussed and rehearsed for days and weeks and months. All the relevant staff have walked through the programme several times, with Sir Lewis, more red-faced than

usual, directing the proceedings and Auberon languidly surveying progress from as great a distance as possible.

On her way to the entrance hall Diana sees Hermia directing
people to their positions for the royal welcome. A blush rises
rapidly from her neck, suffusing her fair face. And OH BLISS,
*Hermia is abandoning her duties and moving in my direction and, yes — yes
— coming to talk to me.* Seized with irresistible irrational happiness
at the chance of speaking to the girl she's not seen for at least
thirty minutes, happiness intensified by Hermia's eagerness and
Diana's awareness of her own glamour this evening and by the
rushed intimacy they're enjoying in the midst of so many
indifferent people, Diana is transfixed . . . She takes Hermia by
the shoulder and gently turns her face towards her, searching
her with her eyes — although what exactly she's asking, she
doesn't know. An impulse propels her to turn and just behind
them she meets the thunderous face of Lucian. Following
Diana's gaze, Hermia also turns towards him. She, too, starts
and blushes. The three stand immobile in an unhappy triangle
until the crowds push them apart.

Back in Industrial Revolution, the lobster preparation is as
complete as it ever will be. Two-thirds of the lobsters are
approximately perfect, though many look rough round the
claws where they have been pulled apart in a frenzy of stuffing.
Garnish in the form of parsley and lettuce leaves from the
emergency supplies disguises the worst gashes. Some lobsters
have spinach only, some have lobster pâté only, a few strays have
neither, but Gustavus has found some ersatz caviar, which has
been dotted gaily if indiscriminately around the plates. The
effect is strange and not altogether appetising. 'Harlequin
Lobster,' he says. Nobody laughs. Mr Rupert's face has lost all

colour at the amateurishness of all this, amateurishness such as Angel Cooks has never witnessed except on the evening when the catering tent collapsed half an hour before a dinner. His jaw is set rigidly. 'For God's sake, make sure the top table and the Director's table get the proper lobsters,' he says. 'It's my fault, I should have known this menu was too ambitious for four hundred . . .'

They are working on the Beef Plantagenet, which with luck will be heated in time since the electricity supply is reconnected and the ovens (bar one, which refuses absolutely to oblige) are again functioning. The beef is being carved by harassed chefs, sweat trickling under their white hats on to the food. The *foie gras* is the finest of its type, rich, thick, smoothly packed with goosey entrails, but is has been overchilled and has to be cut with heated knives. The thinnest slices of *foie gras* are inserted precisely between the slices of beef. 'I'm sure the beef will be OK,' says Mr Rupert to Gustavus, 'though there's a lot of work to do. But it's quite straightforward.' *If only it were*, he thinks: nothing could be less straightforward. As for the puddings – well, that preparation has not even started, nor has the savoury, but after all it's only seven thirty and the guests won't be eating their pudding until ten . . . two and a half hours away, ages, really . . .

Mr Rupert thinks Gustavus is OK but he's not quite convinced: at least he looks self-controlled as he darts around the room, commanding, cajoling, encouraging, sometimes shouting (but not too often). From time to time he's still sipping his glass of water. 'At least,' he remarks to Mr Rupert as he runs past, 'the tables won't collapse.'

'That's one thing that's never ever happened,' says Mr Rupert, in a chuckling sort of way. Being superstitious he tries to touch wood, but finds only Formica.

★ ★ ★

The entrance hall is full, burstingly, magnificently, richly and sonorously, chatteringly and glitteringly full. Many of the people there see members of the Royal Family repeatedly, some dine or sleep with them, but tonight even the most *blasé* are caught up in the mood of anticipation. At the front door, where John Winterbotham now stands guard, a little reception party is formed by Sir Lewis and his wife, the Mayor of Lambeth and her husband, and Auberon. Behind them the people being presented are ranged in two lines, while the Head of Special Events, wearing an expression of fierce resentment over her deconstructed and safety-pinned black Lurex evening dress and her gold wellington boots, is marshalling them backwards and forwards, slightly to the left and then again a bit to the right, so that they are in the ideal spot. She is making them move around slightly more, perhaps, than she needs to.

For Ted Hoskins, accustomed to such events evening after evening, the prime concern is attention to every detail, to every face that comes close, to the possibility of unforeseen interruption. It's not only the surprise attack he needs to beware, it's the approach by an erratic enthusiast with an unsolicited present or autograph request. Keeping undesirable members of the public away from the royal person is a key element of his job. The ideal event in his view is the one where nobody's present except one uncontroversial foreign head of state and plenty of detectives.

At least this job should be under control, and I've got good close-protection officers in Pete and John. There's not much of a chain-gang here for the Principal to deal with, only the Mayor of Lambeth and husband. A bit of flesh to be pressed, we all know the form. No possibility of industrial disputes here — always one of the worst worries — the place is well run. Given how much territory we have to cover and the numbers in the building, I'll have to work hard on eyeballing the Principal but we know each other so well we can almost always tell what the other's thinking. Not so simple with the Duchess, she has her own little ways, but that's another story . . . Dinner — wonder who I'll be next to this evening. They're not always so easy, my fellow guests. Some of them like the thought of meeting a genuine detective and want every detail about what it's like working for the royal person, others resent being next to a copper. It's going to be difficult to keep a Purple Corridor in the Great Hall, such a lot of people and not enough space, but we've worked out a reasonable escape route from the staff entrance if all goes horribly bent.

They walk up the outside stairs. Not a bad crowd, all well behind barriers. Reception party at the top of the stairs. Mayor clearly nervous but heaving with excitement, funny how these Old Labour types love a royal, it's the New Labour ones who are dodgy. Sir Lewis and Lady B. know them well. Auberon Booth, not seen him before. Indoors now. Bit of a rumpus in here, lot of noise, as usual all goes quiet when we come in. The lighting's a bit strange, odd on Midsummer Night to have all these candles, they obviously want to make a major splash. John Winterbotham being presented. Give him a wink. Twenty-eight hands to be shaken in the hall, all the trustees plus others. We'll try to get the Principal through in four minutes, trouble is he's so good-natured he enjoys meeting people and spends a lot of time on them. Can't push him too much. Eight hands shaken, two minutes up, definitely won't make it on time.

Bit of whispering going on now, but they're mostly engrossed. Passage between the guests has opened up nicely. All the trustees chatting hard, the Principal knows a lot of them, makes it harder to move him onwards when he wants to gossip but there's a lot of ground to cover before we get to the exhibition and HRH wants a proper look at it, says he enjoys the eighteenth century, lots of things lent from the Royal Collection. Over half-way down the line now. Is that woman with the big nose going to try to speak to him? Quick glance at the equerry whispering in the Principal's ear. Goodness, the smell in here is overpowering, what are they playing at? Quite a lively crowd, not all oldies at all, some peculiar dresses, it's odd people don't think they should dress formally for a royal occasion but then some of these girls do look pretty gorgeous even if they're showing all that flesh — no complaints about that, mind you. I've often wondered what would happen if I talked to one or two of these girls in the way I'd like to . . . Enough of that, concentrate, Ted . . .

The boss is pretty nearly at the end of the line. We must make sure we get him out of the room double quick for the next stage . . . Yes, he's finished pressing the flesh. Sir Lewis is doing his business, 'Sir, would you like to . . .?' and they're away, off down the human corridor, Winterbotham at the head, and out of the door. Two minutes over time but that's within the allowance . . .

They've laid out an alternative route to the exhibition, avoiding the crowds, which takes us through all sorts of odd corners. It's very quiet here, strange, low lights, almost like being in a forest with all these odd things looming out at you. God, what dreary places museums are, full of old bits and pieces like exhibits in a law court, though at least there's not much crime round here. Into the main exhibition place, where everything seems in order. Another line of people. Sir Lewis does the honours. Big Japanese man at the front of the queue, Sir Lewis seems keen HRH should talk to him, almost prevents him moving on to the next character, oldish woman, nice face, long red hair. Through the exhibition pretty fast. Stop finally in front of a big picture of a fairyish sort of figure dancing around in a wood, is it a bird or what, or some kind of a poof? They all exclaim with excitement, which is obviously the thing to do — can't see much in old pictures myself. The Principal's asked his opinion by the big Japanese man who seems to have joined the party (rules about not starting a conversation with the Royals have gone completely these days). HRH says, in a jokey sort of way, 'Well, is it genuine?' This goes down like a ton of bricks so then he says, 'What a remarkable picture, Reynolds, is it?' When someone whispers to him he says, 'Gainsborough, Gainsborough, of course, do you know the great works at Windsor Castle, Mr Kobayashi?' Mr Kobayashi seems to like this and says no and HRH says, 'Well, we must arrange something, a special tour with the Surveyor of the Queen's Pictures, I know you'd enjoy seeing them.' Mr Kobayashi smiles and rubs his hands and Sir Lewis grins like a Cheshire cat and they all seem happy. We get a talk about this picture, quite a long one, from a little girl in black who seems to be very important here for some reason. Finish the exhibition. Dead on schedule, now. Off to dinner, arrival scheduled for 2030 hours. Everyone's moving correctly into the Great Hall. Trumpeters bursting to do their fanfare.

Meanwhile, back in the exhibition galleries, *Lady St John*'s been lowered by the handling team on to a wooden trolley. Bill and Anna are in charge of the picture as it's wheeled into a dark side gallery. Friedrich von Schwitzenberg, carrying his infra-red lamp, emerges with Jane from the shadows. 'How much time do we have?' they ask Bill and Anna.

'Five minutes, sir,' Bill replies, grinning nervously. It's all their jobs are worth to be discovered involved in this caper, important though it clearly is.

Friedrich passes the lamp slowly over the surface of the painting. 'Very odd, Jane,' he says. 'I can't see anything. It appears to have no underpainting or restoration at all. Could it be – do you think it could be a completely intact canvas, in perfect condition?' He taps it. 'If only I could take it out of its frame . . .'

'No, I'm afraid not, sir,' says Bill, looking anxious but conscientious. 'We have to take it into the Great Hall in less than two minutes, sir.'

'But feel, Jane,' says Friedrich, ignoring him, 'the canvas layer, it's so thick. When has it been relined?' He scans the picture again and asks that the lights should be put on again. 'I wish I could see the edges. And what's this? Jane, what is this? Is it a signature?'

'The picture was never signed, as far as we know,' she answers.

'But look at this. It's an initial, tiny, look through my lenses, in the hair on the tail of the dog. R, isn't it, and an S? Who on earth could that be?'

'That could be, that almost certainly is, Ronnie Smiles,' she says.

As they gaze at one another, mystified by this discovery, the head of the picture-handling team and Bill edge deferentially towards them. Friedrich inspires some apprehension among the staff.

'If you don't mind, Jane, Mr von Schwitzenberg...' they say.

'No, no, wait...' says he.

'Of course we must go,' says she. 'And we must move quickly into the Great Hall ourselves, Friedrich, or people will notice we're not there. And we shouldn't go in together.'

Friedrich has become very agitated. 'What's going on?' he cries, as they hurry down the dimly lit Gallery of Medieval History ('Yes, yes, but do come along, Friedrich,' she urges.) 'What is the history of this picture?'

He storms his way through the Gallery of Early English History towards the entrance hall. It is strangely quiet, and the blinds over all the windows allow only the dimmest light to penetrate even on this warm, glowing evening. The entrance hall is now almost silent, no guests left there, only a few wenches and swains collecting glasses, removing furniture, picking up nefarious cigarette stubs. From the Great Hall comes a roar of chatter.

'We're awfully late,' says Jane. 'You go in first, I'll follow.'

But in vain. At the entrance to the Great Hall stands John Winterbotham. As he sees them, creeping in like errant children, he nods heavily. 'Been busy?' he asks.

'Oh, just some essential details in the exhibition, you know.'

'Ah,' he says. And he gives, as though humorously, a discomforting smile. 'I hope they really were essential. In any case, your movements will have been recorded on camera. It's double security tonight, as you must know.'

Jane's spine tingles disagreeably as she gropes her way towards her place on Sheridan, embarrassed that the Great Hall is filled with expensively dressed people milling about and refusing to sit down, that the lights are low, that she has to weave her way through the crowds without looking confused or anxious although she's so obviously late. As she advances with what she hopes is not too much of a scuttle, she turns back to look at Winterbotham. He is following her once again with his eyes, and speaking into his walkie-talkie.

The Great Hall always looks impressive for these dinners, much better lit and more seductive than the galleries that surround it, but this evening it is outstanding. The royal coat-of-arms above the stage, the garlands on the walls, the tightly structured pyramids of white roses interwoven with mixed foliage on the tables, are bathed in soft, gently flickering light. Each table is lit by an almost completely convincing chandelier with flowers intertwined in the branches, the pools of light creating sociable islands within the surrounding dusk. In the centre of the room the lifesize statues of True Love and False Love have finally been installed. The two female figures are more beautiful than one would believe possible, extraordinarily lifelike, naked but for a wisp of material around their loins. The coloured lights playing over their bodies give them, for a moment, softly blue heads, mauve breasts, scarlet thighs, golden legs until the colours change again. Each table is a little work of art adorned with a portrait (commissioned for the occasion) of the celebrity it is named after, framed in gold and poised at the summit of the floral pyramid. The linen tablecloths and napkins assert their starchy perfection through the mass of silver, the crystal decanters, the little round glass vase of white roses at each place, the stiff hand-illuminated menus. And the royal table is a sight that even the royalest or serenest of highnesses might admire. The table has been set with a Sèvres dinner service made for Louis XV and presented by him to the ancestor of the present noble owner during his embassy in Paris. This descendant has alarmed the staff of his rural priory by agreeing to lend twenty-four complete settings for the dinner. It's good of him, one might suppose, to lend so generously to Sir Lewis, whom he's never met. The rosy pyramids on this table (George III, it's called, in spite of some doubts about the associations) are twice as high as the pyramids on other tables, their peaks disappearing into the darkness. As Auberon notes with some asperity, there's no doubt which is the top table. The tablecloth on George III has been ruched into bows adorned with silk roses, which alternate neatly with the gilt tapestry-covered chairs from the museum's stores. The guest of honour has been given the gilt chair on which a royal duke sat at the coronation of George III, surmounted by a red velvet canopy. The display cases in Late Georgian and Regency have been emptied to provide the most sumptuous table decorations, dominated by the two Paul de Lamerie épergnes, which have been laden with pale green grapes exquisitely arranged by Mirabel Thuillier. It's a table not to be forgotten, and it won't be forgotten – already it's been photographed for two historic-interiors magazines. Competition to sit at this table has been keen, and several also-rans consigned to neighbouring tables such as Handel or Gainsborough (where Auberon is) are stealing disconsolate looks at the luxury so close but so remote. The lucky persons admitted to Paradise are preening themselves, chattering with assumed ease about the table's adornments, and effusively introducing themselves to one another as they await the royal arrival.

It is perhaps fortunate that the happy guests cannot see what is happening in Industrial Revolution. Although the lobsters have now all been plated, in the process the correctly stuffed ones have become confused with the semi-decorated lobsters and the not-at-all-decorated lobsters. Mr Rupert's attempt to sort them out has not been successful. Gustavus is running from beef preparation to lobsters and pleading with the waiter looking after Chatham, where his prospective television producer is sitting, to check that every plate is a perfect one. The waiting staff, all unwilling to give their tables incomplete servings and risk complaints, are surreptitiously replacing B- or C- with A-lobsters on their trays and shaking them about as they do so, while Fred (still persecuted by his mobile) guards the royal crustaceans. As for the beef — well, the beef is ready for the ovens although some of the cuts look as though they've recently been involved in a rugby match.

'He's arriving,' the word goes round Industrial Revolution. The trays are finally put in order under Mr Rupert's stern eye, accompanied by noisy complaints and covert kicking of shins by staff whose A-lobsters have been stolen. 'Consistency! For God's sake, keep your tables consistent!' cries Mr Rupert, though he knows consistency has vanished. 'As long as every plate on each table is the same no one will notice, they're too plastered to care.' The forty waiters are lined up, so that when Mr Rupert shouts, 'In!' they will enter the hall in a long procession. As they wait, the ones at the front can see the guests standing to greet the royal party, the Duke unmistakably tall at their head. The fanfare of trumpets blares through the hall.

★ ★ ★

The royal party sits down. The royal table sits down. The other tables sit down gradually, like ripples receding on a beach. There is another fanfare of trumpets, and the orchestra strikes up with *The Arrival of the Queen of Sheba*, immediately inaudible in the chatter, which rises like a cresting wave then abruptly halts as, to a further burst of trumpets, *Lady St John* is wheeled into the room. The spotlight on the picture follows it along the hall but flickers slightly so that the figure of Puck seems to be moving. Auberon has particularly dreaded this moment — the whole business is so dreadfully unprofessional and theatrical, he's sure colleagues in other institutions will mock, though it does have a certain dramatic effectiveness. In front of the humming expectant hordes, the huge object is lifted on to hooks by the handling crew (dressed in rustic Georgian outfits like Stubbs's peasants) and raised on ropes operated by invisible hands. *Lady St John* judders a little as she approaches the right height, is lowered again (out of the corner of his eye he notices his Chairman staring forward with a fixed grimace), rises once more and is finally steadied — upon which a new floodlight bathes the picture in soft warmth and the trumpets sound yet again. The guests burst into applause. Sir Lewis's grimace broadens into a complacent grin.

No complacency for me, thinks Auberon. *Been to lots of dinners here but never has so much depended on the evening, for me or the museum. I wish I knew nothing about Sir Lewis's plans, not even their outline: what's proposed for* Lady St John *worries me, it's not illegal but the idea of the picture being lent to a Japanese museum for a long period immediately after it's been shown here makes us seem faintly disreputable. What the hell is this bread? Tomato, tarragon and garlic — for God's sake! Anyway, nowadays can we realistically associate museums or even universities with moral standards or the search for truth? Aren't they commercial operations, now? Are moral standards relevant any longer, now old absolute values have been abandoned? Museums are just extensions of the marketplace, dependent on commercial or political pressures. Why bother with serious issues, when all the public want is interactive videos and period prurience? God, this bread is disgusting, who wants to bite into a chunk of fresh garlic? All I am is an impresario, using scholarship and intellectual integrity like animals in a circus.*

Olivia's at the next table, I can see her if I turn my neck just a little. She looks delicious, the slit up the side of her dress just revealing a hint of that fabulous leg . . . If I look at her just briefly, now she's turning away from that odious newspaper magnate and opening her bag, she might see me. She's taking out her lipstick . . . she's caught my eye . . . she's smiling faintly and looks a bit embarrassed to be seen attending to her makeup . . . she's blushing. Those few moments in my office this afternoon, such pleasure, such abandon, such closeness, intimacy . . . her suggestion that I should go round next week when the husband's away . . . Shall I? Do I dare? It's potential headline stuff, could ruin my career, then again it could make it . . . Odd, dinner's taking a long time to arrive, longer than we expect from Angel Cooks.

He has a second sip of white wine, is surprised to see his glass almost empty, he must make sure he doesn't drink too much, though it's wonderfully soothing. But as he begins to let himself feel anxious about the dinner, Mr Rupert's celebrated grand entrance is again enacted. Led by Mr Rupert himself, wearing some extraordinary eighteenth-century concoction with a three-cornered hat, the waiters troop in again in their two perfect files.

Auberon turns to his neighbour on his left and amiably opens conversational proceedings. She is one of his favourites among the museum's patrons, a wealthy lady of singular sweetness of disposition, who finds consolation for her widow-hood in dispensing large sums of money to her favourite charities and prefers paying for the essential things that other rich people dislike supporting. Such people make the odious business of fund-raising supportable for Auberon.

'You seem anxious,' she says.

'I am anxious this evening,' he replies. 'Of course, it's my job to be anxious – but I'm sorry if it's obvious.'

'Probably only to me,' she answers. 'What are you anxious about? Everything's going swimmingly. You must be delighted.'

'I am, of course,' he says, and she laughs.

'Exciting about the Nowness of Now,' she goes on.

'Mm,' grunts Auberon.

She laughs again. 'Are you wanting a modest contribution from me for that one?'

Auberon is not able to reply quite at once.

She looks at him seriously. 'Do you think it will happen?' she says. 'Of course, you may not be here to deal with it. Do you really want the Bloomsbury?'

So obviously everybody's talking about my application, it's taken for granted. Do I really want the job? Will it mean more of this artificial hospitality, trading culture for cash, night after night? No doubt at all, it will . . .

The lobsters arrive. Auberon looks routinely at his plate and again more searchingly. There is a hush as others peer at the menu to see what they're supposed to be eating. Most of the lobsters have a windswept look, as though they had been walking along a beach in a storm, and some have gathered a strangle sprinkling of black dots. 'Caviar?' says Auberon's neighbour doubtfully. 'With lobster? Gilding the lily, isn't it?' Auberon, realising he is frowning, pushes up the corners of his mouth and looks at the top table in case of trouble. But Sir Lewis looks contented – the top-table lobsters must be OK.

'Perhaps it's an eighteenth-century way of serving lobster,' remarks Auberon lightly. But as he wonders once again how one's supposed to tackle the thing – they never had lobster when he was a child – there's an interruption. From the further reaches of the hall emerges the tall, white-clad figure of a wild-looking chef, moving at speed. In his hand he holds a plate, his other hand curved protectively around it. Advancing like a flurried Doom from a morality play, he clearly has a target. Auberon knows he should not be staring across the room but feels it's his duty to know what's going on. The target turns out to be a tall residual Bohemian, recognisable as the director of a television production company. The chef seizes this man's plate from under his fork and thrusts the plate he's been holding into its place. The producer stares furiously at the chef, who gives a sickly smile and disappears.

There is further movement from behind the top table. Mr Rupert, who has been overseeing the service of His Royal Highness, is off.

'Well,' says Sir William St John to Jane, 'who'd have thought we'd meet again like this? D'you still see many people from those days?' When she'd stumbled to her table in a flush of embarrassment, she'd known him at once, with the alarmed pleasure felt by those who re-encounter people they knew twenty or thirty years before. She could still see why she'd liked him all those years ago. He looked at her consideringly and gave her a kiss. 'I remember you very well, better than you might suppose,' he said, and looked at her quite tenderly. Could she ever have been Lady St John, she'd wondered, and how would it have been?

'Some,' says Jane, 'mostly from my college. A frightening number have become senior civil servants, or headmistresses. Tremendously worthy. I went to a Gaudy the other day, it was fun but sad too...'

'Why was it sad? Just *tempus fugit*?'

Jane does not answer. Instead she says, 'What do you feel,

seeing *Lady St John* set up in triumph?'

'Good, this lobster, isn't it?' he replies. 'Though mine looks quite different from yours. I seem to have green stuff in mine, spinach, I suppose.'

'I've got pink stuff — can it be lobster pâté? I think that's what they intended to put in it.'

'Regional variations, I suppose. What do I feel about seeing *Lady St John* here? Not narked, no, not really. We had our time of grandeur as a family. It's no good looking back.'

'I mean — has the picture changed a lot since you last saw it, whenever that might have been?'

He does not answer directly. 'To be honest, I was a bit surprised when I saw her again in the exhibition. Hadn't seen the picture, actually, since it was sold to that chap Denzil Marten, d'you know him? Never quite sure about him. Anyway, it certainly looks different now from how it was at home, not that we ever looked at it, we just kept it in the attic.'

'Oh, yes,' says Jane eagerly, 'in what way different?'

He hesitates before answering. 'Shinier, I suppose, and brighter, and just . . . different. Still, Marten was so persuasive . . .'

'I hope you got a reasonable price,' remarks Jane innocently.

He smiles. 'If you're anxious to know . . .'

'Oh, no, not particularly, I just wondered.'

'Since you're such an old friend, I'll tell you . . . but not tonight. It was a useful bit of money, but Marten assured me they'd have to spend a huge amount to make it look OK. I mean, it did look a bit odd, after the fire and all that. I suppose I shouldn't be telling you all this, in fact I had a call from Marten telling me to stay quiet, hadn't realised it was so important . . .' He looks at his lobster and grunts a little. 'Well, to tell you the truth it does make me rather angry to see this performance here tonight, wheeling the picture in for goodness' sake, as though the thing were a sacred icon when it's only my naughty old ancestress who's been through the wars, cleaned up to look expensive.'

'It was in poor condition, was it?' ruminates Jane. 'You might be interested to know it's now insured by Sir Lewis for ten million pounds.' She hopes this will provoke him into indiscretions.

'What?' says Sir William, dropping a little lobster on his shirt front. 'Ten million? Ten million pounds, not dollars? I've been done.' His handsome ruddy face clouds over.

'Something's been done, anyway,' says Jane.

He broods for a while. 'I hope Burslem enjoys it,' he says, not very convincingly. 'I suppose he's been done too, in a way. Never liked Marten, shouldn't have trusted him. I'll tell you something, Janie. I mean Jane. Oh, well, to hell with it, Janie. I think this may interest you. The fact is, when I say the picture was not in very good condition...' He stops as they hear a muffled sound from offstage, followed by the noise of clattering and shouting. A door closes and the sound is blotted out. Then Sir William is claimed by his neighbour and Jane has to wait.

She looks about her. *In this huge room, amid this theatrical spectacle, four hundred mouths are opening and shutting; eight hundred eyes assessing their surroundings, their table companions, the dresses, the decorations, the lighting, the statues, the hosts, the royal duke, the Gainsborough, the food; four hundred minds seeking amusement, influence, gossip, mention in a newspaper. Are they all enjoying themselves, or deceiving themselves? Lady Burslem, for example, smiling and talking so easily to HRH up at the top table — is she aware of her husband's penchant for dear Helen, now seated (and just why is she at a better table than I am, after all she's considerably my junior at the museum?) next to Mr Kobayashi to whom she's dutifully cooing? Is Tanya aware that Auberon's fascinated by someone not younger but more glamorous than she is, richer, more smiling, thrillingly unobtainable (I suppose)? What's Alan Stewart thinking about this event, and the possibility of becoming a museum director? And Auberon, who's confused by what's going on in the museum now and doesn't know which side he's on or, indeed, which side is which — what's he experiencing? Does Sir Lewis, surveying the scene from up there, find his moment of triumph as satisfying as he'd hoped? Or is he subject like so many of us — why not be moralistic? — to unease and disappointment over success? And all these other people, concealing so many hopes and ambitions and anxieties, so many blossoming and wilting affections beneath their silk fronts, what are they deriving from this exercise, from all the words exchanged this evening between these chatterers? God, how many words will be spoken in this room this evening, at least two million and most of them garbage or banalities. If only we spoke less and thought more . . .* Professor Hilary Ironside beside her claims her attention with an oblique reference to his most recent publication and she promptly replies with a flattering allusion, making it clear she has read it.

At other tables they are talking about publications too. At Walpole, 'What is the next novel about?' Diana asks her neighbour. He is a successful novelist she has not met before.

'It's about global warming,' he answers. 'Ordinary people, humble but serious working people, and how our planet is being destroyed.'

She cannot think of a sensible reply to this. There is a silence. Then she rallies. 'That sounds good,' she says wanly.

'As you may or may not know,' he says, 'my last book was about the destruction of a family by paedophilia, a father molesting his daughters and his son, set in a deprived community in the North of England. It was intensely painful to write.'

'It's been very well received, hasn't it?' says Diana, who has not read the book but has seen a précis prepared by Special Events.

'It's doing well,' he says. 'I'm afraid it just shows what a cancer this child abuse thing is ... Terrible, terrible ... We've sold over forty thousand copies to date, film rights under negotiation ...'

'Your novels are always searing, aren't they?' asks Diana.

He looks huffy. 'I hope they're strong but not formulaic.'

'No, no,' she says. 'I mean you always deal with the most difficult problems in a fearless way.'

This remark goes down better. 'Novels today have to be fearless, don't they?' he ruminates. 'And they need to be about ordinary working people, not élitist, privileged people. After the global thing, I'm doing a black saga set in inner-city Manchester. Should be a winner.'

'A winner?'

'I mean, it will confront some of the most acute problems of our days, for a broad but thoughtful audience. Look at Dickens — face the problems, get the readers. If you want to change society, it's no good writing endlessly about neurotic women in middle-class suburbs.'

Diana has decided she dislikes him quite strongly. 'I never read novels,' she tells him, 'and I'm afraid I've never read any of yours.'

'Oh, that's all right,' he replies, looking deeply offended. There is a pause. And then, to her amazement, he looks at her body intensely from her chin downwards and asks, 'Have you got a boyfriend?'

Denzil Marten, sitting next to Helen, is having an easier time. Turning towards the Gainsborough, he remarks, 'She looks good, doesn't she?'

'She looks wonderful,' says Helen. 'Lewis — Sir Lewis — is a great judge of art. It's remarkable, isn't it, in a man who has so many concerns, and has to worry all the time about huge sums of money, that he can give so much attention to pictures?'

'Remarkable,' says Denzil. 'What do you think of the Gainsborough yourself?'

'It's superb, one of the finest of his later – period portraits,' she says.

He looks at her sharply. 'Oh, good, I'm glad you like it. You must come into the gallery one day and have a look at my stuff,' he says.

'Sir Lewis tells me you have beautiful things,' she answers politely. 'He speaks very highly of you, says he can always trust your advice. I'd love to come in.'

'Come and have a spot of lunch. We do quite a nice little lunch at the gallery.' He looks at her sideways, charmed by her long sleek body and the heavy black eyelashes adorning her pale face under the shining black hair coiled on her head. *She's like a fox*, he thinks, *there's something feral about her, under all that clever poise.* He'd like to put his hand on her knee and work it slowly upwards . . .

There seems to be a lot going on in this room, Ted Hoskins considers, *more than I'd expect of this sort of dinner. And speaking of the dinner, that lobster was a bit rough – mine looked as though it had been struck by a blunt instrument. It still hasn't been cleared but at least they've poured the red wine – pity I can never touch a drop at these events – let's hope the beef is coming soon, we're slipping behind schedule. Odd, that chef appearing from the kitchen, what on earth was that about? And why is John Winterbotham running around, taking messages to someone, looks like that man Bankes we met in the exhibition, and why's Bankes standing up and leaving the hall? Don't like this kind of unexpected activity. The Principal, though, is having a good time . . . chatting away to her ladyship . . . Must keep on talking to my neighbour, wife of the chairman of a large company, about her travel plans and what the*

Principal did when he went to Canada recently and her children's school and my own children . . . What on earth's happened to that beef? We've been waiting ten minutes now. One thing the Principal does get cross about is being kept waiting, and the schedule's pretty tight, we must be home by twelve fifteen, we may have to cut the pageant — no great disaster, though the kids will be disappointed — and I have to drive home but of course that's the least important thing . . . Lovely girl three places down on my left, wish I could give her a lift home . . .

Lucian is sitting next to a woman who's unimportant except that her husband's one of the richest men in England. On her other side is the secretary of a large grant-making trust, whom he's keen to charm. He has to talk across the uninteresting lady (while pretending to include her in the conversation, which annoyingly she wants to participate in) to the man in his sights, while trying to suppress his anxiety over the progress of the interesting little plan he's involved in. On Lucian's other side is Baroness Shawe, who's negligible politically just now but might wield influence if the government changes. He needs to give her adequate attention and laugh moderately at her quips while not seeming too friendly (facing him on the next table is a government minister who could have a major impact on his own future). This evening he finds Lady S. not too bad, in fact — there's a certain vigour to her dark features that is almost appealing, and he's never minded a faint moustache on a woman. On her other side sits a business friend of the Chairman, who also needs attention, and could be touched for money. All this requires concentration and more's needed for his struggle with his lobster (what on earth are Angel Cooks up to? His looks as though it's just arrived economy class from Tokyo). In the midst of all this he's surprised to find John Winterbotham leaning over his chair. John wants a word, urgently. When Lucian returns to the table five minutes later and Baroness Shawe asks in a jolly way if anything is wrong, he has to reply, 'Nothing that can't be sorted out, I hope. A little security problem.' But he looks furious.

Meanwhile Sir William has just finished his story to Jane. 'My God!' says Jane, and stares at him in horror. 'How disgraceful – everything except the dog – how ironic!' She feels almost inclined to laugh, though when she catches the eye of Lucian resting on her from two tables away she does not feel amused at all.

Ronnie Smiles and Mirabel Thuillier are on Hume ('Who was Hume, anyway?' says Ronnie. 'Oh, really? Wish I could have had someone a bit more Rococo – like Madame de Pompadour'). They have finished discussing the decorations and Mirabel has successfully revealed no trade secrets at all. They have enjoyed a satisfying (though loyal) gossip about Sir Lewis and Lady Burslem, with only the most discreet giggled references to his love life. 'Did you see the nice young lady's sitting on the royal table?' Ronnie burbles. 'A bit brazen, isn't it? But then Elizabeth's so good about it, I don't really think she minds, do you?'

'She'd have an awful life if she did,' chuckles Mirabel, 'but you know the funny thing is how well the two of them get on, they're really happy, you should see them choosing curtains together . . .'

'How are things going on the royal table?' asks Ronnie. 'I can't really see from here.'

Mirabel, trying to suppress her rage that she's not sitting there (when she's worked so hard and given them a substantial trade reduction), peers towards it. 'HRH was talking to Elizabeth,' she says. 'Now he's moved on to the woman on his other side . . . Lewis — well, Lewis is not looking very relaxed, poor man, I suppose it's because he has to make a speech. But he seems to be having a nice time with Lady St John, who looks good — I suppose it must be the candlelight.'

'Very odd, this lobster, isn't it?' says Ronnie. 'It tastes all right but my claw seems to be filled mostly with spinach.'

'Mine's mostly lobster pâté, no spinach at all,' says Mirabel. 'I wonder why they don't take the plates away, time's going by. Perhaps that's why Lewis looks unrelaxed.'

In the Gallery of the Industrial Revolution, people are unrelaxed too. The power supply for the ovens has failed, apparently irreversibly. The beef is as ready as beef could be, the *foie gras* perfectly layered between the slices of meat. The vegetables are done, the sauces prepared. But they are all stone cold. Fred has hurled his mobile phone into the corner of the room where it has hit one of the wrapped-up museum objects with a disturbing thud, and is shouting, 'Fuck! Fuck! Fuck!' Gustavus is not to be seen. There is an uneasy silence.

The chefs and the waiting staff cluster around Mr Rupert. This is a moment for decision, he thinks. It is possibly the worst moment of his life: he's lost control. 'Well, the show must go on,' he says, in a cheerful manner. 'We must serve the food cold. Say nothing to anybody, no apologies, no explanations. From now on, a cold entrée is what was always planned, cool food for a hot evening.'

Fred stops saying, 'Fuck,' and instead asks, 'What do we say to Sir Lewis?'

'Nothing,' says Mr Rupert. 'Leave that to me. If the rest of the evening goes well, he won't really mind and he'll mind even less when I cut fifty per cent off the bill. OK, everybody? Lobster away. Claret's poured. Then it's Beef Plantagenet *frappé*. And where the hell is Gustavus?'

The waiters are in line. The doors open. 'We haven't told the trumpeters we're ready,' cries Fred, one of whose many jobs it is to co-ordinate the music with the dinner. He is distracted just now by his wife's extremely clear-cut pronouncement that unless he is back home within an hour she is leaving with the children and going to her mother's, probably for ever. With their silver dishes held with one hand above their heads, the forty waiters advance into the Great Hall, announced a minute later by an only slightly ragged fanfare of trumpets. Mr Rupert, trying not to look conspicuous but hampered by wearing an enormous ribboned wig and a silver court dress coat, remains close to the service door, not anxious to be behind Sir Lewis when the plates of cold beef arrive. It's not long before he's summoned to the high table by a po-faced footman. As he walks he looks ahead to gauge the mood of the great man. It seems curiously subdued. The flashing eyes and whirling hands of the Chairman's worst moments are not in evidence.

Instead he's confronted by a slightly menacing jocularity, possibly considered more suitable in mixed society.

'Ah, Mr Rupert!' says Sir Lewis, turning in his chair and speaking with sinister softness. 'Anything wrong in the kitchen? Some of the lobsters looked as though they'd been hit by a hurricane.'

'Yes, Sir Lewis.' Better not to offer an explanation.

'And the beef is cold.'

Make something up? Tell him this was a period touch? Admit the truth? Blame someone else?

'The power failed. I'm very sorry. There was nothing we could do.'

'No emergency generator?'

'The emergency generator failed too. Everything failed.'

Judicious pause. 'You might speak to the museum staff about it.'

A nasty one for Sir Lewis, though he isn't prepared to acknowledge the fact. He maintains his savage smile, but he's silenced for a moment.

'The beef's disgusting, cold. We shall have to review our long-standing relationship, Mr Rupert.'

Mr Rupert cannot bring himself to be courtly. 'With great pleasure, Sir Lewis,' he says.

Lady St John, sitting beside Sir Lewis, shows signs of wanting to listen to the conversation. Sir Lewis flicks his hand imperiously to dismiss Mr Rupert and turns to her urbanely, remarking that cold food is so appropriate for a warm evening. Mr Rupert leaves, telling himself that nothing will persuade him to work for this horrible old party again. He feels, all the same, that he has to explain himself to Auberon.

Auberon is clearly not enjoying his beef. 'This meat is not one of your great successes, Mr Rupert,' he says. But seeing – to his amazement – tears welling into the eyes of the great caterer, he goes on, 'Not your fault. Idiotic menu for this number of people, anyway. And the canapés were delicious.'

'Thank you, I appreciate that,' says Mr Rupert.

As he speaks, a waitress runs up to him. 'Mr Rupert,' she says, 'there's been a disaster. I mean, there's a little problem. I mean, we need you – we need you urgently. Gustavus... Gustavus...' But she is unable to say what is so serious about Gustavus.

'What about Gustavus?' asks Mr Rupert. He reminds himself that in the Army much worse things could happen. 'What about Gustavus?'

'He's ... he's rather tired.'

'We're all rather tired,' says Mr Rupert. 'What's special about his tiredness?'

'Well,' she says, 'he's fallen into the raspberry coulis. The coulis in the big vat. He doesn't seem to be able to get out. In fact, he seems to have passed out.'

'Will you excuse me?' Mr Rupert asks Auberon.

The dinner remains buoyant, more or less, sustained by the rivers of alcohol. Not many people mind particularly that the beef is cold, since the menu does not suggest it should be hot. The claret chosen by Sir Lewis is of such spectacular quality and poured with such generosity that merriment spreads uncontrollably. *Are we just drunk?* Auberon wonders. *Is the sociability we think we're enjoying artificial?* He does not like the way this conviviality is presided over — ironically, as he sees it — by the portrait of Lady St John. In the golden spotlight, her teasing smile seems to quiver, her eyes to interrogate him, the wooded hinterland behind her is more mysterious than ever. Looking at her, he sees in her features — for the first time — the pure beauty of Olivia Doncaster.

His attention is torn away from the portrait by new activity. John Winterbotham has reappeared. He is moving purposefully towards someone — who? Jane? He is speaking to her, holding the back of her chair as though to help her. She does not seem eager to move. He looks insistent, even bullying. She is standing up, she is leaving . . . What on earth? He hides a lump of *foie gras* under his knife and fork and asks his neighbours to excuse him. As he stands up, Lucian appears at his elbow.

'We had to ask Jane, as chief curator, to come and look at something in the exhibition, Auberon,' he says. 'Small matter of conservation, slight damage to an object, reported by my staff. Just thought it should be attended to immediately.'

'Shouldn't I come?' asks Auberon.

'Oh, no, no need at all,' says Lucian. 'Just a little problem with a manuscript, nothing serious. It's all under control.'

The entrée is not under control. Piles of beef and *foie gras*, of discarded vegetables, congeal on the plates of the four hundred guests. Over the stiff white tablecloths red stains and little heaps of salt appear. People are leaning back, tilting their chairs and talking to friends at neighbouring tables, fingering the flowers in the huge table decorations, resting their hands not just on the backs of chairs but on the backs of their neighbours. More than one hand, it seems, has wandered into a nearby lap. More than one cigar has been illicitly lit. More than one bread roll has been tossed, and tossed back. There is a sense of bubbling anarchy.

Ted Hoskins isn't happy. *This is getting out of hand, the party's loosening up too much. And we're way behind schedule.* He catches the eye of the Principal, who raises his eyebrows and rotates his left wrist as though to indicate the time. Ted nods and shrugs. But at last something's happening: Sir Lewis is walking towards the microphone.

Sir Lewis hates the annual general meetings at Burslem Properties unless no questions are asked; only if the audience is silent can he begin to savour his powerful position at the centre of the platform. He equally abominates having to attend the Friends' AGM at the museum, when all sorts of fuzzy history enthusiasts not wearing suits ask unexpected questions. Even today, at the apogee of his triumph, at an event which (he is confident) should help him towards the title he's deserved for many years, he'd much sooner not be making a speech. But a speech must be made – first by him as chairman, then by the Royal Guest, then again by him as sponsor of the exhibition, and finally by the Director. His speeches have been rewritten and rehearsed many times, and contain a number of jokes and one startling announcement.

The first speech goes well. He proclaims the success of the museum and the exhibition, thanks the lenders, thanks the patrons, thanks the sponsors (loud applause, here), thanks the designer, 'the incomparable Mirabel Thuillier'. He says a few words about the importance of exhibitions to the museum, how they are its lifeblood. He announces – to even louder applause – that that very afternoon the board of trustees has agreed to commission a feasibility study on a new project, the Nowness of Now, and – to tumultuous applause – that £14 million has been raised already. Then (more confident in the face of so much clapping) he lowers his voice, and with more expressions of gratification than it seems possible to crowd into a minute, welcomes the Royal Guest.

The Royal Guest is an accomplished speaker, and his private secretary an accomplished speech-writer. His lead joke is genuinely funny and the laughter hesitates for a second, as though surprised at the idea of being spontaneous. Many more thanks, many more congratulations, many more references to the excellence of the museum and the dinner (only one or two slightly hollow laughs at this). The guests burst into cheers.

There is a further fanfare of trumpets. In the distance the waiters re-emerge like a row of clockwork dolls, carrying above their heads large silver platters laden with cheese. From his seat on the platform Auberon can see a tall figure dash towards them, waving its arms. The front waiters stop, the waiters behind don't. The liveries sway and push and curse, metal clatters on the parquet floor, and hundreds of kilos of Queen Victoria's Cheese Platter hit the floor. The waiters retreat higgledy-piggledy through the service door, leaving the trampled cheese behind them.

Sir Lewis stands up again. He is so happy to be supporting this exhibition, which he'd have wanted to sponsor even if he hadn't been Chairman of the Trustees. It's given him a wonderful opportunity to help the museum ... and such a chance for his company ... the largest property company in the UK, extensive interests in Australia, New Zealand et cetera, bringing architecture and building together ... Burslem Properties, 'dedicated to people, dedicated to quality ... We look forward,' he concludes, 'to another wonderful millennium for Britain.' Bow, smile, wave of the hand, second bow, he sits down at the back of the stage. Thunderous reception from the audience.

It's the Director's turn. A lot of speeches tonight, think the guests, as they slip out for a discreet visit after all that wine. Auberon thanks his staff and his Chairman. He gives a brief account of the exhibition's themes and academic purposes. He does not mention *Lady St John* – she's written into his speech but he's sick of her. He also sits down to loud clapping. From the corner of his eye he can see Lord Willins of Plympton, clapping hard. Bloomsbury looks a step closer.

The applause dies down and the speakers return to their seats. It's time for the community pageant, the moment nobody in the audience has been looking forward to. Announced by yet another fanfare of trumpets, several tiny children dressed as flowers run on to the stage and burst into a pretty song. But for only a moment, since a voice, a much louder voice than all of theirs put together, interrupts them.

'Shut up!' the voice shouts at the children. Aggrieved, or possibly not understanding him, they sing rather louder. 'Shut up, you little bastards.' This person is evidently not fond of children. The audience hisses at his brutality. The children hesitate, several burst into tears, and the singing peters out. The pageant has not started well. The tiresomely insistent voice goes on. 'Sir Lewis, tell us about the Gainsborough. Hasn't the picture been dramatically restored? Isn't most of it done by restorers? Isn't all this fuss sheer hype?'

Sir Lewis waves his hands distractedly in the air. 'What?' he says. 'Be quiet! No questions, please!'

'Answer me,' shouts the voice. The guests stir and crane and chatter and try to spot the speaker. It's a man, but who? Youngish, in a black shirt, intense, anxious-looking, determined – who the hell is this?

'Isn't it true,' he says, 'that you're sending the picture to Japan, and making lots of money out of the deal for yourself? This whole event's a promotion exercise for your property. Can you deny that?'

Ted Hoskins is looking in the direction of the Principal, who just for the moment is pretending to be happy with this development. *This is not going well, not one bit. He'll be wanting to leave soon, we'll have to get out of the place as discreetly as we can.*

'Shush, shut up,' cry some of the guests, but not many, since this interruption is compensating splendidly for the deficiencies of the dinner as well as halting the pageant.

Tense moment for Auberon. He loves to se Sir Lewis embarrassed and floundering. He's fairly confident of being able to deal with Valentine Green better than his chairman can, even though he's not quite sure what Valentine is suggesting. But the general atmosphere is not promising.

The children on stage try once again to burst into their song and dance routine ('We have a mania, For dear old Britannia'). Auberon pushes them gently but firmly offstage. They look fiercely resentful and one or two utter some very unflowerlike words as they go. 'D'you want to speak?' he asks Sir Lewis.

'No,' says Sir Lewis. 'Get rid of the man.'

Auberon takes hold of the microphone and says, in a jolly way, 'I'm sorry, everybody, this is not a press conference, it's a dinner. Some journalists never know when to stop!' There is some uncertain laughter, which halts when John Winterbotham and one of his men take Valentine by the arms.

'Go on, Auberon,' he shouts, as they drag him off, 'you tell them, you tell them about the Gainsborough . . . Let me go, this is a free country, let me go, you pigs . . .' but a guard places a hand over his mouth and he is led out of the room.

'Thank God,' says Sir Lewis. 'Intolerable . . .'

'Don't thank God yet,' says Auberon, as the voices in the Great Hall rise in a raucous crescendo. To a further fanfare of trumpets, strong, confident and extremely loud, the line of waiters, their liveries slightly crumpled now and some of their wigs missing or at a strange jaunty angle, re-emerge with their platters above their heads, heaped this time with fruit. They are greeted by thin applause and a few jeers. 'Shall we go back to our seats?' Auberon asks his Chairman, noticing uneasily that at the royal table movement is going on. A large solid-looking man has mounted the dais and is whispering into the ear of the Royal Guest. The Royal Guest has stood up and now advances to shake the hands of the Chairman (who looks like a disappointed child) and the Director (who doesn't). The large man and His Royal Highness vanish. They are followed a moment later by the minister, who does not shake any hands. *Oh, God, there goes our grant-in-aid increase*, thinks Auberon furiously.

Jane has disappeared and Valentine has been taken away, Diana realises. *Goodness knows what they've done with them. I may be the next to be spirited away. And some of the most important people are leaving. I have to do something, say something — it has to be done now, in public, at the dinner, we can't rely on action tomorrow, which might be suppressed, just as we might be . . .*

Auberon is completely confused by these developments. *Have I been deceived by the Chairman?* he asks himself. *Is this stuff of Valentine's justified?* But his thoughts are interrupted by another loud proclamatory voice. *It's like a meeting of the Seventh Day Adventists, this dinner,* he thinks. *Who now?* A clear female voice . . .

'When it gets to Japan, the Gainsborough is being sold by Sir Lewis,' the voice says. 'Sir Lewis has made an arrangement with Mr Kobayashi, to sell him the Gainsborough for twelve million pounds.'

Sensation.

Sir Lewis seizes the microphone. 'This is rubbish,' he says. 'I have no intention . . . I mean, nothing has been decided — anyway, the picture belongs to me . . .'

Auberon realises who the speaker is. Diana — competent, calm Diana. Why on earth? And where does she get this strange information from? Can this stuff conceivably be true?

'And what is more . . .' she is saying, when Lucian jumps out of his chair and seizes her from behind by the arms, in an intimate yet threatening gesture.

'Enough!' he shouts. 'Enough!'

Around them the guests are being plied with seasonal berries by the waiters, by now determined to deliver their wares. Many of the guests are standing and whispering incredulously to one another.

'Let me go, Lucian!' Diana cries. 'There's more to say. This is where the money for the Nowness of Now is coming from, not from anyone's generosity. And Lucian Bankes is involved, for a huge fee. Let me go, Lucian!' she shrieks, as he grips her neck. He releases her, he stares around him at the gaping faces. He scuttles to an emergency exit and disappears.

Sir Lewis's blood is now as up as blood can be. He shouts into the microphone, causing acute pain to the ears of the people nearest the loudspeakers. 'Yes yes yes, it's true,' he bellows. 'Yes, I am selling the picture, and I'm proud of it. It's my picture. I've a right to sell it. I'm not selling it for myself, but for this museum. Yes, for the museum. From this sale I'm making a donation of ten million pounds for the Nowness of Now. I wanted it to be a secret but since I'm being treated like a criminal, I want my generosity to be properly acknowledged, not vilified by an ignorant reporter.'

Auberon takes the microphone and tries to think of something dynamic to say. He fails. What should they all do? Sit down? Pretend nothing has happened? Eat their pudding and propose toasts?

'Let's get off the platform,' says Sir Lewis to Auberon. 'This is all new to you, Auberon; I should have told you but there are one or two complications, export licences and so on, I would have preferred to keep it quiet. Anyway, it's all out now ...' There is a triumphant yet faintly manic look in his eye. Auberon, mystified, stays quiet.

But as they make for the steps, they're again prevented. Through the door from the entrance hall bursts an Amazon, long red hair flowing behind her, green velvet dress torn at the arm. Behind her run two men in security uniform. As they enter the Great Hall they stop, embarrassed by the hundreds of eyes on them.

'Get away!' Jane shouts. 'Get away, leave me alone. I've something to show you. All of you, all of you here ...' and she advances like a warrior of ancient times towards the platform.

So rapidly yet majestically does she move, with such dishevelled assurance, that nobody dares stop her. The chatter hushes: the only sound comes from the last plates of dessert being smashed on to the disordered tables by the furious waiters.

Jane mounts the stage. 'I am Jane Vaughan,' she cries, in a thrilling tone. Mrs Siddons would have admired her. 'Jane Vaughan, chief curator of this museum. I have something to tell you all. It's about the Gainsborough. This picture we've all been admiring, this masterpiece, it's hardly a Gainsborough at all. It's the pretence of a Gainsborough!'

Sir Lewis is back on the platform. 'It is not a pretence,' he says, in a strange panic-stricken voice. 'It's a great masterpiece. It's a top masterpiece by one of the greatest British artists, Sir Thomas Gainsborough.'

'Maybe it once was,' she says, 'but not any more. Friedrich!' she calls.

Friedrich von Schwitzenberg is on the platform beside her. 'We have good evidence,' he says, 'that this picture has been so much restored that it is hardly the work of Gainsborough.'

'No!' cries Sir Lewis. 'Don't damage my beautiful Gainsborough. No, no, no!'

'I won't damage it,' says Friedrich, 'at least, not the original picture. Look!' He stands on a chair. And with a scalpel he cuts, vigorously, the top and sides of the painting. The piece of canvas on which the image is supported rolls slowly forward. There is a groan from the audience, such as you might hear at a public execution. Auberon finds himself giving a feral gasp, high and warbling. He tries to restrain himself, and notices he is not succeeding.

'Look!' cries Jane. 'There's the Gainsborough underneath, the real Gainsborough.'

Under the fine intact canvas which supports the glossy

portrait of Lady St John, is now exposed another canvas. It is black, mottled, with great ridges and cracks – hardly a picture at all. Only in the bottom left-hand corner can an image be recognised: it is a dog, a non-communicative greyhound, with its tail slightly drooping.

'Different, isn't it?' cries Jane mockingly. 'That's the picture that was going to be sold to Japan for twelve million. That's all that's left of the Gainsborough, after fire damage. It's hardly worth twelve pounds.'

There is a strangled scream from the top table. The scream is in Japanese and few people can understand it precisely, but it is generally clear that Mr Kobayashi is very upset indeed. Then there is no more sound from Mr Kobayashi.

Into the appalled silence Jane looses a few more words. 'They stuck a new canvas on to the old one and painted the picture again,' she announces, to the world in general. 'This isn't Gainsborough 1780, it's Ronnie Smiles 1990.' She laughs cruelly. 'What price Ronnie Smiles now?'

She stands triumphant as Sir Lewis, staggering towards her, clutches his side, utters the words, 'My Gainsborough . . . my Gainsborough . . .' and falls heavily on to the floor.

At this moment the two statues of False Love and True Love, who have been extremely well trained by their agency and have remained immobile for the past three hours, decide they have endured enough. They step down gracefully from their pedestals and leave the room.

THE BOARD ROOM,
TWO A.M.

Only a moment ago Angel Cooks were still in action clearing the Great Hall and the Gallery of the Industrial Revolution under the weary but still decisive command of Mr Rupert. Fred, having disappeared for an hour or so ('I'm sorry, I had to go, it was Samantha, major crisis ... no, I was able to sort things out, she's fine ...'), returned and seemed calmly detached as he assessed the damage to the new tablecloths. Gustavus, recumbent in the coulis for three hours, awoke dripping with scarlet juice but with a beaming face. 'Was I asleep for a minute? It was all that vodka,' he proclaimed joyously. 'If it's really good quality it knocks you out but you feel fine when you wake up. So, where are we at, how's the dessert doing? Oh ... oh, God ...' as he recalled the events of the evening. A moment or two later, changed into his Vatel outfit, he reverted to cheerfulness, as though relieved of a burden. He was remarking to Fred, 'Ah, well, no television programmes for little Gustavus just yet,' when a call came through on Fred's ever-busy mobile, inviting him to participate in a programme on chefs' disasters the following day. He said, 'No,' and then, a second later, 'Yes.' As Fred and Gustavus were leaving the room, Fred caught Gustavus's eye. Gustavus rolled both eyes in return. Fred giggled, Gustavus giggled louder, and the two of them burst into an orgy of uproarious laughter.

'The beef,' they cried, 'and the *foie* fucking *gras*,' and 'You should have seen yourself lying in the coulis,' and Fred was vividly describing the waiters' repeated attempts to serve the pudding ('without any coulis, but it didn't matter a toss because everybody was shouting and nobody wanted the fucking stuff') when they were quenched by Mr Rupert. 'Come along, boys, it's been a long night,' he said. 'I just hope it's not the last night Angel Cooks are ever employed.' Now, after the last slamming door, the last laugh, the last flurry of lipstick-stained napkins retrieved from dark corners, the Great Hall is swept and quiet.

The human detritus was more difficult to manage. It took quite a while to remove Sir Lewis. Diana was able to despatch her Jonathan with a few curt words ('Too much to worry about, can't come back with you now' – 'Wouldn't it cheer you up to come home?' – 'No, it wouldn't, I don't need cheering up thank you, and I have professional responsibilities too, you know,' though as she snapped out the words she regretted being so disagreeable). It needed much longer to clear most of the guests, who milled around discussing the evening's mysterious events and fingering the torn remnants of the Gainsborough. Only when the lights were turned on at full strength did the sign of their raddled friends persuade them to move on. On the way out they were bemused to be offered party favours, neat little bags containing scent and catalogues and postcards of *Lady St John* and information about Burslem Properties, even though the exhibition posters showing the now discredited face were already being taken down.

Despatching the guests was complicated by the suspension of John Winterbotham. At this delicate moment, he was thought to be too closely involved in the plot to continue his duties. He was told to stay in the control room under the supervision of his own staff — the ultimate insult, as far as he was concerned — before being sent home. Ian, who took his place, disliked this obligation and was even sorry for him. They had a little conversation in the control room a while ago. 'I thought I was doing the right thing,' said John. 'Sir Lewis is the boss here, after all. I was doing what he wanted, wasn't I? They told me Jane Vaughan and the rest of them were trying to create mischief, so I kept an eye on them.' Ian shrugged and offered him a cigarette, a wholly forbidden action in the museum. 'I mean,' John went on, 'how was I to know Sir Lewis was planning to sell a picture to Japan, and even if he was... well...' He took the cigarette. 'I mean, when you're trying to do your best for the place you work for...'

It was Lucian's movements that particularly interested Diana, now acting Head of Exhibitions. She was to begin her duties at six in the morning. Had she got rid of him at last? What's more, he was no longer a rival for Hermia, who in any case can't have liked him much... She noticed that Helen, who was surely implicated in Sir Lewis's plans, hadn't dashed out of the room like Lucian, but made an elegant withdrawal with all the other guests. Perhaps she wasn't seriously implicated, in spite of appearances? Or was she just being very cool about it all?

As soon as the guests began to shift, the trustees and senior staff convened in the board room. 'Like the last meeting of the provisional government in the Winter Palace, isn't it?' remarked Alan Stewart, as they fell into chairs or leaned wearily against the panelling, 'though let's hope not equally disastrous.' John Percival, as acting Chairman, called them to order. The exhibition would proceed as planned, he announced, obviously minus *Lady St John*. All the posters and publicity material showing her image would have to be withdrawn and destroyed, and replaced with another image immediately. A press release would be issued the following morning. 'The show must go on,' they all said sagely.

'I offer my resignation,' Auberon announced vigorously. 'I think I should leave.'

'Your offer is not accepted,' said Percival. 'But we'll want to consider what's happened very closely. Clearly, serious mistakes have been made. Of course there'll be many questions to be asked – particularly why nobody spotted that there was a problem with the picture much earlier. I think I speak for everybody in saying you have our confidence.' And they all nodded, all except Mrs Hobson, who treated Auberon to one of her hatred looks.

The telephone rang and Mary Anne answered it. A moment later – 'It's the *Daily Telegraph*. They want a story at once – every paper in the country is trying to reach us. Will you speak to them, Mr Percival?' And half to herself, she breathed ecstatically, 'The attendances are going to be sensational.'

'Very well,' Percival answered. 'Auberon, you and I must issue a joint statement.'

'And there's a television crew on the way, should we let them in? I hardly ever get television for anything positive,' Mary Anne muttered, 'but let's make the most of it.'

'Someone told me,' said Auberon, 'that Ronnie Smiles is the press's new rogue hero, and has given six interviews already. He's billed as the new Tom Keating.'

'Little creep,' said Jane.

'Ah, Jane,' remarked Percival, 'outspoken as ever. We owe you a special thank you.'

'And Diana too,' she said stoutly.

'And Diana too. Many congratulations. We won't forget what you've both done. Very incorrect procedurally, of course, but then there was some pretty incorrect behaviour going on here, wasn't there? We have some tricky days ahead of us, ladies and gentlemen, but I'm sure BRIT will survive.'

The telephone rang again, and Auberon answered it. He spoke for a little while. As he put the receiver down, he said 'That was a surprise call. It was Lucian Bankes.'

'Lucian Bankes!' they exclaimed. 'Where is he?'

'He's at the front desk. He said he was on his way to Dover when he realised how foolish he'd been. He said he'd disgraced the museum he loved. He wants to apologise, and face the consequences of his behaviour.'

They gaped at him.

'And he's on his way up to the board room, if that's OK by you.'

'Shall we drink a toast?' suggested Trevor Christiansen.

'To the Nowness of Now?' asked somebody.

'To the Thenness of Then,' someone replied.

AROUND LONDON,
THREE A.M.

Bill and Anna are asleep, together. They were brought even closer by their joint adventure, notably their information to Ian, which had such unexpected consequences, and their release of Jane and the others from the Medieval Manuscripts store in which they had been locked. When they finally went off duty at two a.m., it seemed natural for Bill to ask if Anna would like to be escorted home, and natural for Anna to agree, and natural for Anna to ask Bill in for a nightcap, and even more natural for them to subside on to Anna's futon almost as soon as they were inside. It will surprise them when they wake in the morning to find that they fell asleep immediately in each other's arms, and are almost fully dressed.

Diana is at home, her hair rather on end, too tired to take off the dress that has earned her so much admiration. She is excited to be appointed acting Head of Exhibitions. She is exhilarated that Jane has triumphed, and even more so that Lucian has vanished. But as for Hermia — well, she does not know about Hermia. When the state of the painting was exposed, Diana felt a strange uncertainty. Was she really in love with Hermia, and was Hermia in the least bit attracted by her? As she stood motionless among the confusion of the Great Hall, she found Hermia beside her. She said, since it seemed the only thing she could say, 'Do you have a lover?'

Hermia replied, 'That's a very old-fashioned saying. Yes, of course I have a boyfriend, but he is in Milano, why do you ask?'

Suppressing her flooding disappointment, Diana asked, 'Do you still want to be my friend?'

Hermia answered delphically, 'You are a wonderful person, Diana, I admire you so much.' What was one to make of that?

Now back in her little flat, she contemplates her diamonds and pearls with disgust. *Better paste than these glittering rocks, paste that at least doesn't pretend to have value. Do I understand myself any better than I did before today? Will I go back to Jonathan and his like, to unenthusiastic affairs with uninteresting men? Or have I really changed? Am I — yes, am I — liberated?*

The telephone rings. Who can this be? 'Diana,' says the voice, 'it is Hermia. I cannot sleep. I had to ring you up . . .'

Jane, meanwhile, sits in her study, still in her torn green velvet, unable to contemplate bed. This — ah, this — is indeed a moment when a lover is needed. But, then, so many moments are. She looks at her books with a cold eye. She looks at the catalogue of ELEGANCE, still open where she left it this morning — what on earth will they do with the sixty thousand copies they printed with such pride, all worthless and laughable now? She thinks about the way she behaved today. Was she courageous? Foolhardy? Is this what her grandfather, the general, would have done? And what about the Chairman — or ex-Chairman, probably? He can't have known that the picture was a fraud — she's almost sorry for him. She feels overcome by a sense of anticlimax and gloom. In three hours she'll have to go back to the museum, to repair some of the damage, but now she can't bring herself to go to bed.

The telephone rings. Auberon. 'Jane,' he says, 'I'm sorry to ring you at this nocturnal hour, have I woken you up?'

'No,' says Jane, 'I can't sleep at all.'

'Nor me,' says Auberon. 'But I wanted you to know how pleased the trustees are with you. Much more than they are with me, actually, which isn't surprising.'

'But you haven't done anything wrong,' she says.

'I haven't done anything right, either. After you'd left, Percival said I was to ask if you'd consider accepting the position of Deputy Director, for a period of five years.'

'What do you mean?' she cries. 'I'm due to retire, you know that.'

'Not if you take that job, you aren't,' he answers. 'No reply needed for a while. Just thought I'd let you know.'

When he has put down the receiver, she thinks, *Deputy Director? Five years! The little house in Oxford delayed for three and a half more years! This calls for brandy. I certainly won't accept this offer.* She has some brandy. *Well, maybe I will.* She drinks a little more. *On the other hand, do I want to work for those trustees? Do I really care about the place, after all this? Is there any point in working oneself stupid for a bunch of self-seeking ignoramuses?* And she drinks just the tiniest drop extra, and goes to bed undecided.

No telephone calls and no brandy in the Burslems' flat. Lady Burslem has returned only minutes before from the hospital. Lewis's heart-attack was a mild one and he will be home in a day or two. Of course she will be there to look after him. She sits at her dressing-table for a long time, brushing her hair, and looks at herself pitilessly in the glass. Then she tears her tiara from her head and hurls it violently at her husband's Renoir. Both suffer damage — the Renoir, on balance, rather more.

★ ★ ★

Auberon, in his elegant bedroom, still in his evening clothes, still too stimulated to sleep, lets his mind range over the day. Does he want to stay at the museum, after all this? Doesn't he look like a public idiot? Will anyone respect him? Is it worth his while going to the interview at Bloomsbury? Will anyone take him seriously?

He throws off his tail coat and does not pick it up from the floor. *Not like me to do that*, he notes. And does he really love Olivia, isn't that a fantasy? Tanya was so kind and supportive this evening, so gentle when she found him. How had she guessed where he was, having a little cry in his office? Has he been wrong about Tanya? Has he been deceiving himself over Olivia, just as he's been deceived over so many other things? Isn't he a fool, gullible, easily distracted, unserious? Hasn't he been seduced by glamour, and forgotten the questions that absorbed him when he was young? When this business has sorted itself out, shouldn't he take a good serious look at himself? He lifts *The Imitation of Christ* from his table and stares at the spine without opening it.

He thinks he should leave the place. He's made a total fool of himself. He'll resign the day after tomorrow, when everything's calmer, and this time he won't allow his resignation to be declined.

The telephone rings. Who on earth, at this hour? There've been enough calls for today, surely.

'It's Valentine Green,' says the voice. 'I've been released from the cleaners' cupboard where your staff decided to put me, and I'm writing a story about this evening's events. It's due in shortly, but I wanted to invite you to comment.' He sounds more vituperative even than usual, but Auberon does not care.

'Sorry about the confinement, not my doing, I assure you,' says Auberon. 'I hope you weren't too uncomfortable.'

Valentine snorts furiously. Perhaps Auberon doesn't sound sufficiently concerned. 'Do you have any comments on this evening's events? It might be to your advantage. The story isn't very favourable to the museum, as you might expect, or indeed to you.'

'No,' says Auberon. 'No comments tonight. It's just been a midsummer folly, hasn't it?' And as he puts down the receiver he falls asleep on his sofa.

Back at the museum, there's no activity at all. Ian, sitting in the control room and hardly able to stay awake, looks in turn at all the cameras — which now, he reflects, belong to him. Young Ralph is walking through the exhibition galleries. Norman is progressing through the Gallery of Early English History. The Great Hall is empty. The entrance hall is empty. The streets outside are empty too. If anyone were passing the museum, they would never guess that anything ever happened behind the closed bronze doors.